Viviana Valentine Gets Her Man

VIVIANA VALENTINE GETS HER MAN

A GIRL FRIDAY MYSTERY

———◆———

Emily J. Edwards

CROOKED
LANE

NEW YORK

Published in the United States by Crooked Lane Books, an imprint of The Quick Brown Fox & Company LLC.

Crooked Lane Books and its logo are trademarks of The Quick Brown Fox & Company LLC.

Library of Congress Catalog-in-Publication data available upon request.

ISBN (hardcover): 978-1-63910-182-5
ISBN (ebook): 978-1-63910-183-2

Cover illustration by Rui Ricardo

Printed in the United States.

www.crookedlanebooks.com

Crooked Lane Books
34 West 27th St., 10th Floor
New York, NY 10001

First Edition: November 2022

10 9 8 7 6 5 4 3 2 1

*For brave kids in places where bravery
should not be demanded.*

*For ways to help, resources are available
on my website.*

Day 1

It was a scorcher that day, and my saddle shoes were in danger of melting to the pavement as I ran back toward the office building, cursing the fact that our landlord wouldn't spring for a fancy air-conditioning unit like they had at the movies.

Feeling the singe of the New York City sun on my skin, I pounced up the stoop, only to narrowly avoid being whacked with the front door, pushed open by a hulking galoot with a familiar mug. He was clearly in a hurry to get away from a building that—judging by his tailoring—was much below the standards of his usual haunts.

"Well, pardon me, mister," I said, not watching my tongue. "Coulda opened your eyes to not knock into a girl."

But my words were ignored as the man hurried into a shiny black car that screeched away from the curb, kicking up a cloud of street dust and a crumpled-up beer can. I watched it careen down the avenue and make a hard left without even slowing for the stop sign, and I continued into the building.

With a paper sack full of food and two bottles of Coke, I climbed up a flight of stairs and waltzed into my boss's office, where he was waiting with a smile.

"So, Dollface," Tommy said, snagging the bag and leaning back in his chair. His shirt was already open and flapping, now that he was alone, exposing his white undershirt. He ripped open the paper and twiddled his fingers in anticipation, plucking out two hefty sandwiches. He frowned and weighed his choices, roast beef or pastrami. He chose pastrami, and I smiled to know I was getting exactly what I wanted for lunch. "Were you in time to spot our special guest?"

"I recognized him. I've seen him in the papers before," I said, hopping up onto a clear spot on Tommy's desk and unwrapping my own meal from its soggy white paper. It was exactly how I liked it—rye bread, ice-cold beef, and horseradish hot enough to melt a car bumper, so you had to slow down and think while you ate it. "I didn't know a man with that much money could be so damn rude." I fished around in the bottom of the bag for my pickle and frowned to see that it was warm and a bit floppy. I ate it anyway.

"The ones with that kind of money are the rudest," Tommy said, cracking open his bottle of Coke with his teeth. The trick made me wince every time, and I think that's why he did it.

"And he really has an eighteen-year-old daughter? The one that's always in the tabloids?"

"Money makes you rude, but it *can* keep you young. Explains why I look like this." Tommy was being cute, goading me to spill the beans on what I thought, but I was A-okay with making him wait as I slowly chewed on the crusts of my rye. He pulled a face in a final attempt to get me to laugh, but he didn't look half bad today—the split lip he had collected last week had healed nicely.

Tallmadge Blackstone was the son of a gun who had nearly knocked me flat without even so much as an "excuse me," and that's what money will do to a man, I suppose. And Tal Blackstone—if the papers are to be believed, and I have no reason not to—had plenty of it. His bank accounts were flowing over, thanks to a one-two punch of being the owner of one of America's biggest diamond importers as well as, they say, the railroads that ferried things to and fro' the mines, I think back in some part of Africa.

Now, do not get me wrong. Plenty of regular folks made good in the war too, but Blackstone wasn't ever regular folks, not a day in his life. His daddy left him a nice big cotton fortune to boot. He was a good old-fashioned American success story, starting out successful to begin with and then padding his bank accounts with more and more success as the years ticked by. He had success coming out of his eyeballs.

Because of this, the Blackstone name was all over Manhattan—from tiny, shiny plaques on benches in the park, next to the cast-off art in museums both up- and midtown; the name was even on new wings at some of the plushier hospitals in the borough. The Blackstones were everywhere one could see and be seen by the proper social set, and had been for generations.

So, Tallmadge Blackstone was here in our dinky little office in the bowels of Hell's Kitchen to gripe about his daughter, the recent debutante Miss Tallulah Blackstone. Regular girls like me didn't "come out" anymore—we just kissed boys until we found one maybe good enough to marry, or maybe not good enough at all—but girls with papers like a pedigreed bitch still did. I suppose it saves time and effort, but seeing all the fuss and muster made me wonder if the whole charade was worth it.

Blackstone's only child, Tallulah was the hottest ticket to come out in years, given that whoever she chose to marry was set to inherit *Mister* Blackstone's family estate. The papers had a lot of conflicting information on Miss Blackstone—her schooling, her favorite flavor of ice cream, even her current beau—but one thing they didn't disagree on was the detail that she herself was set to inherit zero dollars and zero cents of her daddy's money in her own name. It seemed unfair to me, but if the *Herald-Tribune* saw it fit to print, well, it must be true.

Another detail not up for debate was the fact that, thanks to the endless evidence of tabloid snaps, Tallulah Blackstone was also a hell of a beaut. She would have no issue finding a husband. She could probably order one to be delivered to her door like a brand-new, custom-made chinchilla coat.

"So, what's up with the kid?" I asked. "She would be a little hard to blackmail. Walter Winchell practically publishes the color of her garter belt every night."

"Boy, ain't that the truth. She's been eighteen for what, six months now? Has there been a day since where there wasn't a camera in her mug?"

"Not as far as I can tell. And don't think it started after she was legal either. Those photographer types have a tendency to skirt the rules."

"Since when have you had issues with boys who skirt the rules?" Tommy asked, pinching me on the thigh, so I hit him with a stack of napkins. "But trust me. Daddy could've sued every rag in town to get them to stop hounding his daughter, but I got the *distinct* impression that it was good for his business. Everyone wants something connected to the rich, salacious, and famous."

"Some beau lay a hand on her?" I asked. "He knows we're not hit men, right?"

"No, no, I didn't get the impression anyone touched her," Tommy said, giving a knowing glance at my cheekbone where, just a few weeks back, I said I'd fallen into a doorknob. "Only monsters blame a dame for that, and while her dad seemed the type, that wasn't mentioned. If his goods were ever damaged, he'd mention it."

"So, this probably isn't about blackmail or violence. She stealing from the till?" I asked.

"Would the bastard even notice?" Tommy wasn't above taking potshots at anyone, even the folks paying the bills. Once they were out of earshot, of course. "But while she remains unmarried and under his roof, the mountains of greenbacks are almost as good as hers. She's still his dependent."

"There's no way it's about money, and I doubt someone *that* rich is a Communist," I said, giving Tommy a sly eye.

"I don't think Joe McCarthy is the president of her fan club," Tommy said. "But I doubt she's under investigation. If she is, that's a bit too hot for me." He grabbed a chewed-up pencil and made a note on a scrap of paper, as if he was really going to ring up the FBI to get notes on the politics of Tallulah Blackstone.

"Okay, so provided she's not a Ruski, it's gotta be about love."

"Those are your only choices?"

"Tommy, I've been keeping your confidence for how many years? It's never anything else. Money, politics, and love. That's it. Those are the choices."

My boss barked out a laugh and choked on his sandwich. I reached out and smacked him on the back.

"Okay, okay. Obviously you caught the photos of her in virginal white, being presented to society?" Tommy asked.

"You know I did—you tease me about reading the rags at lunch at least once a week."

"And all those dapper young penguins standing around, eyeing her like she's a tasty mackerel?"

"Enough to make my skin crawl." It wasn't often that I was happy to grow up dirt broke, but if that's what rich girls have to go through, I counted my lucky stars.

"She's promised off, but it's not to a young scion, I can tell you that."

"Not too many young scions left, to be honest," I said. "Which is bum luck for me."

"I pity any stuffy, little rich boy that'd try it with you." Tommy laughed. "But that's not what I mean."

I pondered for a bit while trying to suck a caraway seed from my back molar.

"Nothing to do with money?"

Tommy shook his head.

"Location? He from overseas?"

"There are fewer young scions left in Europe than America, Viv."

"Not money or location, so it's gotta be . . . age?"

Tommy smiled.

"Oh, so the rags are right again!" I said, smacking my teeth as the seed came loose. "Her daddy's got her carriage hitched up to his partner!"

All the gossip rags hinted that Tallulah Blackstone's debut had just been a formality, and Blackstone had promised her off to his reclusive business partner, Webber Harrington-Whitley, long before she came of age, even though Web was forty years her senior.

"She hasn't done the logical thing and run off yet, has she?" I asked Tommy. If he ever asked me to run an errand while a client came in to chat again, I swore to myself then and there that I would outright refuse. It was exhausting to ask this many questions.

"No, she's safely ensconced in her daddy's big apartment uptown," Tommy said. "He says she's barely allowed anywhere without at least two bodyguards, though all those photos in the tabloids would say she's rather good at giving them the slip. We're in no danger of losing her. Physically, that is."

"That's good. A girl from those circumstances wouldn't be long for this world," I said, using a new phrase that I'd picked up weeks ago from some spine-cracked romance novel like the ones left in every nook and cranny in my boarding house, with titles like *The Next Starlight* or *Valley of Obsession* or some other such nonsense. "So, if she's still at her daddy's, what's the big problem?"

"This day and age," Tommy said with that damn twinkle in his eye that made me prepare for what was coming, "girls got all these big ideas about what they should be in this world. And Tally—that's what they call Tallulah—Tally's got this idea that she doesn't have to marry a man she doesn't care to marry."

"She's right."

"I know she is." Tommy's sigh said he wasn't exactly a stranger to the situation of wanting to marry a girl who didn't want to marry him.

"So, again, I ask you—what does Daddy dearest want from you, ol' Tommy Boy?" He hates it when I call him *ol'* anything, but he always lets me get away with it.

"Tallmadge has this big idea that she's got her eyes on someone else, and he wants me to find out who."

"So you can knock some sense into him?"

"It's a little something like that."

"You're gonna get cheap on me with information?"

"For right now. I gotta do some footwork before I share more." Tommy drained his soda and put it on top of the empty sack. That was the sign that I should gather up the napkins and head on out of his office, but as I gathered, I decided to try my luck.

"You need anything before I pack up for the day?" It was early, but I couldn't see anything else happening on the horizon.

"Yeah—you got that case file on that city councilman?" he asked.

"You bet." I plucked a file from the pile on my desk and handed it on over. "Any ideas yet on who's put the heat under his heels?"

"I got a few ideas," he grumbled. "The hard part is proving it."

"Well, if anyone can pin the tail on the ass, it's you, ol' Tommy boy."

"Thanks, Viv," Tommy said, letting me go. "Do you need money for a cab?"

"No, thanks. It's still light out—I'm okay to walk."

"You watch your six, though. I'll see you in the morning, Dollface."

"See you in the morning, Tommy."

I sauntered my best saunter back to my desk, closing his door behind me with a click. Gathering my purse, I took a look at the office and smiled.

I had a good thing going here with Tommy.

A jitter of the door handle broke me out of my stupor.

"Mr. Fortuna in?" A man about my height had stuck his head through the crack.

"Yes, sir, but for appointments only."

The face scowled. "Fine, I'll make one."

"You need the number?"

"Nah." And with that, he was gone. We get a fair amount of lookie-loos, and Tommy told me early on that anyone who can't bring themselves to make an appointment isn't ready to learn whatever they want him to find out.

It's like God himself delivered me to Tommy one day. I'd spent my last nickel on a Coke and was wondering if I was *ever* going to make an honest living when I looked up at the sky and instead found myself looking right into a grimy window in the heart of Hell's Kitchen, watching a galoot in his shirtsleeves and sporting a shiny watch ruffling around on his desk, looking for something in a stack of papers and empty fifths of whiskey. Even from the sidewalk I could tell he was perturbed, throwing things and stomping his feet and making a great big racket.

Most girls would've run away, but I just mustered up my courage, walked right in the front door, up the stairs, through the *conspicuously* empty space where there ought to have been a secretary, and into the office where Tommy was standing half naked and angry, and I asked, "What can I do for ya?"

Tommy just about jumped through the plaster ceiling, and when he landed in his big boots, he said, "A green folder with a coffee stain at the corner," and sat down hard in his leather chair, the cushion letting out a big burp of air and about a million dust mites that'd one day grow to be a thorn in my side.

It took me about three seconds to see that coffee stain peeking out from underneath his desk, and when I swooped down to get it, Tommy caught me by the arm, and I'd be lying if I said that my stomach didn't do a Tilt-A-Whirl.

"I can't afford to pay you much," he said through his teeth, his face just inches from mine.

I looked him right in the baby blues and told him that all I needed was sixty dollars a week, which would cover my living expenses and my rent, and maybe, if he was kind, a kitty at the office so I could buy a few sandwiches for lunch. A man like Tommy is much easier to deal with when his stomach isn't griping.

"Sixty dollars a week?" he roared back, letting go of my wrist, but I held firm as I stood and whacked that missing folder right down on his desk, now a reminder of what I could do that he couldn't.

He was trying to cut the figure of a rough-and-tumble boy, but the piece on his wrist was the genuine article—I could tell from across the desk—so I figured at the very least he could afford to keep me on for a month or so. The room I rent is only fourteen dollars a week because it doesn't have a window, but he didn't need to know that.

"Mister, if you want a girl to show up powdered and smiling and *alive* every day, she's gotta live at a place that's nice and safe and clean. And that costs more than you think, this day and age." I put my hands on my hips to let him know that I wasn't budging from my price *or* his office.

He must've considered it a reasonable argument.

"What's your name, Dollface?"

"Viviana Valentine."

"That can't be your real name," he mocked.

"Swear on the Bible, up and down, it is, and I got the Social Security card now to prove it," I said, and I caught the first of many laughs starting to spread across my boss's face. "And you are?"

"Tommy Fortuna."

"And what is it that you do here, Tommy Fortuna?"

"I'm a private investigator."

"That's rich, coming from a man who couldn't find a folder."

"Swear on the Bible, up and down, I am, and I have the New York State license in my pocket to prove it, Miss Valentine."

"Well, then, nice to meet you, Tommy Fortuna, PI. I think I'm your new girl Friday."

He must've agreed, because he shook my hand, sent me out front to dust off the typewriter, and told me to get myself put. And I've been put ever since.

★   ★   ★

Thanks to the endless light of a New York summer, it was still a beautiful day when I popped onto the sidewalk and started heading back toward my apartment building.

I've grown pretty sharp over the years in the city, and of course, as soon as I got to the corner, my eyes scanned the crowd and focused on one man toeing the opposite curb.

I never saw a real one, but I swear it, that dirty old man had eyes like a wolf.

He was stalking this pretty little thing standing in front of him on the sidewalk. A big, wide street, sure, but I could still see him. Dirty face, but not the kind you get just from living. *Mean* dirty.

She must have been new, you know, walking with a shoulder bag like that, not even paying attention. Not that anyone deserves to get their earnings pinched, of course, but my mama would have said she was as innocent as an angel but one great big fathead, bless her. I could see him put his ratty claws right in top there and pluck something out. Not too much movement, just quick, like a rattlesnake. He didn't even take the time to shove her coin purse in the pocket of his coveralls. She just kept carrying on like she didn't feel any of it, and I knew right then and there that she couldn't've been in the city longer than forty-eight hours, to not be able to feel the weight change in her handbag when that great big, bulging coin purse was plucked right out of there. No girl in the city carries around that much metal—your back would be griping after just a few days.

The signal changed.

The girl and the big bad wolf both started moving, like nothing happened—a great big, yellow-eyed creep following a little innocent lamb who was none the wiser. And I felt the folks on my side start to cross, but I knew he was coming my way, so I waited, while all the men on their way to and from work bumped into me, not ever changing their course.

The wolf was picking up speed as the crowds moved, and he was watching for something else, so he didn't see me keeping an eye on him. Who am I, really? Just some dame who looks like she grew up in the sticks because, honest to God, I did, and I won't ever shake the look, no matter how much I might want to. But I've been here in New York City long enough to spot a bad man coming my way down the sidewalk, and I was ready for him.

He was rushing my way, that big mean face looking so pleased with himself, licking his lips like he had himself a great big lamb dinner with all the fixings, dirty fingernails stroking the satin cloth that held so many quarters, dimes, and nickels. I just popped out my right shoe, and he went flying, scattering his catch all over the gummy sidewalks and cursing a blue streak as he got the wind knocked out of him good and proper. He didn't even have the mind to put out his hands as he went crashing to the ground, scraping his cheek on the pavement and some bone in his face making a nice, loud crack.

I tapped the new girl on the shoulder just as she swanned by me.

"You're gonna want to pick that up, hon," I said as sweetly as I could. "It's all yours."

She must've been real green, because instead of just bending down and picking it all up or kicking that wolf a little bit right there in the ribs, what do you know, she started bawling. It was nothing to cry about—maybe some of the people around us had picked up a few of the coins, but they couldn't have gotten more than a buck. But she was blubbering on and on, so—with one foot on the wolf's back to keep him pinned—I just scooped up as much as I could and pushed it back into the bag she was letting dangle in the wind for all the world to snitch from.

By now we'd drawn a crowd, and a sweaty-looking cop in dark blue wool was one of them.

"Officer," I said, "I saw this man pinch this sweet girl's wallet across the street. He tripped when he got over here, and the whole thing went a-scattering." The cops like it when you play innocent little girl, and after the past few years, I knew just how to turn any one of those lugs into soup.

Since now was the time to look a hero in front of not one, but two simpering dames, the cop just hoisted the dirty man off the sidewalk. The wolf was bleeding from his snout as the cop marched him down the street without more than a gruff, "You'll have to come too, miss," to the crying girl.

I never get a thank-you, but I'm used to it by now. The traffic lights cycled, and I crossed the street, heading back home.

★ ★ ★

Home is Mrs. Svitlana Kovalenko's girls-only boarding house, where I've been ever since I moved to the city. Mrs. K has a big brownstone in Chelsea, close enough to Tommy's place that I walk most days—unless it's snowing, raining, or Tommy tells me not to—and she keeps her girls in line. My room's got a good working radiator and nice thick walls to keep out most of the hubbub of the house—and most of the summer heat. Breakfast and dinner at seven, morning and night, and it's a pretty good life, all things considered.

Mrs. K is real sweet and has always looked out for me since I arrived in the city at an oh-so-sweet sixteen, so I try to brighten up her week when I can. On the way home, the Italian market was selling beautiful daisies, fifty cents for a whole great big handful, so I nabbed some, and the boy behind the counter wrapped them up. I'm good with money, I have to say, and I've made a nice little egg for myself, so it's easy for me to treat Mrs. K for everything she does for us girls. Nibbling on a greasy bag of zeppoli on my way home with the flowers, I caught Mrs. K sitting on the stoop, fanning herself and enjoying the afternoon in a black sundress with a parasol to match. I sat down next to my landlady and put my purse and keys next to my feet on the stairs.

"Howdy!"

"*Dobryden*, lovely girl," she said back, her smile growing larger as I handed her the flowers.

"Want a doughnut?" There were a few left tumbling around in the bottom of the greasy sack that I shook in her direction.

"No, thank you. I'm watching my figure." Mrs. K patted her stomach and smiled. "It is a beautiful day, *no*?"

"Yes, very. I feel like I should spend the rest of it outside!"

"Sit with me. Others will be coming home soon. Ah, first, let me put these in some water." Mrs. K hustled inside to find a vase for her daisies and to check on the house dinner, and I leaned back on to the hot brownstone to enjoy the breeze and the sounds of the Dodger game at Ebbets Field coming in over a radio somewhere on the block. By the sound of the crowd, they were doing okay.

I hadn't been too much younger than Tallulah Blackstone when I'd managed to make my way to the city; I'd paid for my one-way ticket out of Nowheresville after I squirreled away some hard-earned clams for a few years. It was rough doing, and I'd had my fair share of scrapes, but in the end, I wouldn't have changed it for anything.

I had my regular racket, and on top of that, I did almost anything a kid could do on the right side of the law: baby-sitting jobs, recycling cans, shopgirl stints, and just good, old-fashioned scrimping, saving, and even more scheming—I didn't look back for even one second as I rumbled my way in to Penn Station. My mama sends me letters now and then and says my father sends his love. They're good people who knew I was never going to stay.

Part of Mrs. K's rules was that every girl in her board-ing house had to work, and by that, she meant during the *daylight* hours, if you catch my drift, and I try as hard as I can to not get in her hair. She isn't too keen on me working in Hell's Kitchen or for a private investigator, and I think her hair would go full white if she knew what kind of hellraiser I'd been before I showed up on her doorstep. But she's met Tommy loads of times, and he's got her convinced I wouldn't ever do anything dangerous for him, though I don't think he got her blessing without a bottle of something good and laying on the compliments thick.

While some of the girls who have come and gone over the years got special permission at times to be waitresses or baby-sitters when things got tough, most of us, now, have lovely little nine-to-fives that keep the house respectable and Mrs. K's bills paid.

Betty is a nurse and has the big room in front on the second floor. She's addicted to radio soaps and writes weekly letters to her family upstate. Dottie—older than the rest of us, bordering on spinsterhood and running toward it with a smile on her face, from what I could tell—teaches second grade, and mostly keeps to herself. Phyllis models for one of the agencies uptown, and while Mrs. K didn't outright approve of the profession or the people of all sorts of stripes that she brings back to the house for late-night get-togethers, Phyllis makes more money than all us other girls combined and takes the two most expensive rooms on the top floor of the house, no problem. She's holding her breath on a gig that would bring her to Paris, which to me was about as likely as going to the moon.

On most summer evenings, the girls trickled in and out, coming home from work or heading back out with dates. Phyllis was uncurled like a cat in the sun, near the front door, but obsessively checked the wristwatch on her slender arm.

"Whatcha waiting for, Phyl?" Betty asked.

"I have a party tonight at nine," Phyllis replied. "It's going to take some time to prepare."

"Must be nice," Betty said back. "It's a work night."

"You can come if you want," Phyllis said. "It ought to be quite the shindig."

"You mean it?"

"Sure," Phyllis said. "Just be on your best behavior. You wanna come too, Viv?" She pointedly didn't address Dottie, but I don't think the teacher minded much, with her nose stuck into her grading.

"Sure—why not?" I'd been on the periphery of Phyllis's friend group before, and even if they weren't welcoming, it was good for a lark.

Dinner was nice and casual as we sat out front, sunning ourselves on the steps or in chairs we propped up on the sidewalk. Cold roasted chicken, with potato salad and corn on the cob to boot. Though Mrs. K still had plenty of habits left over from her old country, she threw herself headlong into American food, and all of us girls appreciated it, as did her teenage son, Oleks, who easily put away a whole bird himself. I was full and happy and sipping on a Coke when I spotted a familiar silhouette walking toward us on the sidewalk.

Betty saw too.

"Hey, sweetie, do a girl a favor?" she called out to me in a loud, clear voice that ricocheted up and down the front of the neighboring brownstones. "I can barely move, I'm so full. Will you run to my room and get my comb for me, Viv?"

Quick on her feet, that Betty, and she was doing her best to save me from the embarrassment.

"You bet, toots." I grinned back. I grabbed my purse and made a retreat into the house to my dark room. I knew Betty would fill me in on the details later, and for now I needed to take a powder.

There was no reason for Sandy to be coming back this way, and the whole house knew it.

NIGHT 1

I sat in my room, waiting for all the girls to come scurrying inside. I pored through my wardrobe, looking for anything that would suit for one of Phyllis's parties, and set about repairing a rip in the hem of my favorite dress.

There was no real sense in getting upset over Sandy's reemergence before I knew what was up, so I concentrated on not poking my fingers with the needle. Someone had come in from the dinner party on the sidewalk and hopped into the shower, and now the scent of lavender wafted through the brownstone. Sandy always gave off the stink of cedar; he said he had a gig cleaning up at a pencil factory in Greenpoint, but I pushed that out of my mind in order to think about poor Tally Blackstone, who probably got to take lavender baths every day, but was looking at a real bummer of a future standing and waiting for her at the end of a church aisle.

There were worse fates for a girl, but not too many, this day and age.

Tally Blackstone, the Diamond Princess. Everyone in the city knew her mama, Madeleine, passed away almost as soon as I'd moved to the city, when Tally must've been just a little girl, still in white dresses and pigtails and small enough to be photographed as a dutiful daughter whenever her daddy was off doing something for charity or watching horse races, or whatever else rich people do to get their mugs in the paper.

Madeleine was young, too—not much older than thirty when she died. It seemed like most of New York, class be damned, set their gums flapping on how they knew the dearly departed Mrs. Blackstone from the Club or boarding school or any old place they could think of, just so they could share in some of the romantic glory of dying young, rich, and beautiful.

Too many of Tommy's ne'er-do-well associates came by the office to talk about the shock of the city, and they said they were sad the missus never gave Mr. Blackstone a boy to take over the family business. Tommy agreed and laughed and laughed, but let me tell you, it burned me up to hear that kind of talk, so I gave Tommy a piece of my mind about him being down on Little Miss Blackstone as if she was no good to anyone just 'cause she had the bad luck to be born a dame. To his credit, there was never a peep like that out of Tommy again.

I remember half the city shut down for the funeral at St. Jean Baptiste, the front stairs of the building draped in white lilies, and people dressed in black. The police had to set up barricades outside, and they guarded the sidewalk from people trying to push their way in, but I couldn't ever tell if all the hubbub was because of grief or good old-fashioned morbid curiosity. When the better gossip rags ran features on who attended the big to-do and the wake afterward at the Waldorf-Astoria, complete with secretive snaps, the real crummy papers said the dearly departed woman was buried in Dior. Or was it Chanel? I always forget.

But then, wouldn't you know it, as soon as she turned sixteen a few years later, the young Miss Blackstone started showing up in the papers. Sometimes she was donating money to the VA while standing next to her old man in a prim and proper tweed suit and veil; other times she was caught at swing clubs, surrounded by admirers *en déshabillé,* as Tommy would say, trying to make me squirm. Tallulah Blackstone was a character, all right, and it didn't surprise me that the only way she was gonna marry a man of nearly sixty was if you dragged her to the church, kicking and screaming.

No, I couldn't blame the girl one *bit.*

★ ★ ★

There was a knock on the door jamb, and when I turned, I saw Betty's grinning face.

"Close call, huh, Viv?" Betty asked while pulling off her shower cap. "You doing okay?"

"Yeah, thanks so much, hon, for getting me out of there." She came over, and I gave her a pat on the hand. "What did Sandy want?"

"Exactly what you'd think," she said. "Stopped to chat and to get dirt on you."

"What'd you say?" I ran my fingers through my hair to, as Tommy would say, *"feign nonchalance,"* but it wasn't going to work, not with Betty.

"Whatever I could!" Betty said. "We didn't want to chat as much as you didn't. Don't worry. We said Tommy was gonna be 'round to pick you up, so Sandy skedaddled pretty quick."

"Ahh, you shoulda left Tommy out of it, Bets."

She looked like a scolded puppy. "It did the trick, though. Did Tommy give him a talking-to after . . .?" She gestured at my face, and my cheekbone smarted.

"No, the men in my life don't mix," I said. "Sandy always asked me questions, but then got as bristly as a hairbrush when I answered him, talking about Tommy and all his investigations. Good riddance to bad rubbish, I say."

"How long were you two even stepping out?" Betty asked. "It didn't seem like that long."

"It wasn't—two months, tops. And then he pulled his stunt," I said. "At least he showed his colors early."

"Well, you washed that man right outta your hair, you did. Come listen to programs with me while we get ready," Betty said. "You wanna call that dreamboat boss of yours to come with?"

"We're not even supposed to be at that party," I chided again, knowing full well she just wanted to find out if she should be sitting on the stoop, all casual-like, to catch Tommy's eye if and when he came rolling through.

I did sometimes offer cover for Tommy when he was digging for information in some of the more respectable joints about town. He liked to fluff my feathers and say he wouldn't be allowed into some of the finer establishments in the city without a lady on his arm. The girls in the house always seemed to think Tommy and I were more than just boss and secretary, but it still didn't keep Betty and Phyllis from batting their lashes at him when they could.

I'd never quite thought of ol' Tommy Boy as a catch, but the other girls sure did. He ticked off all the boxes of what Madison Avenue thought an American man should be, though. War hero, for one thing, who came back home after getting knocked out with some shrapnel to the hip at Midway. I'd seen the jagged white scars myself when I cleaned the man up after he played punching bag to an underestimated goon. And now he spends his days fighting for justice—or at least for the justice of whoever is signing his checks. And the cherry on top is that he isn't some stodgy cop, he was a twangie-boy private detective who knew all the best bars and clubs in the city, most of them unlisted and all of them guarded by a bouncer with a discerning eye.

Then, of course, there's no denying that he's a tall drink of water, with square shoulders and brown hair that stuck out every which way when he was thinking, and bright blue eyes. But I never get a good look at 'em because half the time they're swollen shut after he gets his lights knocked out sticking his nose somewhere it did *not* belong. Got a nasty habit of walking around the office in his undershirt whenever he worked up a sweat thinking about a new case, too, his suspenders hanging from his waistband and arms flapping in the wind.

But even I admitted that those arms *were* on the strong side. The man ate his Wheaties.

"What are you listening to tonight? I can swing by and do my hair while jawing with you."

"Just a rerun of *Light Up Time* with Frankie," Betty purred. I guess she carried a torch for dopes with blue eyes.

"Count me in!" I said.

After she left, I gathered my makeup kit and headed into Betty's room.

"Have an okay day today?" I asked, curling up on the floor in front of a pile of *Life* magazines. I opened one up and tossed a pile of hairpins into the center fold for safekeeping while I went about my twisting.

Betty looked a bit grave. "Well, someone had an emergency, and I had to handle an ambulance all by my lonesome for a while. Something happened at the fish market."

"Was it bad?"

Betty's face was grave. "There was a lot of screaming. And blood."

"Oh, Betty, I'm so sorry," I said. "You did everything you could. I'm sure that everyone's okay, but I'll keep my eyes on the paper for any details, see what might've happened."

"Got anything to take my mind off it? We've got five minutes until Frankie."

Part of me was leaping at the chance to tell Betty about Tallmadge and Tallulah Blackstone, but I felt as if I barely had any dirt to spill.

"Nothing new," I fibbed. "Summer in the city can be pretty dull. All the criminals get the hell outta Dodge, I bet."

We sat in silence, flipping through the magazines and painting our faces, until we heard the telltale fanfare on the radio and an announcer reminded us that there was never a rough puff with Lucky Strikes.

★ ★ ★

Betty snuck out quietly, and one whiff let me know what she was up to. I let out a holler.

"Betty, are you in my perfume again?" I knew I smelled L'air du Temps. Heels clicked back to her room, and a bright face was peering at me, more than a little bit sheepish.

"I am, but I promise I'll get you a new bottle," she said, shaking the empty glass vial in her hands. "I'm sorry, Viv, but I just need it to go dancing. It was a day."

Mrs. K bustled up the stairs, looking for me. "Letter," she said, shoving a thin, white piece of paper into my hand. "Oleks just found it under the door."

There was no envelope, so it must've been hand delivered. The edges were taped in just one spot in the center, so I knew both Oleks and his mother had read the contents—one of the corners was already creased and smudgy from where they'd pulled the flaps apart to snoop. I broke the Scotch tape and saw just a few lines in a bold, blue pencil:

Viv—

Don't ever run off like that again. I'm done with you when I say I'm done with you.

See you soon—you can bet on it.

Sandy

I crumpled the note into a ball and sighed. Mrs. K gave me a look.

"It's nothing," I assured her. "Absolutely nothing." I went downstairs to wait for Phyllis and get going to a party

I hoped would knock me from reality for at least a few hours.

★ ★ ★

The three of us descended the stoop into the hot night air.

"Where we heading, Phyl?" Betty asked. She was decked out in a bubblegum-pink frock that looked girlish and young with her bright, bottle-blonde French twist and green eyes. She wore white lace gloves and carried a white patent-leather clutch, and it took me a second to notice her dress was a bit worn around the edges, the crinoline overskirt noticeably mottled by a cigarette burn. But she looked plump and young and lovely, and I wondered if she had been prom queen at her high school, but didn't think it was the time to ask.

I'd done my best to dress for the occasion, in a deep-green, nipped-waist dress, whose belt I'd adorned with two golden dragon brooches Tommy'd been paid with after he figured out who was skimming off the top of an import-export business down in lower Manhattan. The dress itself was rayon but looked near enough to silk; the pins were gold plated, but not tarnished, and the whole look was finished off with black lace evening gloves and my favorite black patent peep-toes. Betty and Mrs. K oohed and aahed over my jewelry until Phyllis joined us outside, looking every inch the model that she was and stealing everyone's thunder.

Her stick-straight, jet-black hair matched her column dress, made of beautiful, real silk, with a wide boatneck, accentuated by a black chiffon cape that trailed from metallic silver bows on her shoulders, each bow bedazzled with rhinestones. Her shoes were open-toe black velvet, and she wore no gloves, letting a simple black velvet clutch dangle from her naked wrist. She looked like she belonged in the pages of *Vogue*.

"My beautiful butterflies," she purred, reaching out her hand to hail a cab. One appeared from the twilight, gliding to a stop at her feet. "I hope you enjoy cruises."

She said it as if I'd ever been on a boat before, and Betty grabbed my arm and squealed. Phyllis held the door open for us and forced Betty and me to do the awkward slide across the bench seat, keeping the curbside door all to herself.

"Chelsea Piers, please," she instructed, and the cabbie took off with a lurch.

★   ★   ★

It was hard to balance on my toes as I made my way down the wooden boards. Betty tripped and stumbled, but her nervous energy gave her superhuman drive to make it to the boat waiting for us in the river. Ideally, without twisting an ankle or losing a heel.

It was technically a yacht. Its rails were illuminated with thousands of lights, and a jazz band in matching tuxedos took up a portion of the deck. Dozens of women as gorgeous as Phyllis dotted the deck, some of them perched like songbirds in chairs and on lounges, everyone laughing, with bright smiles and perfectly coiffed hair. Even the stink of the river seemed to magically dissipate in the atmosphere of that much money.

Betty squealed. "Oh, my goodness, how on earth . . .?"

Even I was making the effort to keep my jaw from dropping open. I thought Tommy had dragged me to some pretty swanky parties in the name of getting good dirt over the years, but this was something else.

"An engagement party for one of the girls," Phyllis said, waving it off. Everyone at Mrs. K's had an outside group of friends and acquaintances, but Phyllis kept the most sets of "girls"—those in the boarding house, those who shared her agency, and other women who populated her artistic parties and social circle. "Cassandra managed to nab herself a minor du Pont."

"What's that?" Betty asked.

"You know those nylons you've got on?" Phyllis asked.

"Yeah . . ."

"His family invented them."

Betty let out a whistle.

Having driven home the importance of her social connections, Phyllis straightened her posture and proceeded down the gangplank, without even a hint of a wobble, until she caught a glimpse of the bride-to-be, whom she enveloped in cheek kisses and light hugs. Without making any introductions, Phyllis was absorbed into the crowd and somehow managed to disappear.

We followed, a candy-colored maiden and an emerald serpent, into a party of New York royalty.

★ ★ ★

A group of young men—from late teens to early twenties, and a handful of square-jawed thirty-somethings, all with slicked-back hair and manicured nails, all in perfectly fitted tuxedos—descended on Betty, and she was pleased as punch to be led to the wide stern of the boat, where raised tables dotted the edges of a dance floor. She stuck out like a sore thumb in her cotton-candy dress, but the boys on the boat seemed rather taken with the fresh meat.

I kept my eye on her and noticed a few men eyeing me while I just beelined for the bar.

It's always a bit risky to be a dame drinking alone, but I knew what was up. Two glasses of something, anything, *maximum*, and I reckoned I could jet to the cabstand up the block in less than a minute, if I ditched my shoes. Tommy taught me, first and foremost, to know my exits, and even though the gangplank was a narrow escape, the likelihood of anyone getting into any funny business here was pretty slim, considering the number of flashbulbs that were now sparkling like jittery fireflies from the boardwalk. The paparazzi were starting to trickle in.

An older man in white tie and white tails slid up behind the bar and gave me a kind smile. "And for you, miss?"

His politeness took me for a loop, considering the last time I went out, I was with Tommy, at a joint that catered to the polar opposite of New York City's social set. The barman at that dive called me "Toots" all night, and my order of white wine ended up being just a highball glass filled to the brim with dry vermouth. Neat.

"Oh, I'm not sure. What would you suggest?" When in doubt, ask the barman to decide so you don't look like a fool. The last thing I needed was to order a whiskey and get a sneer out of the hired help.

"Most seem to be enjoying the Champagne, miss."

Glad I let him make the decision—I'd never have thought to ask. The manicured man lifted a bottle of Champagne from an ice bucket, wiping off the green glass and the gold, shield-shaped label with a white linen napkin. The pale, straw-colored liquid fizzed and jumped as it swirled about a cut-crystal coupe. It wouldn't be my first sip of French Champagne, but it'd probably be my best.

"Miss." He handed the glass to me and I took it gently by the stem, hoping beyond hope that he didn't notice my cracked and bitten fingernails.

I leaned against the bar to survey the scene.

The gender split was mixed, maybe a few more young women Phyllis's, and presumably her friend Cassandra's, age. The parents and grandparents and their high-falutin' friends were seated, enjoying the band while politely chatting and dripping with heavy jewelry, none of it fake and all of it insured to the hilt, I assumed, based on the crowd. Even if a choker went into the murky drink of the Hudson River, no one would be out the cash.

There were no small children—likely all left at home with governesses, though there were a few teenage girls, who could be of marrying age if their parents agreed to let them marry before they came of age—or perhaps forced them to. But by and large, the population consisted of well-heeled twenty- to thirty-somethings, and the air was thick with Big Band music and expectations.

The trumpet wailed its way through every dance standard I could think of and a few numbers I couldn't quite place.

"Don't Get Around Much Anymore" blended into "Yacht Club Swing," with "Polka Dots and Moonbeams" taking it away into a slow dance. The band leader had clearly assessed the crowd—or, more likely, had been specifically instructed to stay away from anything too modern, too cool, too under-ground, or just plain too bebop.

Near the gangplank at the bow, there was a rustle, and the cameras lit up like the Fourth of July. The band slowed and began playing softly, just some little ditty that came to their heads, then stopped altogether; the upright bass took a breather from his constant thrum to shuffle his instrument out of the way of the moving crowd. Whispers made their way through the boat, and out of the corner of my eye, I watched as Cassandra hopped down from her seated perch on a table-top to scowl at whatever or whoever had decided to take the spotlight on her big night.

Dates and wives and women were left standing without accompaniment as a crowd of dinner jackets and Brylcreemed heads worked its way down the deck until the sea of fawn-ing admirers opened. And there, standing in the center of the crowd in ice-blue pleated silk, and with a silver mink stole trailing from her right shoulder to the ground, stood the debutante of all debutantes, Tallulah Blackstone.

She was, in all honesty, stunning, all Betty Grable legs and Jane Russell curves, every inch of her accentuated to attract attention. Shining chestnut curls were pinned in a twist by dazzling diamond clips, framing a translucently pale face with gleaming eyes. Her lips were painted the softest peach, a color so perfect for her that you couldn't even buy it at the counter at Bergdorf's. Her décolletage was bare, as were her arms to the wrist, where she stacked dozens and dozens of platinum bracelets that shone with pearls and aquamarines. And plenty more diamonds.

"Cassandra!" she shouted, enunciating every syllable with the accent only rich people manage to get. She tossed her arms to the air and the mink to the floor. Her wrists rattled with a gentle tinkle of metal on metal as she moved, though the luxuriant silk didn't make a rustle. "You beautiful girl!" Tally glided forward and embraced the stunned bride-to-be, holding her gently by the upper arms and kissing both her cheeks, like French aristocracy. Cassandra stood stock-still until the heiress let go.

"Oh, my, Miss Blackstone," Cassandra politely cooed to her social superior, a raging blush breaking out over her face and a hint of tears in her eyes. A man stood at her side, pale and a little sweaty. Sipping my Champagne, I imagined the minor du Pont was far better acquainted with Tally Blackstone than his intended. Cassandra was trying not to stir the pot, and her eyes were shifty.

"It's Tally, you know that. Aren't we old friends?" she said, clipping her words just short of sniping at the girl. But the storm quickly left her face, and she was back to her beautiful, pearlescent smile. "Congratulations on landing such a wonderful catch. And don't worry, my love, I didn't *exactly* show up empty-handed. Your gift will be delivered to your townhouse in the morning. It's for your wedding night, sweetheart. I know you'll love it. Chinese silk." Tally turned and walked toward me, leaving Cassandra to blush and smolder.

As Tally wafted toward my general direction at the bar, it was all I could do to get out of her way in time.

"I like your dragons," she said, her eyes starting at my toes and beaming up the length of me, stopping at my brooches before meeting my eyes. She held my gaze for a moment, daring me to speak to her, before turning her attention to the barkeep. "Champagne, *s'il vous plaît.*"

He delivered with lightning speed.

"To Cassandra and her *Prince* Charming. Cheers!" she shouted to the frozen revelers on the boat. They responded with a roar, and the horn player took it as his cue to start up again.

Tally looked around briefly before tapping an anonymous gentleman on the shoulder. "Excuse me," she purred. "Would you mind grabbing my fur?" She glanced in the direction of the dead animal, and the man scurried to scoop it up and bring it back to her crooked left arm, where it draped like a waterfall. "Thank you, dear." With a slight turn of the shoulder, she indicated that that was the closest he would ever be to Tallulah Blackstone's bare-naked skin ever again.

Tally continued to sip the French alcohol, surveying the party, all the while looking quite pleased with herself and the commotion she'd caused.

For just a few moments, I was left gaping at the debutante, before I felt a tuxedo sidle up next to me. I sighed, ready to turn and tell him to scram, but the breeze shifted just enough so that instead I smiled. Cigars and coffee and a hint of old whiskey.

"Hey there, ol' Tommy boy," I said before turning to find my boss standing at my elbow.

"Dollface." He leaned in close to give me a peck on the cheek, his skin smooth without a hint of a five-o'clock shadow. The kiss lingered as he whispered into my ear clandestinely. "You're looking lovely tonight. See anything interesting?"

He held a crystal coupe that matched my own, but his was nearly empty, so he placed it on the bar to get an almost immediate, magical refill from the bartender, who eyed us with a rising level of suspicion. The man stopped just short of demanding, "You're not from 'round here," like a barkeep in a John Wayne movie.

I'll give the old rough-and-tumble boy this: Tommy cleaned up good. He was in full black tie, square shoulders outlined in the night by twinkling city lights. He might have looked like a million bucks, but I knew he had gotten the dinner jacket on a five-finger discount, because I was the one who had sewed up the ripped lining. In its previous life, it had been used to hide pilfered ones and twos at a gambling den that also ran girls, which Tommy had busted up a few years ago in Little Italy. Domenico, the fixer who ratted out his boss to Tommy, snitched threads from the back room before the police took stock. I never did ask what else the rat managed to filch. Probably the ones and twos from the lining.

"Did you see our princess's decree?" I asked.

"I did." He sipped his Champagne and eyed me over the rim of his glass, waiting to hear what else I had to spill.

"And you're wondering how I'm here?" Tommy knew all well and good that I was not usually a member of this jet-set crowd.

"No, I already saw your housemate Phyllis holding court among the du Pont cousins on the stern. Tell Mrs. K to get her adverts ready—that one's aiming to get hitched, and fast." Tommy's eyes get real sweet when he smiles. He placed his glass on the bar and signaled to the bartender that he would take no more refills. "I'm heading back to the crowd. You give a holler if you need me, okay?"

"Gotcha, boss."

"Goodnight, Dollface."

With another kiss on the cheek, he disappeared like handsome mist into the blackness, leaving behind the scent of cigars and whiskey.

With a sigh, I downed my Champagne in a gulp, winked at the bartender, and went to find a place where I could powder my nose. Maybe for the rest of the night.

★ ★ ★

"You were standing next to Tallulah *Blackstone!*" Betty shrieked as we piled into the back of a cab. Her hair had come out of its pins after a particularly energetic bop on the dance floor. Slamming the door shut, I noticed, but didn't point out, that her lipstick was also quite smudged. Phyllis had found me after the great commotion and Tommy's disappearance, to let me know that she'd be spending the night with Cassandra at the bride's parents' home, comforting the girl as the bride-to-be flipped her lid about the heiress crashing her party. Phyllis said Betty and I should grab a cab without her. Sooner rather than later.

"Tally came to stand next to *me,*" I said. I wasn't quite as impressed as my housemate, and wanted to make it clear that

I wasn't fawning after the gossip-rag girl. But Betty was as hopped up as a canary on bennies.

"That was bonkers! And she was all decked out. Did you see that dress? I first saw it in *Vogue* months ago, while I was at the hairdresser's. *Christian Dior.*" She put on a snooty French accent to say the designer's name, so it sounded like *Kwis-tee-ahn Dee-aww.* "How many diamonds do you think she had on tonight? What was it like standing *near* her?"

I could tell Betty was going to get miles out of this gossip on the ward tomorrow, or die trying.

"Like standing near anyone else," I said. "It's not like her money is contagious. She's a gorgeous girl, but that display was some corny business. Imagine how it felt to be Cassandra!"

"But she'll be able to say Tallulah Blackstone gave her a wedding present!"

"Who would want *that* kind of a present from Tallulah Blackstone? Or anyone?" I looked at her.

The girl fell quiet, but I could tell she was still flipping her wig, as if the run-of-the-mill millionaires she'd been party-ing with—and smooching—before Tally arrived were noth-ing special.

I pulled a notebook out of my evening bag and licked my pencil, scribbling down everything I could remember from the night, in order to tell Tommy *my* observations in the morning.

DAY 2

I woke up the next morning, nursing a small hangover, and I really wasn't in a great mood to head out to the office. Both Tallmadge and Tallulah Blackstone had put a sour taste in my mouth, and I hoped Tommy's case would be a quick one so there would be no more chance encounters with either of them.

Now, Champagne goes right to your head, I'd heard, but I'd rarely had the opportunity to try it out. I ignored the scent of frying bacon coming from Mrs. K's kitchen in the basement, the thought of the hot meat making my head go all whirligig.

I dressed for the day as quickly as I could, in my comfiest blue-and-white-striped sundress and worn-in saddle shoes, and pulled out my sunglasses—white pearlescent Lucite with rhinestones at the hinges, which I had splurged on the summer before.

I was preoccupied with thinking about the Blackstones as I skipped down Mrs. K's steps, and my toes slipped on something on the stoop. Catching myself before I fell and kissed the sidewalk, I found my keys where I'd left them the night before in my rapid flight from Sandy. Thank goodness I'd found them, or else it would have taken forever to pick my way into Tommy's office, which was locked up about as tight as Fort Knox.

I hightailed it to my favorite Italian bakery, to feed the banging monster clamoring in my temples, looking for a breakfast something that was the exact opposite of Mrs. K's bacon and eggs.

"*Ciao, bella!*" The sweaty man behind the counter gave a wave. He was far too friendly for the hour in the morning, but then I remembered he probably woke up at midnight to get started on his day.

"*Ciao*, Emilio!" I smiled. "Hot enough for you this morning?"

"My son—he does not understand! I am an old man. I cannot stay by the ovens much longer," Emilio replied, shaking his head but still peeking to see if his theatrics were having the proper effect on me. "But he—he says he had to become an accountant. Who am I to stop him?" By the look of his eyes, I could tell Emilio had, in fact, tried his absolute best to keep his son from pursuing a desk job, and would probably never stop.

"That's the way the cookie crumbles sometimes," I said with a shrug. "One black coffee and *un ciambella, por favore.*"

The old man smiled and handed me my pastry. "*Ciao, bella.*"

"*Ciao*, Emilio. I'll see you soon, okay? Don't work too hard." The man smiled and waved, and prepared his sob story for a mother with two small children, entering the bakery as I held the door open for her.

I walked my way to the office, the sidewalks filled only with my fellow working stiffs. The secretaries—fleets of us scurrying, trying to make it to our desks before the boss could arrive—kept their eyes down and hands on their purses, a few nibbling at toast squirreled away from the breakfast table. Butchers and florists dumped buckets of dirty water at our feet, never noticing if they splashed our new satin pumps with water flecked with blobs of fat or slimy, rotting leaves. The sidewalks were a river of garbage, and the distinctive sound of scraping push brooms provided the rhythm of the neighborhood. The diesel engines of moving trucks pumped plumes of smelly, black smoke into the sky, and the stationary vehicles unloaded pallets of frozen meat and cans into the street with deafening booms and plenty of yelling from the men. One lone old man with a wheelbarrow dumped ice on top of dead fish, the day's catch already smelling in the heat.

It was a quiet Thursday morning, and it felt like every person in New York City who could leave was gone, probably heading for the shoreline to get a breather from the suffocating blanket of hot, muggy city air. Only bakers, cabbies, cops, maids, waitresses, bus drivers, street sweepers, and secretaries—all the people who kept the wheels of society turning—remained behind, to keep the place clean and tidy 'til the white-collar set dared to return.

I turned onto a narrow street lined with three- and four-story brownstones. I couldn't imagine Hell's Kitchen ever being considered chic, but there still was something charming about the faded awnings, rusty fire escapes, and forever-damp sidewalks in places where people had to work for a living.

Tommy's building stuck out for the fact that it had obviously been crammed in—it took up the narrow space between two larger, older buildings, the front of it barely twenty-five feet wide. It looked as though it had been squeezed from a toothpaste tube to fill in the cracks of the city, and surprised that the trick had worked.

Because there were few windows and the roof was shaded by the bigger buildings on either side, the lobby was cool, the tile floor giving the whole vestibule a nice chill like an icehouse. A narrow staircase hugged the right side of the entryway, with creaking, splintering wood boards that looked like they'd give way any day.

I knew the downstairs tenant—a Mr. De Lancey, an architectural draftsman and real piece of work—had skittered off with his family to the Poconos for a few weeks. The lawyer—a Mr. McAllister, who stank like alcohol, maybe because of all the ambulances he chased, lived at the top and had roof access. He tried his damnedest to avoid any and all contact with the other tenants, who were literally beneath him. He'd managed to take a family place in the Hamptons, though I'd wracked my brain as to how he could afford it, and had come up empty.

All that was left were Tommy and me, the working stiffs, right in the middle.

Up the stairs and across the mezzanine, once I was on the second floor, I found the heat everyone else had escaped. But

I choked through the humidity, and winging open the door, I heard a scrape.

Someone'd shoved an envelope through the crack between the door and the floor.

I held my paper coffee cup in my teeth and swooped down to nab it, flicking on the ceiling fan with my free hand, then tossed the envelope on my desk for Tommy to open when he got in. The fan immediately began to squeak and sent great big balls of dust floating in the sunlight filtering through the blinds.

"He'll have to get his own damn coffee," I said, scowling at the percolator and hot plate. There was no way I was adding extra heat to the office today.

I couldn't wait to hear what Tommy thought was going on with Tally. The case seemed pretty open and shut to me—if there wasn't a serious beau that her father didn't know about, there were plenty of boy toys in the wings for a young girl livin' the high life. Obviously, she didn't want to marry someone almost old enough to be her grandpa, or give up whatever rights she might have to oodles of green. All Tommy had to do was get the girl to spill her beans. I don't even like sharing my L'air du Temps perfume with Betty when she's got a hot and heavy date, so the idea of Tally giving her fortune to a future hubby? No, thank *you*.

I set about compiling my daily to-dos. Tommy had been alone in his office for so much of the day yesterday, all my papers were in order and all the humdrum busywork of invoicing, mailing, filing, noting, and depositing was finished. But generally speaking, when the easy stuff was done, it was time to start on my worst project of all: tidying Tommy's private office. The swamp that had gotten me into this whole situation.

First thing, as soon as I was in the door, I pulled out my bucket from the coat closet, checking its contents. Rubber gloves, a ratty feather duster, my canister of Bon Ami for the glued-on gunk, and my trusty sprinkler of Renuzit for all the stink that that man somehow managed to work into the place, what with those sweaty nights and horrible cigars. I kept begging for him to spring for a Hoover, but no luck yet. I grabbed the mop, broom, and pan from the back corner of the closet and kicked the door shut with my toe.

Tommy's private office was more than twice the size of the front, and he liked it dark. He owned no more furniture than his desk, his beat-up leather swivel, and two wooden chairs for clients. Those chairs were straight out of a principal's office too—my guess is, Tommy liked to keep some of his less savory guests *un*comfortable.

But don't get the impression the place was empty—*no, no, no.* That garbage dump was usually filled with mountains of old newspapers and files not meant for my eyes, and you never knew when there was going to be a mysterious package, all tied up with string, taunting you from the corner. Once I had walked into the office and nearly died of fright when there was a painting of a rather unashamed lady, sitting propped up against Tommy's desk, where no one could miss it.

On twisting the squeaky knob to fling open the door, it bounced right back into my mug, hitting a great big something Tommy had left in the middle of the floor the night before. I put my back into it and shoved—nothing was going to keep me out—and I steeled my nerves for another sighting of flesh.

The door pushed open enough for me to get my little self on through, my toe hitting something squishy and soft right beyond the threshold. Truth be told, I dropped everything and let out one helluva scream.

A man I had never seen before was lying there, right in the middle of the floor. And from the looks of things, he wasn't breathing.

I didn't even stop to check to see if the man was alive. All I knew was that I had to get someone here on the double. Tommy and I were on friendly enough terms with most of the local coppers, even though we didn't care for police detectives coming and snooping around under normal circumstances. But when you've got a mysterious lug lying flat on his back on the floor of your boss's locked office, it isn't normal circumstances, and there was no choice but to bring in the boys in blue.

I ran back to my desk, and shaking like a wet puppy, I spun the rotary and waited for my connection to the closest station house.

The line had barely stopped ringing before I cut off the desk sergeant announcing the name of the precinct.

"There's a body at Tommy's! On Fiftieth!" I shrieked. Putting the situation into words made my blood run colder, so I sat my keister down in my desk chair while all my limbs went numb.

The stoic, gruff voice on the end softened just a bit. "Aw, damn. It isn't Fortuna, is it, Viviana? You hold on tight—I'll get some guys there on the double."

I couldn't tell which officer had picked up, but I was calmed to hear that he at least knew me. There's nothing normal about anyone calling to report a dead body, but he wouldn't think I was a total crack-up.

"It ain't Tommy," I said, a sob hitching in my throat. "I don't *think* it's Tommy. I only got a glance. I don't know who the heck he is. I ain't never seen him before in my life!" I knew I was beyond flustered because I was speaking bad English. I glanced over my shoulder toward Tommy's cracked door. It seemed quiet back there, and I could make out the crown of the man's head and an ear.

No blood, I didn't think. *But head wounds, and bodies, almost always come with blood.*

"Okay, Viv, just calm down. We got some flatfoots heading your way now. You wanna stay on the horn with me 'til they get there?"

"You bet I do," I said, trying to get my composure back. "I didn't look around or nothin', so I don't know if anyone's still here with me!" I calculated that if a prowler hadn't attacked me yet, he likely wouldn't do it while I was on the phone with the cops, but in this day and age, you could never know. And in my saddle shoes and sundress, I wasn't exactly dressed for a rumble, but I grabbed my letter opener just in case.

I heard boots running up the stairs. Without even trying to see if it was unlocked, the first cop slammed open the door, splintering the jamb, and it went careening back so fast it hit the wall and shattered Tommy's window, a great big pile of glass and gold leaf tinkling to the floor.

"You okay, ma'am?" the copper heaved.

I rolled my eyes, pinned the receiver between my ear and shoulder, and thumbed the sweaty beat cop to the back room. "The stiff's in there, buddy."

"What was that crash? You okay, Viv?" asked the voice on the phone.

"Yeah, yeah, I'm just fine," I said, picking up a pencil with my free hand and writing down the series of events in the likely case that someone asked me what happened: *9:06 AM: Copper broke Tommy's window.* "Same can't be said for the office, though. Someone's gonna owe Tommy a new door. And last time it was replaced it cost fourteen fifty."

"Sorry, but that isn't my department. But give me a call back if you need any more help. You can expect a detective to show up soon too."

"Oh, yeah, I'm sure. But you know me, I know how to *handle* a detective."

I hung up on the desk sergeant as he chuckled to himself.

Turning around, I watched the two cops try to push the door to Tommy's office open, against the body. Eyeing their backsides, I determined that if there was a thug lying in wait, I could outrun at least one of the policemen, so that worked in my favor.

But they weren't exactly champing at the bit to get their eyes on the carcass, and the one that stormed in now, guns practically a-blazin', looked a little green around the gills. The heat and humidity of the office wasn't helping me keep a cool head either. I breathed in deep, and there was a new scent mingling with the usual office stink of cigars, coffee, and whiskey, and I recognized it as the tang of panic.

"You big, strong men need a hand? I got farther than that all by my lonesome!"

The two junior police officers—neither one of them looking old enough to even shave—blushed darker than Phyllis's face after a photo shoot.

"No, ma'am," one said. This one was tall with black hair and a square jawline, who had that comforting scent of Aqua Velva about him, and was the kind of young man who moved up the ranks because he looked good in a uniform. I took a moment because he did look *awful* good. He took off his hat and held it between his mitts, standing as straight as an arrow.

"*Ma'am?* Do I look married to you?" I realized I was still clutching my letter opener like a shiv, and I let it clang back down onto my desk.

His blush went darker.

"No, Miss . . .?" Guess the sergeant didn't radio all the necessary details before sending him off to Tommy's—including the name of the dame who rang in the report.

"Miss Valentine," I said, extending my hand. "Viviana Valentine."

The tall, dark, and handsome fellow's hand was almost on mine when he was beat out by his flush-faced compatriot, sweating out a fog of what must've been half a bottle of Old Spice. This one was shorter than me by a long shot and fair skinned, with a rash of orangey curls sticking out from under his uniform cap. And, as he gripped my fingers, I realized he also had clammy palms.

"That's a hell—a *heck* of a name there, Miss Valentine," said the ginger.

"Easy to remember too. You are?"

"Officer O'Malley, miss," stammered the one still holding my paw. His fingers tightened around mine as he spoke. Guess he was nervous.

"And you, bub?" I winked at the tall fellow, and O'Malley's hand gripped mine harder.

"Officer Leary, Miss Valentine," he said. He went to shake my hand but saw that his partner still had me in a vise grip, so his hand fell back to his hat brim.

"Okay, Officers Leary and O'Malley, now why don't you get to doing what you came here for?"

Leary put his hat back on and stalked back to Tommy's door, with O'Malley skittering close behind. The tall and the short met, planted their feet, and shoved hard. The body on the other side slid along the wood floor.

To all of our collective surprise, it also let out a breathy groan.

"Aw, gee whiz, he's still alive!" O'Malley said. Whatever color there was in his pale face now left it, and I thought he was ready to upchuck on Tommy's dirty floor, just adding to the whole mess.

"You just graduate La Salle?" I asked, eyeing my mop.

"No, Miss Valentine. Regis. Class of '48."

"Close enough. You want to use the phone to call the ambulance?"

"Yes, please, Miss Valentine," Leary replied. "They're expecting a corpse, and I don't want them to dillydally."

I led Leary back to my desk to use the phone, and left O'Malley crossing himself in Tommy's office.

As Leary dialed, I heard another set of shoes coming up my stairs. Not heavy rubber soles like the flatfoots, but leather, tapping away at the tile.

"Miss Valentine, what do you have here?"

The voice was so low it thrummed through my chest and almost made my newly set curls frizz. It was a familiar purr—just loud enough to ring through every corner of Tommy's office and make the two officers stand up straight and stop their fretting.

"If it isn't Detective Jake Lawson," I said, turning to stare at his familiar mug.

He was dressed as he always was—far too casually for his title, I'd say, in wide-legged pants; a plaid jacket in all the right shades of green, to bring out his eyes; and an open-collared shirt, like he was going to be stopped at any moment by *Esquire* and asked for his thoughts on men's fall fashion. Even though it was darn near ninety degrees outside, he didn't shine with sweat. He had cultivated a sandy Clark Gable mustache since the last time I'd seen him, but all that manufactured charm sure was wasted on me. He politely removed his straw fedora as he entered, and another quick sniff revealed that he was still addicted to Vitalis Hair Tonic.

"It's me, babe—your knight in shining armor. What's going on? Tommy get into some trouble last night after hours?" That horrible mustache just highlighted his crooked smile, keen as he was to catch Tommy up to some dirty tricks.

"Don't 'babe' me," I said. "And you better head on in there—you got a live one who might need some looking after, and all poor Father O'Malley seems able to do is anoint the dead."

That got Detective Lawson to put a sock in it pretty quickly, and he tossed his hat onto my desk, to hurry back into Tommy's office as medics ascended the stairs, clean and shiny and both looking like the Good Humor man, carrying a canvas stretcher between them.

"In there, fellas." I motioned to my growing audience, the scent of antiseptic and three different men's colognes filling the office and making me slightly dizzy. "Alrighty. Who wants coffee?"

No one answered, but I set about making the pot.

★ ★ ★

"And you said you never seen him before?" Lawson asked. The medics had left with the man hours earlier—who never managed to make another peep—and promised to ring both Tommy's office and the precinct when he regained consciousness.

So far, not a single jingle.

Police photographers came and went too, snapping every inch of both the reception area and Tommy's office in black and white until Lawson gave them the boot. Tommy wasn't going to like this kind of invasion of his privacy, but I didn't have much of a choice. A big pile of sooty, spent flashbulbs was sitting on my desk.

"I told you a thousand times already, he's a mystery to me." I tried my best to look cavalier and picked up a nail file from my desk, but I'd bitten my nails down to the quick while no one was looking, and now there was just no point.

"But you two specialize in mysteries. And I should know—you've stuck your noses in plenty of *my* cases over the years. When's Tommy showing up, anyhow?" Lawson was leaning against a tall filing cabinet, pencil stub in his manicured hand, leafing through the pages of his notebook like he was gonna catch me in a fib. He was playing cool, but the purple bags under his eyes didn't lie. If someone didn't show up with answers by the morning, this case would forever sit open. He could fingerprint every surface in here, but there wasn't going to be much else to go on.

"Beats me," I said with a shrug as I made another round, pouring him and his pair of young cops fresh cups of coffee, the three of them each holding in their mitts one of Tommy's chipped coffee mugs. I've tried to scour those mugs clean a million times, but they still had brown-as-tar rings around the bottom. I was out of Chock full o'Nuts now too, so I hoped they were going to leave soon; or else I'd have to call the grocer that delivered, and that would just mean more dirty shoes trodding across my floor and more good-for-nothing men in my office.

"Aw, yeah? He tell you to say that?" Lawson gave me an eye that implied he was just pulling my leg, but after the morning I'd had, a gentleman should know when a lady just wasn't in the mood. I had pretty thin patience for cops to begin with, plus I hadn't been to the bathroom all day.

"Oh, for the love of Christ, Jake Lawson," I said, slamming the aluminum percolator down and watching, out of the corner of my eye, O'Malley cross himself because of my blaspheming. "You know Tommy doesn't stick to a schedule, and I ain't his keeper. Or his mother, or his *girl*."

"Testy, testy, Viviana Valentine. What's got you all worked up?" Jake Lawson strolled over to me and brushed a curl off my forehead, and if I hadn't been so worked up about Tommy, I would've slugged him right in the kisser and gone to the slammer with a smile on my face. Detective Lawson had never laid a finger on me while Tommy was within line of sight, but if Tommy wasn't here to stop bad behavior, Lawson usually saw it as a green light to do as he pleased, and what gave him more joy in the world than anything else was riling up girls, with a strategic pinch to the backside or an accidental caress of hand to breast.

"I'm worried for my boss, Detective," I said, breathing through my nose to the count of ten as his hands lingered and I waited to see where they'd land. "If he doesn't show up, how am I supposed to make my rent?"

This got a guffaw out of Lawson, and he shoved his roving mitts into his pockets. The laugh forced an echo of a chuckle out of O'Malley. Leary stood all the straighter—the strong and silent type, I supposed, the kind that's just strong and silent enough not to ruffle his boss's feathers.

The detective took a deep breath. "What kind of cases are you working right now?"

"Nothing that'd leave a body."

"Oh, yeah? I know Tommy's been poking his nose into Tino—don't deny it."

"Sure, poking, but nothing more!" My blood was up. "Tino's ties to the Sicilians are strong as new rope. Tommy's dealt with the mob, of course he has, but Tino is too much for him right now, and even he knows it."

"Okay, Viv. Because we all know he's got eyes on Tino the Conderoga, and if you see him before I do, tell him to back off."

"You want to take him in. I get it." I folded my arms over my chest and glared.

"If that's what you want to believe. Let's let this little girl be for a while," the detective said, dropping his mug on the filing cabinet and plucking his straw hat off my desk. "Can't work with women when they start to get hysterical."

He strode out of the office, and O'Malley followed. Leary stopped for a moment in the doorway.

"Miss, would you like someone to walk you home? You could ring the station later and . . . someone would be happy to assist you." There was just enough hesitation in his voice to let me know this wasn't official police protocol with regards to dames deemed crazy who were stuck all alone at a crime scene.

"No, thank you, Officer, though it's gentlemanly of you to ask."

He nodded and quietly closed the door behind himself before realizing it didn't have any glass, then beat feet down the stairs.

As soon as I heard the front door close below in the lobby, I blew a raspberry in Detective Jake Lawson's general direction and set about tidying up.

★ ★ ★

I was just scooping the last pile of window glass into the bin when I looked up and saw that it was pitch-dark outside. No one had yet called to let me know about the man who had nearly died this morning amid Tommy's ever-growing cache of empty bottles, books on knives, mutilated hats, and gossip rags he sometimes used to cajole his marks into giving up their dirt.

There was no way I was going to scrub up the whole office, knowing Lawson would think I was hiding evidence, but a little sweep-and-dust action made me feel like I had some control over my surroundings. I peeked into Tommy's space and was relieved that at first glance there wasn't a big ol' pool of blood on the floor, which would only bring the bugs and a whole new mess to deal with in the morning. The scene behind the door—which I realized now was an honest-to-goodness crime scene—would have to stay what it was, for now.

And my boss had never shown.

It wasn't far outside the realm of possibility to have Tommy disappear the day after getting a new case, but that wasn't to say I liked it when he did. He was like a bloodhound on the scent when he got a new mystery, off like a shot and leaving me to collect the pieces. Without a doubt, he'd show up bright and early tomorrow morning, spouting off information about Tally Blackstone that every scandal-hungry hackette in the city would give her left hand to know, and I'd have to scurry around behind him, taking dictation and grabbing every last piece of evidence he pulled out of his pockets and dropped onto my desk while I tried to make sense of things as he yammered.

It was his usual habit.

But it wouldn't be until he'd exhausted his supply of information that I'd be able to get a word in edgewise about the mystery man left to groan away on his floor while he was gone.

I went to the window ledge and slid a great big stack of yellowing, mildewy newspapers onto the floor, where they landed with just about the same amount of order they'd had when all stacked up. Between them and the radiator was a piece of plywood we used to fit over the broken window in Tommy's door.

I didn't feel like staying the night to make sure no one would come in and pilfer the typewriter and any other treasure they could find, so I reached into the bottom drawer of my desk for a small toolbox Tommy had stashed there ages ago. He'd fixed a few rickety chairs in front of me, but I'd also seen him use the monkey wrench to get information out of a reluctant stoolie. A few threatening whacks of heavy steel against the palm of his hand and the reluctant pigeon would always sing, though truth be told, I'd never seen Tommy actually make the connection between someone else's flesh and the greasy metal. Maybe it did after I went home.

I plucked out the hammer and fished out a few rusty nails I knew were swimming at the bottom. Pinching them between my lips I tacked the plywood over the broken window. The last one went in crooked and stained with Max Factor Hollywood's Coral Glow, but it was the best I could do.

I went into Tommy's office and picked up his empty wastebasket. I'd have to confess to my crime-scene tampering should that piece of work Detective Jake Lawson show his face here again. I took it to my desk and in one swoop got all the flashbulbs in the can. If I couldn't have the whole office to myself and Tommy, I'd at least have my desk for me.

Next on the docket: prepping case files—good, orderly work that'd help me get my head on straight. I loved anything that involved organization, planning, or being a general mastermind—one reason why I was such a good fit for Tommy's harebrained mind. I pulled a new folder from the supply in my desk and got out my black marking pencil.

BLACKSTONE, TALLULAH

All caps and all one line on the tab, just like Tommy preferred. He said it was easier for his old eyes to read, but Tommy wasn't older than thirty-five, so I think it was because *he* only wrote in all caps.

The moves were rote and comforting: the blank piece of paper sliding onto the carriage of the typewriter, the whir of the gears, and the slamming of the paper bale reminded me it was time to focus.

First and foremost, a dossier about the client, who was requesting the work—and who I would bill.

CLIENT NAME: *Tallmadge Blackstone*
OCCUPATION: *Millionaire*
REQUEST:

I hovered for a moment. What did he want exactly? For Tommy to spy on his daughter. To find out whether she intended to marry the man to whom she'd been betrothed.

And to find out if there was anyone else in her life. That's what he'd said. It all felt fishy, so I left it blank, for Tommy to decide.

TARGET: *Tallulah "Tally" Blackstone, 18. Daughter;*
    intended bride
RELATED PARTIES: *Webber Harrington-Whitley, 57.*
    Business partner to Mr. Blackstone; intended groom

That was the best I got out of my short and sweet conversation with Tommy, so I pulled the paper from the typewriter and set it in Tally's folder, where it'd wait for further notes from Tommy the next morning.

But to be on the safe side, I slid another folder out of my supply and again reached for my black marking pencil.

UNCONSCIOUS MAN

All caps and all on one line on the tab. I could change the folder once we got more information.

Another blank piece of paper slid onto the carriage of the typewriter, with a whir of the gears and a slam of the paper bale.

NAME:
OCCUPATION:
REQUEST:

To find out who beaned him good and proper and left him to die in Tommy's office, I guess. But I didn't write that down.

RELATED PARTIES:

I stuck out my tongue as I typed the terrible words: *Detective Jake Lawson. NYPD Investigator. Midtown North.* .

I placed the sheet in the folder for Tommy to take a gander at in the morning.

I gathered up my purse and shut the blinds, turned off my lamp, and started for the door. But before my hand hit the knob, I was back at my desk, lifting the heavy black receiver to my ear and spinning the dial.

"Midtown North Precinct, desk sergeant speaking," said a gruff voice.

"Is Officer Leary still in? This is Viviana Valentine."

"Aw, yeah, Viv—let me grab him."

"No, no, don't. But please tell him thank you for me, and let him know I'd appreciate a call in the morning with any new info he might have on the stiff . . . I mean, the gentleman in Tommy's office."

"Yeah, sure, Viv. I'm sure he's looking forward to giving you a call." The sergeant hung up, and I realized then and there my stomach was all in flutters.

Oh dear.

Unnerved, I dialed the operator to send for a cab and waited in the lobby, tapping my feet impatiently against the tiled floor, until it showed. The ride was slow and still. The cabbie didn't play the radio, and instead I was serenaded by the squawks coming from dispatch.

Day 3

"Tommy Fortuna, private investigator," I said into the receiver. I picked up a pencil and paper, prepared to take notes. I had never been trained in proper shorthand, but I always managed to get Tommy the pertinent information.

"Miss Valentine?" There was a low, reassuring voice on the other end that didn't make my hair stand up. It wasn't that scoundrel Jake Lawson.

"Speaking?" I tossed the pencil back on my desk, and the eraser caused it to bounce up and away and under the desk.

"This is Officer Leary," he said with a slight hitch. The poor boy sounded nervous. "I wanted to call and . . ."

"Tell me how our mysterious stiff is faring?" I crouched down to pick up the pencil that had inconveniently rolled as far as it could toward the dusty baseboards.

". . . check in to ask if you needed anything," he finished.

I stood up too fast and whacked my head good and proper, and tried not to curse a blue streak into the receiver. "Aren't you a dear."

There was a huff on the other end. I think he'd expected me to swoon and hadn't yet picked up on the fact that I'm not the swooning kind. And even if I was, I was going to do my damnedest to make sure I wasn't the swooning kind for the likes of Officer Leary.

"Thank you, miss."

"You can call me Viv—everyone else does."

"Thank you, miss."

"But no, I'm fine. Everything's quiet in this neck of the woods." I declined to add that I was sweating through my girdle at the moment and felt a goose egg emerging on the back of my head. I had a whole bin of number-two pencils on my desk. Why I'd felt the need to chase after this one was suddenly beyond me.

"Wonderful. Do you need someone to replace your window?"

"I'll call our window man out, thank you. I have one who offers Tommy a discount for repeat business."

"Okay." There was no sound of laughter, but worse yet, there *was* an expectant silence on the line.

"How's the stiff?"

"Alive, Miss Valentine. Breathing, but he hasn't, um, been able to talk."

I picked up my pencil again. "Got a name?"

"Not yet, miss, and his eyes are still all puffy, and we think he has some broken bones, among other injuries. So we can't tell who he is, or if he was known to anyone. We'd like to get pictures circulating around at the precinct."

"It isn't Tommy," I said to assure myself as much as the cops. "Tell me where the guy is, though, and I'll come down and confirm it isn't Tommy. I've seen him in all stages of bruising. But also, the hair's all wrong." The coppers didn't have to know that he was also alive and well, and tracking our mark all over the borough—and to fancy parties just a few nights ago.

"We assumed you'd've known."

There was a pause. "Anything else, Officer?"

Another pause before the question came out. "Is Mr. Fortuna in yet today?"

"No, not yet, but I'll let him know you were looking for him."

"But call me—uh, call the Detective—if he shows up or if you can think of anything you may have remembered since yesterday. I"—there was a tumult on the other end of the line—"I gotta go."

"Thank you, Officer Leary."

"You could call me Alan."

"Thank you, Officer Leary." I hung up the phone and immediately called Tommy's glazier to schedule an appointment for his earliest convenience—but the fastest he could skedaddle my way was the following Tuesday.

I flopped down in my chair and put my feet up, unhooked my underpinnings just a bit around the waist, and set about thinking what I'd tell Tommy and how I'd tell him that we needed fourteen-fifty to replace yet another window.

I'd managed to almost fall asleep in the heat before I spotted the envelope stuffed in the door crack the day before. Stretching to get my blood pumping again, I grabbed my letter opener and slit open the seal. Inside there was a note, quickly scrawled in pencil on a piece of soft, cream-colored paper:

i have to go out of town for a few days. please keep an eye on things.

tommy

Keep an eye on things, my foot, ol' Tommy boy. He had some nerve running away like that.

I set to balling up the envelope out of frustration, when I felt the weight of something floating around in it. As I tipped the contents of the envelope into my hand, a sparkly hair clip fell into my palm. Just another bit of Tommy's evidence he threw on my desk, with none of the wire I needed to make sense of it all. There was nothing to do but log it.

Placing the clip on my desk, I went to Tommy's giant wooden cabinet, which looked like an old library card catalogue, nearly as deep as it was wide. I counted down, yanking open the drawer in the fourth column, third from the top. It was filled almost to the brim with all sorts of office trash, loose bullets, and rubber bands, but I crouched down to angle my body and shoved my arm into the gap as far as I could, until I was in up to my armpit. Stretching my fingers, I felt the telltale groove and pushed.

The false back of the drawer flipped on its spring and fell neatly out of the way.

"You need to clean, *ol'* Tommy Boy," I said to the empty room.

I could hear his usual reply in my head: *"If I clean it, it won't be good for hiding nothin', will it?"*

I smirked as I strained even harder against the recess, my fingers landing on the hard leather I was looking for. Through sheer determination, I managed to pull it from its hidey-hole.

The Land camera.

★   ★   ★

Two years back, Tommy had returned from a jaunt to Boston with no evidence that we could bill for, but with a smile as big as a possum's in a garbage can. He pulled what looked like a giant, leather-wrapped flask, with a purse strap, from his jacket pocket and laughed.

"Open it up!" he said and watched while I fumbled with the latch on the front.

"What is it?" I asked, bending a nail on the metal clasp.

"Open it up!"

Finally, something clicked and the flap fell open, revealing the silver face of a box with a lens in the middle. On the front, stated in simple lettering, was "Polaroid: Model 95."

"What is it?"

"It's a camera!"

"Doesn't look like one," I said, extending the front and feeling the accordion folds expand.

"That's because it's not just *any* camera," Tommy explained. "It's an *instant* camera."

"I don't get it." I held the viewfinder to my eye, and Tommy plucked the camera out of my hand before I could click the shutter.

"It makes photos immediately! You don't even have to bring film to the store. You load the roll, take a picture, and a minute later you have a photograph!"

"Who needs a picture that quickly?"

"Everyone," Tommy said with a humph.

"Don't get huffy," I said. "It's awful interesting. How much did it cost?"

"That doesn't matter." Which meant "a lot."

"What are we gonna use it for?"

"Stakeouts, angry customers, anything we'd need a picture for," Tommy said. "Catalogue every piece of evidence we get in the office, add instant pictures to the files. This thing will pay for itself!"

Earlier this year, I'd told Sandy about the camera one night over cannoli, and I thought he was gonna accuse me of witchcraft. Said no one ever needed pictures that often or that quickly. Ever since he'd said that, I got to thinking it was pretty neat.

★ ★ ★

I set about positioning the spangly barrette in the light, for the greatest effect. Two photos would be needed—one of the front and one of the back. As soon as both pictures were developed, I taped them into the folder and clipped the hair clip alongside them for safekeeping.

Where could Tommy be? He knew Tallulah Blackstone was out and about, gallivanting in New York City, gate-crashing engagement parties, and who knows what else. Presumably, her father was in town too, considering we'd seen him the day before yesterday, as fit as a fiddle and telling Tommy he needed answers, lickety-split, about his tart of a daughter. So he wasn't trailing any of them around, or else he'd be . . . right here.

As far as I knew, Tommy didn't have another open case, but Lawson had been asking me about gangsters just yesterday. A funny pit in my stomach opened up, and today I couldn't blame it on pricey wine.

★   ★   ★

I couldn't help but feel there was a ghost in the office, with Tommy's closed door taunting me. I knew for sure there was no second body behind it, but curiosity was getting the better of me despite my dicey stomach. I needed to go in and poke around.

Tiptoeing to the door—even though I was the only soul in the whole building—I pushed it open while holding my breath. It was a mess, just like I'd left it—papers scattered on the floor, wastebasket missing, Tommy's usual disarray. This time, that included a few half-empty inkwells, a sealed pack of Luckies, crumpled-up forms, and a pulp novel with a half-clothed broad on the cover, surrounded by the words *The Dangerous Thirst*.

What kind of dames was he bringing around after I left?

There was nothing I hadn't noticed before except for a big splotch of ink where someone had crushed a fountain pen, leaving a craggy footprint in a puddle of ink from Tommy's favorite Dubonnet Red—too bright and cheerful to be blood, but unsettlingly crimson nonetheless.

"Now how am I going to get that out of a wood floor?" I asked the universe, and I thanked my lucky stars that I didn't get an answer, or else I'd have a whole new can of worms to deal with.

Receiving the peace of mind I needed from the uninhabited office, I went back to my phone with an idea in my head. I spun the dial, and a man's voice came over the line.

"Midtown North."

"It's Viviana Valentine. What hospital is the stiff in?"

"Aw, Viv, I'm not supposed to give out that kind of info to civilians."

Boys in uniform could get awfully cagey at the worst times. The fib just tumbled out of me without thinking. "Yeah, well, Lawson asked Tommy to meet him at the bedside, so what am I supposed to do? Schmooze up every nurses' station in Manhattan 'til I find the one?"

"He's at St. Luke's," the voice said. "But don't tell anyone you learned it from me."

"Your secret's safe," I said, rolling my eyes at the mystery man on the other end of the line.

★   ★   ★

The door was still shut, so I just hiked up my dress to redo my underthings without heading to the bathroom upstairs. There was at least one benefit to Tommy being out of sight.

Grabbing a few empty file folders and slinging the Land camera over my shoulder like a Continental soldier, I careened down the stairs from Tommy's office, skittering to a stop on the tile of the building vestibule. A flutter of papers could be heard from behind the closed door of the first-floor office. Before I could knock, the door wrenched open beneath my waiting knuckles, and the architect—laden with tubes of paper and a pencil behind his ear, nestled into a head of silver hair—ran out, sliding a bit in his scuffed, tan-and-white brogues, which matched his shoddily cut brown suit and pitifully dented watch.

"Oh!" I couldn't stop the shriek from tumbling from my lips. The man stopped dead in his tracks.

"Miss." His full arms meant he couldn't reach to his hat brim, so he nodded in my direction.

"Afternoon. Not sure if you recall—I'm the girl from the middle office, Viviana Valentine," I explained. "Can I lend a hand?"

The draftsman was fumbling for something in his pocket—presumably his keys—and he threw the armful of papers at me without so much as a "Yes, please."

"Have you been back a while? Perhaps since Monday?" I asked. "I could've sworn Mr. Fortuna said you were away for a summer respite, Mr. De Lancey,"

"Young ladies shouldn't swear," he muttered back, finding a ring of keys in his jacket and violently stabbing a chosen piece of metal into its lock. "You're as hopeless and uncouth as that man you work for."

"Thanks for the advice, sir." It'd been many years since I'd been told what young ladies should or shouldn't do, and it had never before been from someone who wasn't a blood relation.

He grabbed his papers from me and left in a lurch, slamming out the front door and declining to answer whether he'd been in the building before this morning.

"I hope you're having a *lovely* summer!" I called to his shadow. "You can cool off by taking a long walk off a short pier."

Giving the sour Mr. De Lancey a few moments to walk down the block and put some distance between us, I followed my neighbor out the front door and down the sidewalk. The hospital was a few miles north, but Tommy's office kitty was empty, and I didn't have the dough on me to shell out for a taxicab neither, so it was gonna be a hike toward the park in the heat. It was a hell of a way for a girl to spend a Friday, but maybe the lucky dolt who'd got his coconut cracked in would know where my boss was off to.

It felt so hot you could fry an egg on the sidewalk, but I immediately started heading uptown, stopping halfway at a deli for a Coke to keep me cool. It was only an hour of walking—with the streets empty, I got there in no time flat, without having to elbow anyone out of the way or even grapple with too many lookie-loos, walking blind, with maps in front of their pusses. *Besides,* I reminded myself, *a little sun never hurt anyone.*

★　★　★

The hospital loomed over the buildings uptown. Wilted folders in hand, I eyed the nurses' station, staffed by one rather cranky-looking woman with steel-gray eyes, who could've switched out her hat and been a passable nun. I smiled my sweetest smile and walked toward her.

"Excuse me, but my steady's an officer at Midtown North, and he begged me to bring these"—I lifted the empty files above the desk to show them off—"to Detective Lawson. He should be with an anonymous gentleman who came in unconscious yesterday morning?"

"Of course, of course," the nurse said. "Thirteenth floor. You keep doing favors for your beau like that, and he'll make you a missus sooner than you know it. And there's a ladies' at the top of the elevator, where you can powder your nose." She gave me a smile, as if she was telling me she was a fairy princess granting my every wish, and pointed me toward the elevator.

"Bless you," I responded with a smile, and walked away.

★   ★   ★

The entire hospital smelled of Clorox, and the thirteenth-floor elevator dinged open to a green-and-white-hued hallway, every color just a little bit muted due to a top layer of industrial neglect. Cantilevered windows were opened up and down the stretch, but the ward was still suffocating, with chemical smells and humid air. The ladies' room was, as the nurse said, to the right of the elevator, though I ignored my powder-less nose and read the sign, which indicated the head injury unit was down the hall to the left, also near the men's room.

I dumped my empty folders into the nearest trashcan and followed the signs. The eyes of a workman in a jumpsuit, bearing an armful of tattoos and armed with a mop, following my caboose the whole way. I'm not some Goody Two-shoes, so the ink didn't throw me for a loop, but the art wasn't your usual sailor's swallows and anchors. I couldn't make out all the details, but there was a big, bold numerical 2 above his right wrist.

Rows of dull aluminum beds lined the ward, the lofty ceilings cooling the room slightly, and big industrial fans in the center doing the bulk of the work to circulate the smelly air. The scent of countless sweaty male bodies awaiting a sponge bath mixed with the stench of disinfectant and laundry starch. A group of cops milled around one fella, and among them was Lawson. When he heard my saddle shoes tap on the tile, he looked up and spotted me.

"Miss Valentine?" he asked. I saw Officer Leary straighten up, and Officer O'Malley twisted around to greet me with his chipped-tooth smile. A few of the other uniforms gave me the up and down, but I got the impression that they were the type to do that to all the dames who walked by, just like the janitor. "I don't want you coming any closer."

"Detective Lawson," I replied, "how's our unfortunate visitor?"

The cops closed ranks around the bed, so all I could see was the peak of toes beneath a white sheet.

"Still anonymous. Made some noises yesterday but didn't exactly wake up or manage to spill the beans on who got him or what he was doing in your office. And he's been out cold ever since."

The bump of the door and the thwack of wet rope made me jump, and I turned to see the janitor had made it to the ward. He was concentrating awful hard on swishing that mop, clearly trying to eavesdrop on whatever the cops had to say.

"Tommy's office, to be specific," I said, turning back to Lawson. "Shame, I'd love to know what he was trying to filch."

"You think he was in there alone?"

"For a time," I snapped back. "Until someone cracked him good and proper, obviously. Or do you think a Bugs Bunny anvil just fell out of the sky?"

"No, I don't." Lawson set his jaw and crossed his arms. "You, scram!" He pointed over my shoulder, and the janitor left the way he'd come.

"You know, I might know him. The stiff. Someone stuck their head in asking for Tommy just before I left. I didn't get a good look at the face when he was in the office. Maybe it's the same fella."

There was a murmur and shudder among the cops, and I wonder what I'd said wrong to make such stalwart men of the law become so uncomfortable.

"We don't need you to make an ID," Lawson said.

"Oh, so you *do* know who he is?"

"I didn't say that."

"Honest to God, Jake Lawson, do you want to solve this case or not?" My girdle, thanks to both a trek through the stifling city and all of this malarky, was now sopping with sweat. My insides squished like a Thanksgiving stuffing, and I was just tired of this official runaround.

"All right, if you insist." Lawson and his cops moved out of the way so I could approach the bed.

The swelling had gone down, but the bruising had gone way up. The man was about as purple as an eggplant, from top to tip.

But even underneath the discoloration and swelling, I could make out that something was deeply, deeply different about his face. From hairline to eyebrows, everything was as it should be, but bruised, for certain. The left side of his face was of a man just past the prime of his life. But his right side was altogether a different story. Where there ought to have been a cheekbone, there was a startlingly concave well; where there should have been a lower jaw, there was a sutured knot of skin.

Half of this man's face was gone.

"He didn't look like this yesterday," I said quietly. "It was dark, but I would've seen this. I swear my life on it."

"No, he didn't," Lawson said quietly. One of his officers picked something up from a small table and passed it to his boss. Lawson held it up. "He was wearing this."

Held in the proper position, I could see clearly it was a porcelain mask, painted delicately with perfect features; the shadow of a cheekbone, a pair of pinkish lips, even the subtlest shade of stubble. There were two leather straps, one to hang from the gentleman's ears, the other to fit tight around the back of his neck. The mask had hidden his injuries completely.

"It didn't shatter" was all I could say.

"Not in the attack or when he fell," Lawson agreed.

"Do you know who made it?"

"No."

Another dead end.

I really felt bad for the man in the bed, and I edged closer to look at him, trying to see beyond the scars.

He was older—older than me, Tommy, and Lawson—but in okay enough shape that he didn't look like he was knocking on death's door before someone decided to expedite his delivery. Well fed, for sure, but I could see he had muscular arms and a big barrel chest. His eyes were closed, and, although thinning a bit on top, his hair was glossy and healthy, with only a hint of gray.

"Any idea what he got hit with?"

"We don't even know he got hit with something," Lawson admitted. "We didn't find anything with blood on it at Tommy's, and there's loads of reasons a man might get discolored like this—poisoning, heart attack even. Did you notice anything missing from the office?"

"Not off the top," I admitted. It was the truth, but it felt like a fib, considering how well I knew every last piece of paper Tommy hoarded. "But I'll look again the next time I'm in the office. What do the doctors say?"

Seeing that I was no longer floored by the victim's appearance, Lawson was back to business, and back to his usual self-assurance.

"I'll tell you when I can lay my paws on one. The hospital's short-staffed because all the docs decided to head out of town for the weekend."

"That's no good."

"No good at all, especially for Tommy," Lawson added.

"Oh yeah? What are you getting at? Besides, anyone who was tussling with this guy could've been doing it in self-defense."

"An anonymous man gets assaulted in your boss's office in the middle of the night, no witnesses, and then Tommy Fortuna, the best PI in the whole damn city, decides not to return the investigating officer's calls? You mean to tell me that's not suspicious to you?" Lawson was looking me dead in the eyes. "C'mon, Viviana Valentine, you've been around this business long enough to know who my number-one suspect is."

"Shut your mouth, Lawson."

"Or what?"

"You're not going to trick me into a threat, you slug." I balled my fists, but I didn't take a swing.

"You'll talk if you know anything—that is, if you know what's good for you. And what's good for Tommy. Chief is putting out a warrant out for his arrest—an APB across the whole tristate area. Might even extend it to Philly."

The young cops gathered around Lawson. Leary stood at the back, his jaw clenched, but there must've been something awful intriguing on the linoleum floor because that's where his eyes were glued.

"I don't know anything about what happened to this man. I don't know anything new today, and I sure don't know where Tommy happens to be." I was balancing on my tiptoes but stood my ground, not daring to break eye contact with the horrible detective. "But I know for certain Tommy didn't do it. You ever think that maybe the man who got his brother has something out for him? No, you'd never think it. Just that Tommy's guilty."

Lawson's gaze pulled away. "Little girl!" he snapped his fingers at a young woman in a candy striper's outfit who

looked terrified at the act of being addressed. "Have the doctor call me at the precinct if this man wakes up. She can stay,"
he said, thumbing in my direction. "But keep an eye on her.
Vamanos, boys."

He and his uniformed thugs headed out, leaving me alone
with the nearly departed.

I walked to the edge of the row of beds and picked up
a metal chair, lugging it back to the side of the anonymous
man.

"It's just you and me now, buddy." I picked up the chart
that was hanging off his footboard and sat down on the cool
metal. "Mind if I have a sip? I've had a hell of a day so far."

He didn't raise any opposition, so I poured myself a glass
of water from a pitcher that was sitting on a tray table next to
his head, and set about my snooping. That water smelled old,
but it was colder than the air, so it was something. Anything
to calm my nerves.

On the left side of the folder, personal details. Scanning
through the information, there was no name and no date of
birth, of course, and I hadn't been expecting to see any. In the
"personal effects" part of the records, the hospital catalogued
the porcelain mask, a full seersucker summer suit, a short-
sleeved white linen shirt, brown loafers, a brown leather wallet with no identification, forty dollars in cash, and a gold
signet ring when he was admitted. Pretty rich equipment for
a snoop, but considering Tommy owned a full tuxedo, I figured it was hard to judge a man by his clothing.

The attendee making notes had gotten bored with the task
at hand and sketched something in the margins; a complicated

doodle of lines within a diamond shape that looked almost like a road sign.

"Boy, tough breaks, my dear," I said to the man. "They didn't even have the decency to steal your hard-earned clams."

As for medical details and diagnosis, John Doe was about six feet tall and a healthy one hundred and eighty pounds, no signs of serious wear and tear aside from the old injuries, the noggin, and the bruising. Four pages of chicken scratch illuminated things like blood pressure, heart rate, respiratory rate, and blood test results.

But the cops had missed one important detail in the fine print.

Upon admittance, the man's pupils were fixed at first examination.

No one'd told Lawson yet this guy wasn't waking up.

I gave my witness the once-over, put his chart back, and downed my glass of water. The camera swung against my hip, so I took the opportunity to snap two photos of the porcelain face mask—back and front—and tucked the instant photographs into my purse.

Nothing good was happening in this hospital today short of a miracle, and since these were modern times, I wasn't expecting a miracle anytime soon.

The door to the ward boomed open again, followed by the janitor and mop, so I snapped a photo of him too, just for kicks. He hunched his shoulders just like Sandy had when I talked about the camera, and then slid down his cuffs to hide his ink. Law enforcement calls those "soft identifying features," so I wondered if he had a warrant. Checking the clock that loomed over the entrance to the ward, I figured half past three was a fine time to quit on a summertime Friday while my boss was out, either hiding out from Johnny Law or, just as likely, having the time of his life, presumably with whatever broad was leaving dime novels around the office.

I didn't get paid by the hour, and Tommy had bigger fish to fry—not like he was ever one to give me the third degree over my hours, anyhow, considering how many times he's made me work into the evening on this or that. Now that he was officially on the lam, bookkeeping was the least of his problems. Squeezing past the custodian and his leering eyes, it was back to the elevator.

I hustled my way to Fifty-Ninth Street and caught a stiff wind coming off the river. The air stank of rotting seaweed and motor oil and whatever else was floating in the murky blue, but the moving air was a lot more enjoyable than the staleness of the hospital.

A summer afternoon in New York City was like nothing I'd ever dreamed of as a kid in the sticks. Back home, when the mercury soared, it seemed like the whole world just up and died—the whole town fell just short of tumbleweeds rolling through the deserted Old West. You wouldn't see a soul walking around. Every last person who could would be indoors with the curtains drawn, and you just knew they were huddled over a big block of ice, wondering why the devil himself was up top and bringing the hellfire with him.

But in New York? It was the opposite, believe me. Sure, people skipped out to head to Jones Beach, but summer in the city was a good, old-fashioned block party.

Though it was a significant detour in my day, I wandered my way to Columbus Circle and took a jaunt through the park, followed by a couple of men in their civvies, straight off a shift at the hospital. It seemed like thousands of people were already on the lush, green lawns and sitting by the fountains, and hundreds more were going to join them by dusk. Buskers lined the sidewalks, playing their saxophones and guitars, and the paths were dotted with men with pushcarts selling Popsicles and pretzels. The entire street smelled like the sour milk of melting ice cream and damp earth. It smelled like summer.

A nickel bought me an Italian ice, and the fresh, sugary lemon tang picked me up as I peeled the cardboard top off the cup and tossed it in the trash, my close proximity scattering half a dozen pigeons who'd decided to check out the offerings of the can. A quick scrape of the wooden paddle across the treat's frozen top, and with one lick, I was in a much better mood. It didn't taste like it'd ever come within three feet of a real lemon, but that didn't mean it wasn't delicious.

The jolt of sugar pepped me right up and brought my attention back to what I'd just seen in the hospital. Not even the cops knew anything. And the man didn't even have a face. How do you ID someone with half a mug made up by someone else?

I never knew Italian ice to be brain food, but I got an idea. I hurried my butt straight to Rockefeller Center, then hooked a left 'til I found the store I was looking for. Even if we were six months out from Christmas, there was always a crowd outside peering through the windows and whining.

If anyone could tell me about porcelain faces, it might just be the doll department at F.A.O. Schwarz.

Pushing my way through all the snot-nosed brats, I swung open the brass door.

"Hello, miss," a polite salesman said. "May I help you?"

"Oh, yes," I said sweetly. "My niece, she just *loves* her baby dolls. Can you please point me in the direction of your beautiful collectible dolls?"

"Of course, miss. Third floor, to your right. It's a rather large display."

"Thank you."

I hopped up the stairs, two at a time, hoping no one would notice an adult without a child, acting like a fool. By the time I reached the doll display, I was out of breath and was immediately confronted by an older woman with a neat suit, pearls, and an overly blued coiffure. Something told me she didn't just sell dolls, but probably had a stuffy one-bedroom somewhere uptown that was lined, floor to ceiling, with dolls no child would ever touch.

"Hello, miss. How may I help you?"

"Oh, I certainly hope you can!" My brain was racing a mile a minute, nervous even though I was about to spell out a harmless lie. "My niece received a beautiful old doll from my grandmother, and unfortunately she cracked the porcelain face nearly immediately."

The woman winced, as if I'd threatened her with the same. "How dreadful."

"I was wondering if your fine establishment had an artisanal porcelain repair shop you'd recommend for such a delicate restoration?"

"Of course, miss. There are several in the Toy Center, naturally."

"I thought this was the toy center?"

She chuckled. "Only to children," she said, more condescendingly than she ought to have, considering that, for all she knew, I was as rich as the Queen of Sheba and ready to buy her out of dollhouse and home. "Most of the industry is headquartered in the Flatiron District, near Madison Square Park."

She gave me an address a few miles south, plus two names to look up in the building's directory—Lars Schaeber and Jannick Christmann. My caboose ached just thinking about walking there. I thanked her profusely as she walked me down the stairs, telling me all the virtues of Dresden porcelain and how upset she was at the city's demise under our dreadful American bombs.

It was Friday around quittin' time, so I knew not to press my luck trying to find anyone at the Toy Center today. Making my way back home from the store through the hot, sticky streets of New York and the hubbub of Times Square, I arrived home to an empty boarding house. All the other girls were still at work or off having fun, while Mrs. K was surely out picking up a few things, and her son was still at his summertime job, heaving crates or moving furniture or some other job that boys built like men seem to do.

I dead-bolted Mrs. K's front door behind me. Anyone else who was coming back would have a key, I figured, so there was no shame in making sure I was nice and secure. I slunk back up to my windowless bedroom and flicked on a fan that I set on my vanity when the New York summer got up to speed in June. The cool, damp air of my bedroom began circulating as I worked my way out of my sweaty clothing.

My dress was the first to go into the hamper. There was no way I was going to sit on my bed in something that I'd worn sitting on that filthy hospital chair, which was probably still festering with remnants of Spanish Flu. Once I was in my slip, I could sit to take off my stockings—my expensive, real silk ones breathed a bit better than nylon in the heat, but that meant I took extra time to take 'em off. Most of the time the silk wasn't worth the trouble, but when the mercury peaked, it made all the difference in the world.

Then the ultimate relief: sliding off that cursed girdle. I tossed it into my delicates bag for Sunday washing, hoping I wouldn't have to pop one on again for the whole weekend.

There are only a few things to do indoors on a hot afternoon, and considering I was all by my lonesome, I figured I only had two courses of action: read or sleep. I rustled around on under my mattress for whatever my fingers could find and came up with a half-finished paperback I couldn't even remember starting.

I flipped to the back cover of *Queen of Shadows* to refresh myself.

Loretta Lovelorn doesn't live for danger—but danger seeks her anyway. Can she stay one step ahead of the man who has Loretta in his sights? Only if she becomes . . . The Queen of Shadows!

Within a few pages, I remembered that it was a barely gripping mystery and before I knew it, my eyes were drooping. My room was always dark—without a lamp on, the only light came from the transom over the door—so I was snoozing my way through the afternoon before I could even put the book back where I found it.

NIGHT 3

I woke up to the sound of knocking on my door, and the clock on my bedside table said it was about six PM—too early for Mrs. K's nightly dinner, but my disoriented mind wasn't agreeing yet with my gurgling stomach. I'm sure there were better ways to kill an hour, but I couldn't think of one off the top of my head.

"Viviana!" Dottie was politely rapping on my door, her diction precise and clear. "Viviana, there is a phone call for you."

If Dottie was waking me up instead of taking a message, it was probably someone important, and hopefully that someone was Tommy.

I tossed on my robe and met her in the hallway, a bit sweaty and bleary-eyed. "Thank you so much," I said, and she gave me a stern smile—if smiles could ever be no-nonsense, it's what Dottie gave every time—and went to her own room in the back of the house.

"Hello, this is Viviana," I said.

"Miss Valentine," a man's voice said on the other line, "This is Tallmadge Blackstone."

My stomach fell to my feet and did the hula.

"Mr. Blackstone—is everything alright?"

"I was hoping you'd tell me, Miss Valentine." He sounded about as angry as a man could get, huffing and puffing and just about ready to blow my house down. "Is your boss dead?"

My innards did another somersault. "No."

"Is he in the hospital?"

"No."

"Is he bound and gagged in a trunk somewhere?"

"Not to my knowledge."

"Then, please tell me why, when I called on Mr. Fortuna's office this afternoon, there was no one there to answer. Perhaps you could enlighten me as to why your employer could not make his appointment?"

I had half a mind to ask him how *he* had the nerve to call *me* at home, but I figured a man that rich had the nerve to do pretty much whatever he wanted.

"I'm sorry, Mr. Blackstone. Tommy, uh, by that I mean *Mr. Fortuna*, sent me on a rather involved errand this afternoon," I fibbed. "And he's suddenly away for the weekend. Family business." Surely a man whose entire life was built on his daddy's money, and who was so obsessed with his daughter's love life, would understand being put out by a family emergency.

"If he's suddenly away for the weekend," Mr. Blackstone demanded, "perhaps *you* should fill me in on the progress of my project yourself, so I know I'm not wasting my money and my time. My house. Eight o'clock. Do come dressed for dinner."

There was another, familiar click, and I was about ready to upchuck on Mrs. K's floor.

"Phyllis!" I hollered into the silent house. "Girls? Phyllis!"

The woman—long and lanky like the gazelles at the zoo—came hurrying downstairs. All raven haired and seductive, she was in a boatneck black T-shirt and black pedal pushers, looking like she was about to go to a beatnik poetry reading at the drop of a hat. Even when milling around the house, you could snap her picture and use it to sell something.

"Viv! What's the matter?" Phyllis's voice was soft and cultured, always with an icy air about her that could chill the fever out of anyone. Which is exactly what I needed.

"I need your help!" My robe had come undone, and I was standing in the hallway in my undergarments, nervous and scared. "I just got invited to dinner."

"Who's the lucky boy?" Phyllis's eyes gleamed.

"That's the thing—it was Tallmadge Blackstone!"

Betty and Dottie joined us out on the landing.

"Wait—Tallmadge Blackstone asked you out on the town?" The jealousy in Betty's voice was only barely contained. He was old enough to be her pa, but still, he had bucks.

"It's not like that," I said. "He hired Tommy to do something for him, but Tommy's out of town. Now he wants *me* to go to his house for dinner and fill him in!"

Dottie took me by the shoulders. "What *exactly* did he say, Viviana?"

"His house. Eight o'clock. 'Come dressed for dinner.'"

Dottie and Phyllis met eyes over my head. Phyllis scowled.

"I don't suppose you have an evening gown." Dottie's words were not a question.

"I have that dark blue Anne Klein," Phyllis dithered, and then she began talking to herself, her long legs folded under her as she sat down on a stair to think. "But I don't think that will do. I wonder if Jacqui would bring over that one Claire McCardell? She does owe me after that Clairol shoot."

Phyllis's scheming was like she was speaking another language. "You're losing me, Phyl."

"Remember earlier this year when I was a blonde?" She looked up and started chewing on her thumbnail.

"Ooh, yeah. That was terrible."

"*That* is why Jacqui owes me a favor."

"And you'd use *that* big of a favor on me?"

"Sure, sweetie." She stood to help me up and shoved me toward the stairs, and I trudged up toward her penthouse rooms by myself. Behind me, I could hear the familiar purr of Phyllis asking for a favor over the phone, in between Betty's excited tittering over my evening plans.

★　★　★

"Phyllis, when have you ever seen me wear something *red*?"

Phyllis held up a dress in a color I could only describe as "fire," and grinned like a fool. The gown was a long, flowing column of pleated silk, with a crossover V neckline and a wide, cinched belt at the waist, like you see on girls in ads for cigarettes from the Far East. It wasn't adorned in any way with beads or ruffles or flowers or fringe—just a subtle gold pinstriping that ran down each individual fold of fabric. It looked like it had taken someone at least a few days to stitch.

"It's either this or that green thing Tally's already seen you in once this week," Phyllis snapped back. "My Anne Klein just won't work for you, sweetie. And the good thing is that in this, you don't need a corset," she soothed. "I'm going to go grab your garters, your silks, and your longline brassiere."

She laid the dress across her bed and went about her errand. Dottie peeked in.

"I'm going to run downstairs and fix you a plate of dinner."

"But I'll barely fit in this dress as it is! Jacqui must be skinnier than a broom handle."

"I assume she looks rather similar to Phyllis. So, I'll bring you a small plate of dinner, then. You can't show up to a formal evening without food in your stomach. There will be cocktails and we can't risk you fainting by the time the first course comes around. That would be rude."

She lit down the stairs and was back with a blob of chicken casserole.

Phyllis returned with my various undergarments just as I was polishing off the pile of mayonnaisey goo.

"It's better than it looks," Dottie confirmed. "Oleks put some in the fridge for you downstairs."

"Thanks." Phyllis turned to me. "Now, off with your whole kit."

"Excuse me?" I wrapped my robe tighter around my body.

"I don't care," Phyllis said. "I do this every day. Or did you think models all got separate dressing rooms?"

It'd never occurred to me that the posh broad in front of me spent most of her days in her birthday suit in front of other girls. Her life had always seemed so glamorous that I didn't realize how much of it was about watching her figure and getting poked and prodded like a breathing mannequin. I dropped my robe and slip and she set about to dressing me up like a doll.

"We'll do your hair and makeup once this is all fitted," Phyllis said with her mouth full of pins. "Just want to make sure you don't destroy the hem. Or else I'll have to owe Jacqui for owing me." She plopped to the floor and set about hitching up a few inches of red silk that trailed on the floor. "You know, you should add more red to your wardrobe."

"I don't know about that."

Phyllis picked herself off the floor and began poking through her train case. "The color looks quite good with your hair." She emerged with a gold tube of lipstick. "Now, hair and makeup. Sit."

My housemate warned me for every moment she'd be yanking on my locks or approaching my eyes with a pointed pencil or mascara wand . At the end of twenty minutes, my scalp was aching and my face felt like it was smothered underneath a layer of Crisco. But, I had to admit I did look spiffy. My hair was pulled into a chignon, and my face was painted and powdered to the point that I could barely see my own skin, but I looked like a porcelain doll.

"Perfect!" Phyllis declared. "Shoes?"

"I don't think I have anything fancy enough."

"That's fine. I do." Phyllis dropped to her knees and fished around under her bed, emerging with a slightly beat-up pair of silver leather sandals with a high conical heel. "You're going to have to scrunch your toes a bit," she said with a frown.

"Fine by me." Once they were buckled around my ankles, she pulled me to a stand.

"Good enough?"

"Better than that," I said, catching a glimpse of myself in the mirror. "I look like a whole different person."

"It's fun, isn't it?" Phyllis asked. "If you ever want to leave Tommy's and start shooting pictures, let me know."

"I can't thank you enough."

"You don't have to," she said, "but you do have to leave *right* now."

If I was going to be on time for Mr. Blackstone—and by hell or high water, I was going to be punctual—it was going to take the better part of an hour, and it was already past seven PM.

I grabbed some cash from my unmentionables drawer and headed downstairs to hail a cab.

It was time to head uptown.

★   ★   ★

A yellow cab was waiting on the curb when I emerged from the house. The cabbie sat in his shirtsleeves, his muscular arms, covered with tattoos, airing out in the open windows. I slid across the green vinyl seat and gave the driver the address I'd written on a scrap of paper. It was a slow, stop-and-start journey through traffic, and I had plenty of time to check out his tats as we approached the address uptown—a whole comic book of illustrations, skulls and knives, plus another big ol' number 2 on his right bicep that musta had something to do with the war, but I couldn't think what. I asked the driver to stop a block short of the destination. The last thing I needed was for the Blackstone's doorman to watch a girl in a borrowed dress and shoes fall out of a cab onto a dirty sidewalk. The fare was steep, but not enough to make me squeak, so I shoved a handful of bills at the driver and made a mental note to have Tommy pay me back for the tab—and all my aggravation.

I was on Fifth Avenue, and the Blackstone residence was in an snooty carved limestone building overlooking the whole park. Granted, this was in the richer part of town, so there were fewer hot dog carts rolling through the paths, and far fewer people dotting the lawns. I guess the help just went home after their shifts were over, instead of milling around on the grass where their boss could see them, and maybe even holler out the windows to ask if they wouldn't mind lending a hand with this or that.

I stepped out of the cab into a gutter with no trash and scurried over a sidewalk that was so clean, it was barely even gray. I knew that being rich had its perks, but I hadn't realized one of them was not having to step over garbage every time you left the house. I went up to the building, and a man in a top hat, green waistcoat, and black trousers bowed his head to me as if I were some kind of princess.

"Blackstones?" I asked, but my voice caught in my throat, and it came out like a sad, little whisper.

"Yes, ma'am," he said and pulled open the wrought iron door.

"You must be sweating something awful in that getup."

"Ma'am?"

"Never mind."

He entered the building after me and escorted me to the elevator, opening the cage and motioning me inside. Another man in a green waistcoat pressed the button for the twelfth floor. The penthouse—not that I was surprised.

"Ma'am," he said, when the car stopped.

"For God's sake, I'm not married," I snapped, though I immediately felt rotten about letting it get to me. "I'm so sorry."

"Miss," he replied.

"Thanks," I sighed. "Do I tip you guys?"

The attendant's muscles loosened a bit, and he lowered his guard. "No, miss. Have a lovely evening."

"Good Lordy, I'll try." I finally met the attendant's eyes, and he winked at me. He was about the age of my grandpa the last time I'd seen him.

"No offense, miss, but you're not the kind that usually comes to visit."

"The borrowed dress give it away?"

"No, miss. The sense of humor." He took a step in front of me in the small car and the cage door lurched open, his old, sinewy hands pressing as hard as they could against the sharp, spring-loaded metal. I shot out my hand and opened the other door before he could, and then raced into the vestibule, as fast as a rabbit, so he could let it all snap closed behind me.

Through the portal window, I saw him smile as the car descended into the blackness.

"Welcome to our home," a soft voice emanated from behind me. "I'm sorry my father is such a bastard."

I started to turn, hoping I wasn't being rude for not waiting at attention and for leaving Tally Blackstone hanging, doubtlessly looking like she was ready for a *Harper's Bazaar* cover in some kind of elaborate swath of silk and her Daddy's discounted diamonds, as effortless as a princess holding court, like in a picture book. With a gulp, I pivoted on my silver heels. In front of me stood the young and beautiful debutante.

She was wearing a red-and-white-checked linen popover shirt and baggy denim pants, cinched at the waist with a thick leather belt like the kind my father used to wear to hold up his Levi's at the mill. Her shiny, bouncing dark brown hair was swept back into a high ponytail, and her bare feet were purple from standing on the cold stone floor.

"That son of a gun told you to get all dressed up, didn't he?" she said, taking me by the hand. No bracelets tinkled on her arms, and her fingers were naked too. I had somehow assumed she wore diamonds like the rest of us wore underpants—that is to say, every day, without thinking twice.

"He said 'dress for dinner,'" I murmured, my cheeks turning the same color as my dress. I broke out into an embarrassed sweat and felt the base on my face begin to ooze.

"Don't worry—this is his idea of a joke." She patted my hand gently. "You aren't the first, though normally I just sit back and enjoy the show too. But let's make sure he doesn't have any fun tonight on account of you. I've got a sundress that'll work with your shoes. Or you could always go barefoot—no one will say anything."

Tally dragged me through a marble-lined foyer that was at least twice the size of my windowless room at Mrs. K's, and into a grand hallway. I took a deep breath and realized the apartment somehow managed to have no smell at all—not even of Windex. My hostess was muttering a tour I could tell she'd rehearsed dozens and dozens of times since she was a kid.

"This is the gallery," she said, waving her free hand to the walls. They were covered with a light beige cloth instead of wallpaper or paint, and a bunch of ancient old oil paintings like you see on postcards at the stands outside the Met. "Granddads upon great-granddads, uncles, and nephews. The occasional grandma. You know the drill."

I certainly did *not* know the drill, but I nodded anyway. Everything was free of dust, and even those ancient old paintings looked like they were in better shape than the poster of a field I'd picked up at Woolworth's last year for a dime and hung in a frame over my bed. Tally hooked a left and traipsed me down a long, long hallway, lined with busts and urns and sculptures, to the rear of the building and into her bedroom. It was soft and girlie and childish—the bright white carpet flecked with gold, the glossy white furniture, and in the very center of the room, a large, four-poster bed with a canopy made up of white lace. The curtains framed a dynamite view of treetops in the park; the curtains themselves were dotted with small, lavender-colored flowers that made the whole room feel like an angelic meadow.

"That's a beautiful dress, by the way," she said as she flung open her closet doors. "Claire McCardell?"

"Thank you," I stammered. "I don't know. I don't know anything. It's not mine. I . . . I borrowed it."

"I don't give a damn if you stole it right off the window mannequin at Saks. It looks good on you." She was shouting to me from the rear of a dressing room that was the size of my parents' living room, her words muffled by the mountains of fabric and shoes and handbags in between her and me. I heard a thump, a tumble of hatboxes hitting the ground, and a curse before she emerged. "You're an itty bitty little thing, so I'm sorry this a bit out of fashion."

It'd been a long time since I was referred to as little, and I stared at the dress with flushed cheeks and no words.

"It's nothing special from a few years ago, but it should fit." She handed me a cotton dress with black and white vertical stripes and a silver leatherette belt. The fabric was soft, like it'd been washed a thousand times, but the hem wasn't fraying. It looked like it'd never been worn.

"Looks like it'll do," I smiled up at the tall woman, and she looked pleased with herself.

"You can change behind that screen, if you'd like," she said, motioning me toward a Chinese-inspired wood and paper partition like all the movie stars have. This one was made with softly shiny paper and covered with half a dozen pale pink birds—legs almost as long as Tally's—flying all around.

"Unzip me first?"

I turned around and felt her cold fingers fumble a bit with the small, nearly invisible toggle at my neck, but with a slight tug, I was halfway to freedom and hurried behind the screen to change.

"What's your name, kitten?"

Good grief. Here I was, half naked in a billionaire heiress's bedroom and putting on her clothes, and she didn't even know my name.

"Viviana," I called out, flinging my borrowed dress over the side of the screen.

"Viviana what?"

"Viviana Valentine." I pulled Tally's dress over my head and buttoned the front placket. It fit nicely—a bit loose in the armpits and hips, considering the difference in our builds, but nothing showy. It would've looked a bit better if I'd worn a girdle to straighten up my posture, but I wasn't about to ask Tally Blackstone if I could borrow her undergarments too. The silver belt hit at my natural waist and did match the heels I didn't have to take off to change. I peeked my head out the side of the screen.

"Let's see you, Viviana Valentine." Tally was lying on her bed, flipping through last week's *Look* magazine. It was an issue in which, I knew already, she appeared in the last few pages, having a gay old time in a two-piece swimsuit on a beach, which, judging by the palm trees, was somewhere that was not in the tristate area.

I came out and did a quick twirl.

"Not bad."

"Thank you for saving me from the embarrassment of being overdressed. I'll change out of it before I leave."

"You'll keep it." She tossed the magazine onto the floor.

"No, no, I couldn't—"

"You'll keep it."

"Are you sure?"

She just rolled her eyes at me. "Oh, real quick." She approached me with a tissue and bent at the waist a bit until her face was level with mine. Her eyes were a soft, light blue, almost like ice. "Let's take one layer of lipstick off that kisser."

She dabbed at my face and blended the remaining cosmetics to soften the look that Phyllis had painted on not even an hour before. She held up a gilded, tortoise-backed hand mirror and I liked that I looked a lot more like myself.

"Thanks."

"*Now* we're dressed for dinner." She took my hand again, and we paraded—now both of us properly dressed—down the hallway, back through the gallery, and into a massive living room dotted with several couches and tables like a hotel lobby, complete with vases of white roses and lilies. Out through the French doors, a man in chef's whites was standing at a barbecue, flipping burgers on a patio that overlooked Central Park.

"We are, at times, *almost* like normal people," Tally said, giving my hand a squeeze. "I'm not sure why Dad invited you, but I'm glad you're here." She pulled me through the doorway and into a summer evening just beginning to chill as the sun went down, and a breeze whipped past the twelfth-floor verandah.

As soon as we stepped onto the balcony, I felt a man's hand envelop my upper arm. Big, thick fingers like hot dogs, for sure, but not even a callous anywhere, so I figured I knew which fancy gent thought he was within his rights to manhandle me.

"What are you doing, Miss Valentine?" His voice was like if a pedigreed poodle decided to growl. Hard to take serious, but I figured since he had teeth, he could still bite.

"Why, Mr. Blackstone, what do you mean?" I turned to Tally's father and gave him my sweetest smile, dripping with cherry syrup like a half-melted snow cone. Tally was standing behind me, reluctant to drop my hand, and she gave my fingers a bit of a squeeze in concern. No matter the reason I was in her house it didn't look good for any girl to be physically commandeered by the host of the party.

"Tallulah," Talmadge said sternly, addressing her over my head in a voice quiet enough to avoid raising the suspicion of other guests, "may I have a moment with Miss Valentine? *Alone.*"

Tally—the cool, calm, and collected woman who I'd seen crash a society party two nights before—skirted off like a scolded child and was taken in by another gaggle of women, all wearing pedal pushers or culottes and enjoying iced tea. They greeted her with light hugs and double-cheek kisses, ambivalent to the violence being displayed by their host.

"Who said you could spend time alone with my daughter?" Blackstone was seething through his back teeth, and if he wasn't such a large man, I would've thought it the behavior of a goon straight out of *Merrie Melodies.* All that was missing was a floppy cigar dangling from his mug. Behind him, two men in dark suits stood watching the situation, surely not neighbors, but hired guns. But the good kind that can almost pass for respectable.

"You never said I couldn't. Besides, she greeted me at that rickety coffin you call an elevator."

"I hired you to do reconnaissance on her."

"You hired *Tommy* to spy on her, not me." I looked down at my arm, where his hand was still clenched. "And I'd like you to take your hand off of me, you horse's patoot."

A mean smile curled up on Mr. Blackstone's lips, but he did as I asked—he'd probably seen too many movies where some classless girl like me started screaming and causing a scene to upset his well-to-do friends, and I don't think he wanted to explain to all the guests, or his daughter, why I was there. "Would you like me to drop your employer?"

"I don't give a darn what you do. I get paid no matter what. I'm here to tell you what I know—at your request, might I add."

"Come to my study."

"I'd rather not, considering what I know is *nothing*." Also, any meathead that didn't mind digging his fingers into my flesh while I was standing in the middle of a party wasn't going to get me alone. Especially since he had backup.

"Fortuna doesn't trust you enough to tell you what he's found out?" He clapped his hands together, thinking he had caught me between a rock and a hard place, and it was the first time I noticed he was at least two and a half sheets to the wind, and rounding the bases toward third.

I suppressed a laugh at the idea that Tommy wouldn't trust me with something as silly as *information* when every day he trusts me with his life. I've stitched him up more times than my Mama has sewed up my best church dress, but I declined to tell Mr. Blackstone that, lest he start to think Tommy's the kind of guy who couldn't afford a doctor.

"Tommy went to work right after you hired him," I said, "and went out of town after his first little look-see." There was no way I was going to spill the beans that he also had the fuzz hot on his tail.

"So tell me, Miss Valentine," Blackstone said plucking a mug of beer off of a passing tray, the silver the butler carried so shiny in the sunlight that it burned my eyes. "Why does Mr. Fortuna keep you around?"

"Beats me, boss," I said again, batting my eyelashes. I've found that if a man thinks you're an idiot and treats you like an idiot, it is usually to your benefit that you keep up the illusion.

"You're not much to look at, that's for sure, but sometimes it's the plain ones that offer a service no other girl can." He drained the beer, and another servant was there to fetch the mug as soon as he wiped the foam off his lips. I'd never seen a crystal beer mug before. "But I don't care where Fortuna is off to. I expect results. And quickly."

"I suspect you'll have answers fairly soon, though you may not like them one bit."

"I suspect I won't." He sighed, but it wasn't in any sympathy for me. "You can stay." He waved me off to the party and walked back inside like he was the Great Gatsby or something. Or maybe the several pints of beer just went through him faster than he'd expected. The goons followed him back inside.

Tally sidled up to me again. "What was that flap about?"

"Your father hired my boss to do something, then my boss got called away on other business. He isn't pleased." It was only sort of a fib.

"Sounds like *mon père*," Tally said with a smile. "He's generally an ass with the occasional bout of just being a plain ol' jerk. Though when he's like this, he can be abominable."

"He seems particular," I said, still trying to be polite.

"Oh, he is. He fancies himself a gangster, but I swear, he's only had one person in his whole darn life that didn't turn on him, and I think that's why he wants me to marry the guy," she said with a smile.

"Not to be rude, but I think I read about that somewhere," I said.

"It's not rude." Tally touched my arm to lead me to the pack of waiting housewives. "Come, I have to introduce you."

The women, some as young as Tally and others nearing or over forty, were introduced to me by name, each with a weak handshake and a full dossier on the man they were married to or fathered by.

"Everyone, this is Viviana," Tally said to the group. Half a dozen smiles with soft pink lipstick smiled brightly, welcoming me to the hoity-toity fold.

"It's a beautiful evening, isn't it?" A blonde woman in khaki pedal pushers and tan sandals offered me her hand, bent at the wrist and displaying an enormous diamond. You could start a camp fire with the damn thing, but I doubted she'd ever be caught dead in the woods.

"Sure is," I said back, grasping the tips of her fingers in my own. My instinct was telling me to either curtsy or kiss the ring, but I figured that was in poor taste, so I just gave her ivory-white fingers a squeeze. She seemed to accept that as a howdy-do.

Another, older woman in madras plaid Bermudas with a matching neck kerchief slipped a glass of pink, milky something off a tray and offered it to me. "You have got to try this," she said, and I sipped it politely. It tasted like melted ice cream—sugary and nutty, but with a hard kick. "It's called a pink squirrel! My drink of the summer!" The women near her burst with polite giggles, and they went about discussing refrigerators with the concern I've seen Tommy discuss hitmen.

All of the wives were polite and gracious and kind, and after what felt like hours chatting about the weather and fashion, and chittering nicely about the terrible things happening in Korea, I tugged at Tally's arm.

"Facilities?" I whispered.

"You can use mine. Know the way back?"

"Yeah. Thanks."

I excused myself and scurried back to Tallulah Blackstone's empty bedroom, now with a few minutes to myself to scrounge the place.

First thing, my hand slid under her pillow and along between the mattress and box spring, any place a normal girl would hide a diary. But Tally, not like other girls, had nothing of the sort. A quick dash to her vanity revealed a few photos of friends—Tally and other beautiful girls at various ages, smiling for the photobooth camera with their arms wrapped around each other—slipped into the mirror's frame. In a hurry, I pulled open drawers—the top left and right revealed nothing but literally thousands of dollars' worth of French beauty creams and more lipstick than I'd ever seen in real life. The bottom left held a hair dryer and hot curlers; the bottom right, hair sprays of a thousand sorts. Peeking behind the oldest, stickiest bottle was a fat wad of envelopes tied with a ribbon, but the handwriting was swirly and feminine, so they weren't from a beau. I slid the drawer shut and made the whole scene look brand new.

Conscious of the fib I had used to excuse myself from the masses, I ran to the washroom and flushed the toilet, just in case anyone could hear. I emerged back into her bedroom and found Tally standing with her arms crossed.

"Hiding?" she asked with a smile.

"It takes a lot of energy to keep up with that lot," I said.

"You're right, but we *do* have to go back," she said with a frown. She grabbed my hand again and led me back out to the verandah for more talking about absolutely nothing.

Once the sun went down, husbands began to come and collect their other halves. No one asked me where I got my dress.

"And how do you know the Blackstone family?" one snake-eyed lady crooned, expecting to enlighten other partygoers to the fact that I didn't belong there. Her words connected, slurring into each other, and—like a high-society werewolf—it was the time of night where claws came out. It was pretty obvious she'd never seen me before in the lobby or at Spence alumna functions, so I thought it was some pretty ham-fisted attempt to embarrass me and out me as a charity case or pet project of Tally's.

"Mr. Blackstone and I are business associates," I said back, and I saw a smile flicker on Tally's lips. The snake-eyed woman, who I'm sure was proud to have never worked an honest day in her life, shut her mouth and sidled away, pretending to need to refill her drink, which hours ago had switched from sweet tea to Sazeracs.

"Marguerite is a real drip," Tally said. "We have to invite her because she's bent out of shape that Dad refuses to leave the penthouse to go live in the country house, and she's left telling her grubby friends they live on the eleventh floor."

"The horror!"

"If you think we have money, you should hear Marguerite talk about how her family was some kind of French aristocracy."

"Didn't they all get their heads chopped off?" I asked. I knew they did, of course—one of Betty's favorite romances was *Love in the Time of Revolution*, and she yakked about it all the time.

"Sadly, they missed Marguerite's family." Tally began to giggle behind her hand. "Oh, I'm sorry, that's just awful. I shouldn't have said that."

"I don't mind."

"Dad's doing some overseas business," Tally said, looking over her balcony and assessing the population. "You wanna get out of here?"

The tall, vivacious daughter of a millionaire was asking me to hit the town with her, and there was not a single bone in my body that was going to say *no*.

"Can I use your phone first?" I asked. "I should let someone know that I might be late tonight. So they don't worry."

"Of course." She led me through the apartment once again, this time past Mr. Blackstone's study, where I could hear him snarling on the phone through the open door.

"Oh, ouch," I squealed to Tally. "Wait a sec? The shoes are borrowed too." I bent down to readjust the buckles at my ankles, taking the time to eavesdrop on the call.

"That's right—Yangon! I said what I said!" He was drunk and furious, and was clearly about to unload on the person on the other end of the line. "I don't care how difficult it is. Make it happen!"

But Tally had a child's impatience. "Oh, you're never going to guess where we're going," she said, hopping like a kid. "Do you want some sneakers?"

"I cannot let this acquisition fall through," her father said in the study. I looked up and our eyes connected, and he motioned for the door to be closed. A body in the shadows slammed it shut.

"No, I'm okay," I fibbed, finishing my useless futzing. "Where's the phone?"

She led me to a kitchen, where a pearlescent white wall phone hung over a jar of freshly sharpened pencils and a stack of notepads with cream paper so plush, each leaf felt like fabric. I flipped the dial and the operator connected me to Mrs. K's. I ran my fingers over the notecards as I waited for someone to pick up.

"Hi, Dottie, it's Viviana. I'm sorry if I woke anyone," I said hurriedly into the phone.

"Don't worry, Viviana. I believe everyone is up and waiting for you with bated breath." Dottie always spoke like a school principal.

"I'll have to tell them in the morning because I don't think I'm coming back until late tonight, after everyone is asleep. I have my key," I reassured her. "Mrs. K can lock up."

"Do be careful, and please let us know if you need anything."

"I shall." Shall? Dottie's squareness rubbed off too quickly. "But I've got enough cash for cab fare back from anywhere in Manhattan, and I can always call on a few of Tommy's friends who owe me some big favors—I'll be okay." I could hear Dottie huff on the other end at the mention of Tommy's circle of trouble boys, but she didn't argue.

As I hung up the phone, Tally perched next to me, now carrying a purse and with a gleaming white pair of PF Flyers laced up on her feet.

"Where you wanna go?"

I smiled. "You mentioned you already had someplace in mind, and nothing I do in this city is all that exciting."

"I *have* always wanted to try this one thing," she led me on. She dug around in a small bin and plucked out a set of car keys. "C'mon, it's gonna be great."

★ ★ ★

Tally pulled open a pantry door. Behind it, where I expected to see tins of beans and dried pasta, a private, hidden elevator car waited.

"Oh, thank God there's no operator in this one," I said, and Tally laughed.

"You're telling me. It's hard to come back from a night out on the town in front of a guy old enough to be your grandpa." She didn't seem to acknowledge how awful it'd be to spend a twelve-hour shift in a broom closet.

She pulled the cage open with a great big clack of hinges and metal. "This is the only one that goes to the garage," she explained as she mashed the single button. "Special little treat for the penthouse. Everyone else has to take the stairs from the lobby. You should *hear* Marguerite bitch and moan."

Every inch of Tallulah thrummed with energy, like a kid about to stuff his pockets and make a run from the candy store. My stomach was fluttering as the car lurched downward; I was standing in close proximity to one of the city's biggest razzle-dazzle girls, sneaking out in the middle of the night for a lark.

I hoped my mug wouldn't end up in the papers where Tommy could see. Fraternizing with the mark wasn't an explicit no-no, but it couldn't be good.

The car thundered down into a repurposed cellar, all dust and cobwebs and sewer smell, the muggy place at least fifteen degrees warmer than the air outside. Twenty cars lined up in the dim light, each one of them covered by its own beige canvas tarp. Tally ran to the car closest to the elevator door and began to tug on the heavy fabric.

"Gimme a hand. And hold your breath."

We pulled, and a plume of dust exploded toward the lights. Beneath it all was a brand new but familiar, shiny, black Cadillac coupé convertible, already waiting with its top down. It was the one I'd spotted on the curb the first day I'd had a run-in with Mr. Blackstone.

She hopped over the door into the driver's seat and thrust her key into the ignition. The scent of burning oil mixed in with the must and dust.

The garage was packed tight with vehicles like sardines in a can, and I couldn't open my door.

"Just jump! You can't hurt it," Tally said, stepping on the gas to make the engine rev. The purr of the engine rose to a growl and echoed off every concrete wall.

"I'll scratch it!" I figured if I dinged the door I likely wouldn't have to pay for it, but Tally would be on the receiving end of some kind of hellfire from her father, who'd already displayed that he had no issue manhandling a girl he *didn't* feel he owned.

"Who cares!" She revved the car again and flicked on the radio, which was just static and whines this far beneath the street above.

I braced my hand on the side of the car and flung my legs up and over the door, landing with a thwack of thighs against the red leather interior.

"That's my girl." The parking brake was off, and she shot forward at lightning speed, tires squealing as she maneuvered the beast up the tiny driveway. The front fender narrowly missed a column as we hurtled to the street.

"You know anything about cars?" she asked. We were flying down Fifth Avenue, swerving around cars driving at normal speed, when Tally took two hard left turns and careened the pricey hunk of metal onto FDR Drive. The tires hummed against the pavement, hitting potholes that sent my teeth chattering, but Tally held the wheel so tightly, nothing could shake her. The only time her white knuckles left the wheel was when she jammed the gear shift and picked up speed. Each time she hit the clutch, the car lurched and clunked and stopped and started, bucking like a bronco trying to shake his rider free, and I felt every single jerk in my bones.

"No, not a lot," I yelled. Next to the roar of the engine, the scream of the wind and the sound of the city, I could barely hear myself. Late-night groups trampled in and out of watering holes while smokers dangled out of bar windows, hoping for a breeze. Taxicabs were stalking for prey, lights on, hungry for someone to pick up, but most of New York was on foot, enjoying the summer air. If you listened closely, you could hear the trains beneath the grates and the steam in the pipes and the sound of a million people all breathing at the same time.

"I hate this car," Tally said, thumping the side of her fist on the dashboard. "It's my father's. It's exactly like him—too big, too showy, and too damn slow!" She flipped the radio dial one more time, and I could hear someone wailing away on a saxophone. "That's Charlie Parker!"

Did I jump into the deep end with this one.

"Don't you want to slow down a bit?" I found myself clutching my purse to my chest and sliding all over the smooth leather bench seat so I ended up in Tally's lap, longing for some kind of belt to keep me in place.

"Don't go chicken on me now," Tally laughed. "If you make it through tonight, you get to tell everyone how Tally Blackstone nearly bopped you off."

"I'm not chicken, I promise. I just . . ." A feeling came over me. "I just think I'm going to be sick."

Returning from my stop at the bushes in front of a small church, Tally patted me on the arm. "Boy, you really don't know cars."

"No." I closed my eyes and scooted down in my seat to lean my head against the door. "My family didn't have one growing up. Since I moved here, I've only ever been in taxis, and they don't go like the devil." The leather was smooth and cold against my temple, and the world was starting to spin a bit less.

"You still want to go out? Or should I drop you home?" She wasn't mad, but she wasn't happy either.

Normally I'm proud to say I live at Mrs. K's, but I was embarrassed to have Tally Blackstone and her four-thousand-dollar Cadillac coupé drive me to what now seemed like a sad little brownstone in a humdrum part of town. "No, let's keep going. I think the fresh air—some *low-speed* fresh air—will do some good."

"Alright, sweetheart. I'll go slow." The car pulled smoothly away from the curb, and Tally switched the radio from wailing, dizzying bebop to a station with Bing Crosby, and he crooned until the station played "The Star-Spangled Banner" and signed off.

After a few more minutes of driving, Tally's voice came out in a whisper: "Have you been through yet?"

There was a dark hole in front of us, and it looked like the planet was about to swallow us in one gulp.

"What on earth?"

"It's the new tunnel," she said. "It goes right under the river."

"Is it safe?"

"I think so. Only one way to find out." The Caddy slid into the darkness, and Tally flicked on her high beams. The air was still and a bit smelly, but it didn't reek of gas fumes like I thought it would.

With another churn of the engine, we were going up a ramp and, without even too much of a change in odor, we emerged from the hot hell of a New York City tunnel in the summertime. An angry, sweaty man was standing at a little metal hut underneath the sodium lamps, and Tally slowed just enough to toss him a dime. We were now officially in Brooklyn.

"Almost there."

"For someone who's never been to where she's going, you sure know the way."

"I've mapped it in my head," Tally admitted, looking away from the hood of the car for just one second to smile at me. "Just needed the right person to go with me."

She flipped the turn signal and headed south, farther than I thought the city could go. The air was fishy and felt cool and damp and wonderful against my skin. Then there was the smell of food and my emptied stomach growled.

"Hot dogs?"

Tally smiled and breathed in deep through her nose. "And . . . cotton candy."

"Roasted nuts and . . . oof, I think that's stale beer." My stomach made a sudden detour again, and Tally watched me to see if she needed to pull over for a second time, but for now everything stayed where it belonged.

"It is, that's for sure." Tally was giggling, and along with the sound of her laughter, I also heard screams, but not the kind from people who are scared for their lives. More like the excited kind, from people who are tickled pink to be terrified.

"Tally—have you never been to Coney Island before?"

"Is it that bad?" She looked embarrassed, a feeling I never thought Tally Blackstone could feel, after seeing too many photos of her dancing on tabletops or spilling out of bars.

"I'm just surprised! You never came here when you were a girl?"

"Never once. *Mon pére* always said it wasn't for 'our kind.'"

My heart ached for the kid sitting next to me in the pricey car; she had all the money and toys in the world but had never screamed her heart out on the Cyclone.

"Pull into that parking lot over there, and let's get the top up," I said, scrabbling around on my knees to pull on the canvas roof. "We're at least getting you on *one* ride before everything closes down."

★ ★ ★

We scurried over the dark sidewalks toward the blinking, noisy, whirring lights.

"You've never been on a ride before?"

"Just one," Tally admitted. "There's a carousel in Paris that I always begged *ma mère* to let me ride. She would give the operator just handfuls of bills, climb aboard the old horses with me, and we would compete to see who could get the most rings. I'm sure she always let me win."

"Do you want to find the merry-go-round here?"

"No, no," Tally said, the memory changing, very briefly, the color of her eyes. "What else is there?"

"The roller coaster, for sure. Steeplechase, The Scrambler. Or the Wonder Wheel." I pointed to the tallest of them all, and Tally's eyes brightened and grew as big as the wheel itself.

"Okay, I think you chose!" I pulled her in the direction of the ride.

We paid for our tickets and ran to the car at the base of the ride. A young man in dark blue jeans and a denim work shirt stood outside, chewing the white plastic at the tip of his cigarillo, the other end of it no longer lit.

"Do you want inside or outside?" I asked, and Tally gave me a look.

"What do you mean?"

"Do you promise you don't get motion sickness?"

"You were the one who tossed in the car." Tally scowled.

"I didn't vomit *in* the car," I replied, doubly loud to ensure the impatient carnie that he wasn't going to have to hose out the gondolas on account of me. I turned to him and added, "Fine, we'll take the inside."

"If you say so," he grunted, and opened the tiny door to one of the blue cars swaying in the ocean wind.

They moved the wheel slightly to free up another car and Tally grabbed my arm.

"What's happening?"

I couldn't help myself—I busted out laughing. "Well, hon, the outside cars, the ones at the very edge, they're welded in place. The inside cars, though—the blue and red ones? The one we're in? These suckers *move*."

Seeing no one else in the darkness waiting for a ride, the carnie pulled his lever, and the whole Wonder Wheel started turning. Our car slid from its stationary position toward the center of the machine, and Tally let out a yelp.

"Oh, my god!" The metal of the car hit the end of the track with a clunk. "We're going to die!"

"We are absolutely not going to die," I said. "Just wait until we get over the top."

The wheel lumbered through its cycle, and the ocean crested through the open-air viewing window. From our vantage point, you could see the entire boardwalk, with the Cyclone lit up along its entire track, and Nathan's Famous's gleaming yellow stand in the distance.

"Are you ready?"

"Absolutely not!" Tally cried.

I could feel us getting to the top of the wheel and braced myself. As we headed back down, the car picked up speed and rocketed toward the edge of the wheel.

Tally screamed.

"Are you okay?"

"I think I want to get off!"

I reached out and hugged the scared girl, patting the back of her head. "Oh, sweetie, we'll just holler at the man when we get toward the bottom. There's nothing we can do from up here." I felt bad, but I couldn't stop my giggles.

"Next time, I'll be better," she promised, whimpering a bit through her own laughs. "Okay, now let me go. I want to see the lights."

★　★　★

"If you thought that was fun, Tallulah Blackstone," I said as we ran down the ramp and away from the sliding cars and blinking electric lights of the Wonder Wheel, "we should come back soon and try the parachute jump."

Tally checked her wristwatch and pouted. "We don't have time for another ride, do we?"

"We probably shouldn't stick around." The streets were deserted of couples and kids; our only company was a battery of carnies shuttering their booths and janitors sweeping up litter. I heard a scuttle against the curb and did my best to convince myself it was trash in the breeze, not rats looking for a midnight meal. "Best not stay for too much longer. Every fair just gets sad at some point in the night, and I think we're about past it."

Tally grabbed my hand again and gave it a squeeze. "Back to the car it is then." We walked our way to where she'd left her daddy's Caddy. She slipped the parking lot attendants a two-dollar tip, and they tossed her the keys with a smile, and we were on our way. In the mirror, I watched a black Nash slink out of the lot and follow us out of Brooklyn. Everyone was going home.

"Top down?" she asked.

"No, I think I need the heat!" A few twisted dials and the blower churned out hot air that only got more comforting as the engine heated up, the leather of the bench seat warming up against my bare legs.

Tally drove slowly back to Manhattan. Even though I'd never sat behind the wheel of a vehicle, I could tell she was making an effort not to take the most direct route. I checked my mirror for the Nash, but the headlights were far enough away not to be concerning.

"Do you not want to go home?" I finally asked.

"Whatever gave you the clue?" The radio was off, and with no one else on the road to honk at us, the cabin of the Cadillac was darn near silent. Though the closest stoplight was half a block away and blazing green, she began pressing the brake until the Caddy slowed to a stop at the yellow. At this rate, we wouldn't be back uptown until daybreak.

If I'd learned anything from my boss over the years, this was the time to open the floodgates and get our girl to spill all her family beans. She'd clung to me from the moment we met like gum to a shoe; a lonely little rich girl in need of companionship she couldn't buy, and for some reason she'd chosen me. One quick question about her brute of a father, and I'd likely have all the dirt we needed to fill the case file, and we could type it all up and send an invoice.

But she'd believed in my friendship from the outset, and all I could think was *She's Tommy's mark, not yours.*

"You know what?" I asked. "We sort of met once before—before tonight."

"Wouldn't surprise me all that much," she said, her voice running just a bit more controlled than it had been before. "I run into an awful lot of people."

"What's a wild story for me probably isn't the same for you," I said with a laugh. "A boat party at Chelsea Piers. Cassandra what's-her-name and her hoity-toity husband-to-be."

"You were there? I didn't talk to too many people."

"No, you addressed the whole crowd at once. I was wearing a green dress. Standing near the bar?"

Tally thought as she casually downshifted for a blinking red light. "Hmm."

"You paid me a kind compliment."

She turned to me with a puzzled look on her puss. "That's nice at least."

"Dragon brooches," I said, running my hand over the patent-leather belt she'd loaned me. "You told me you liked my jewelry."

"They were very pretty," she said, with a smile creeping over her lips and a blush overtaking her cheeks.

"Thank you."

The car went silent, the heat making a sheen of sweat break out on my skin.

The car meandered its way back through the new tunnel and into Lower Manhattan.

"Your father won't worry where you are?" I asked. Considering the man had hired my boss to tail his only daughter, I figured he was a bit overprotective.

"No, no. He drank so much beer tonight, he won't wake up before noon tomorrow," Tally assured me. "And even if he does, he'll just blow his top at somebody else."

"No one will get fired, though, right?"

"Not likely. Funny enough, once all the boys got back from being soldiers, only a select few were happy to still take orders," Tally said. "Especially from a horse's ass like Tallmadge Blackstone. He can't go through help like Errol Flynn went through girls. Not anymore. But the staff that's left is really stuck to him like glue. I don't get it."

"I've only spoken to the man a few times," I assured her, "but I get why someone may not want to work for him."

Tally laughed, relaxing again into the bench seat. "Are you hungry?"

"Starved."

"Here, I know a place." Tally turned her Cadillac up Second Avenue and stopped a short ways away from Cooper Union; the Nash continued on down the broad street. Tally caught me eyeing the car.

"Know him?"

"I don't think so, but someone I knew thought they were the best cars in the world," I said. "Sandy never once shut up about 'the lines.'"

"Really? A Nash is a gangster's car, the same way this Caddy is for grouchy old men."

"I guess gangsters seem pretty rich to some of us." I shrugged.

"I'd go for a Porsche, myself, but to each their own," Tally said. "Come on."

A bright green sign lit up the block, advertising an all-night kosher diner.

"You like blintzes?"

"How can you not?"

"I *knew* I liked you."

★　★　★

A platter of fruit and cheese pastries skidded to a stop before us, the whole dish dusted in what looked like pounds of powdered sugar. Tally and I stopped slurping our egg creams to dig in. The diner was a long, thin corridor with a shiny white Formica counter and hanging milk glass pendants that sent off a dull, yellow glow. It smelled of fry oil and sugar and onions—a not *un*pleasant aroma—and a small radio on the far end of the counter played classical. There were four souls total beneath the lights—Tally, me, and two Eastern European cooks, both leaning on the counter, reading thick textbooks, now that our food was off the hob.

I picked up my fork and twiddled it in my fingers, stabbing a random roll of dough and delighting as the red filling oozed out. As soon as the hot, buttery pastry met my tongue, it melted, and I was thrilled, for the second time that day, to not be wearing my girdle.

"Did you try the apple one yet?" Tally asked, a drip of cinnamon-colored jelly dribbling down her chin. Her mouth was open slightly, and she was fanning herself, the hot, sugary filling clearly burning her tongue. "It is soooo *good*."

I stuffed a second forkful of cherry into my mouth and chewed while shaking my head.

"These are some of the best I've ever eaten," I said, swallowing, "But don't tell my landlady."

"Do you have an apartment?" Tally asked. There was jealousy in her voice, and I was floating.

"Sort of. I have a room in a boarding house. There are three other girls, and the landlady lives in the basement with her son," I explained. "I love having people in the house, but I have a space that's all mine."

"That must be amazing," Tally said. "My father won't even let me put a lock on my door. The only time I ever got to be alone was when my mother took me to France for the summers."

"He let you go?"

"Oh, with plenty of yelling and shouting, for sure," Tally confirmed. "There wasn't *much* he could do—*mon grandpère* has more money than Dad ever will. And that he can respect."

"At least it's something. What part of France?"

"All over. There were apartments in Paris until—" She broke off, and I knew what she meant. "And then the estate in Burgundy. I like the cities, but I was such a little rat when I was a girl. Put me in boy clothes, and I'd be digging up the vines, stalking badgers, coming back with snail shells and frogs and who knows what else to show *ma mère*."

"She didn't find that disgusting?"

"Oh, no. *Ma mère* was a wild one," Tally said with a knowing smile. "That's where I get it from, I assure you. The personality *and* the figure." She shimmied a bit in her seat to ease the tension, but I knew she was putting on a show to break the air of sadness.

The country's most sought-after debutante went about studying the plate of pastries in front of us, and my heart started breaking for her. She'd not known fun for too many years of her short life; she'd never had a day go by without someone needing a report on how she was feeling, what she was thinking, or where she planned to go.

"The boarding house isn't all heaven," I said, trying in my own way to make her feel better. "I have to share a bathroom with two other women."

"Yikes."

"Betty never cleans up after she spits out her toothpaste," I said. "And you should hear Dottie yell about it. Phyllis, the model upstairs, is the only one who has it good—she's got her own bathroom. But for us, it's like going to Barnard without a diploma at the end."

"Did you go to college?" Tally's voice was swooning.

"No, sweetie—I barely went to high school."

College, I thought. *Girls with money have some ideas.*

"Me too, sorta," Tally admitted.

"What?"

"I've never been to school." The heiress's eyes went down to the chipped white Formica.

"You can't just not go to school!"

Tally laughed and her eyes met mine. "Yeah, you can. I had a governess."

"How . . . European."

"That's what you get when your mom is French and your dad is a wealthy, overprotective hawk. I know they thought about Miss Porter's for a while, but my mother couldn't bear to let me out of her sight, even if it was just to Connecticut. And after *ma mére* died, Madame Beauchamp came in every day. The basics, you know—reading, writing, poetry, music, and manners."

"Not math and history?"

"History I got from books. Math . . ."

I laughed. "It's a good thing your dad's bank accounts are endless."

"I'd never be able to keep track of expenses—the business, the autos, the private train car, the Los Angeles estate, the Connecticut estate, the horses . . ." Her sentence meandered off.

"Now I'm glad that my ledger just reads for rent and the occasional new dress!"

Tally brightened up. "Could you imagine? Thank goodness Dad has Web too. He went to Philips Exeter. And then West Point. Then Princeton after the war. The whole deal."

"What a catch!"

"I'm sure he was quite handsome in his prep school uniform," Tally said, wiping a tear from her eye. "Too bad that was before the time of the Great War."

I took the crack as a joke, but Tally stayed silent, and my mind immediately jumped to imagine her in a wedding dress, being met at the end of the aisle by an aged doughboy. I guess it wasn't much of a joke to her.

"Oh, honey," I said, patting Tally's hand. "You don't have to go back there tonight. Come and stay with us regular folk. Mrs. K won't mind if you crash in my room tonight. And she always makes enough breakfast to feed an army."

"That's awful nice of you," Tally said. "Let me go ring home and tell the boys to run interference on Dad if he wakes up too early. He doesn't need to know where I am."

Tally scurried to the pay phone by the restroom and made a long call to her staff, who I think were happier to take orders from the younger Blackstone than the elder. The door swung open, and two men in jumpsuits, getting off a late shift, came in and took the booth by the door. One of the cooks grunted in their direction, and the coveralls with the bald head barked an order for black coffee and nothing else. The one with the dark curly hair went to wait in line for the phone.

When Tally returned, we polished off our blintzes while pantomiming to the sounds of dramatic, rapid-fire Italian coming from the workman's phone conversation. He hung up and caught us teasing him, so Tally, true to form, overtipped for the drinks and snacks, and scribbled a note on the bill to say she'd also covered his. Then we exited into the crystal-clear evening. It was well past two o'clock, and the bars were emptying. Plenty of men now roamed the streets, drunk on summer and cheap beer to boot.

"Where to?" Tally asked as she slammed the Caddy's door shut. The engine in the black car behind ours turned over, ready to hit the road.

"Chelsea."

"How hip," Tally said with approval.

"How *broke*," I said back. "Be sure to lock up tight when we park."

★ ★ ★

Few people on our block owned cars, so Tally slid up to the curb in front of Mrs. K's boarding house.

"This is it!" I said, popping open my door. "Home sweet home."

"It's so pretty," Tally said of the squat, brown building. In the darkness, it looked like a grumpy chicken woken up in her henhouse. The porch light was on—the only blazing bulb on the whole block, aside from the streetlights—but all of the curtains were drawn.

"Mrs. K and her family are on the bottom," I said, lowering my voice as I pulled my key out of my evening bag. "The girls live on the top. Some of the walls are paper thin, so we better be church mice."

My key slid into the lock easily, but Mrs. K must've kept it all unlatched for me, despite my warning to Dottie, because the tumblers didn't click when I turned it. The heavy wood door opened with a small grunt. The door led to a small vestibule that was littered with Oleks's umbrellas and dirty sneakers, then another door that was usually wide open in the summer months. It was closed for now, so I bumped it with my hip and directed Tally with a tiny shove toward the stairwell, dark for the night. The exterior door shut with a tiny thump, and I reached to flick the dead bolt.

We were in total blackness. All I could hear was Tally breathing and the footsteps of one of the girls upstairs in the hall, probably making a nighttime trip to the facilities.

"Come on, and watch your step," I whispered. "I'm just up one flight. Hold on to the railing." I held Tally's hand as I dragged her upstairs, keeping her between me and the bannister on the wall.

"I'm as blind as a bat!" she giggled.

The footsteps upstairs stopped. "For crying out loud, it's just me, Betty. Or Phyllis. Or whoever you are!" I hissed loudly, almost breaking into full volume. "Don't *worry*."

I turned to Tally. "I bet it's Dottie—I can smell her pencil shavings. She's a teacher and, uh, doesn't go out much on Friday nights."

I barely got the words out before heavy, thunderous footsteps came racing down the length of the hall. A door opened up on the landing—Betty, sticking her pretty blonde head out to see the commotion, and squinting like a mole in the darkness—and I could see a silhouetted figure flying down the stairs, where moments before I thought there was nothing but shadow. Tally dropped my hand and I couldn't sense her in the black—it was like she'd evaporated at the sound of footsteps.

Before I knew it, the figure hit me, and I was airborne and careening down the staircase. The last thing I heard was the sound of a woman screaming in the night.

DAY 4

Saturday, June 24, 1950

As soon as I woke up, I saw Mrs. K's pale, round face close to mine, like I was staring at the moon.

"Where . . .?"

"The French Hospital," she whispered. "You are fine—you're awake."

The ward was dark and gray, a cheerless well of a room filled with barely breathing girls. The look on Mrs. K's face let me know that polite society would still consider this the middle of the night.

"*Pretty girl*, it is good to see your eyes," she said, smoothing my hair. Her hands were warm and soft, but they met the hairspray Phyllis had caked on my strands with a bit of a crunch. Mrs. K grimaced and pulled away.

"I've got a hell of a headache, Mrs. K," I muttered. Everything in my body hurt, right down to my teeth.

"Yes, I am sure. Let me get Nurse." Still in a brown plaid housecoat, Mrs. K shuffled away. Even in the darkness,

I could tell that she was the only person with me at the hospital.

Two figures came back my way, and in the flickering light of the enormous infirmary, they couldn't have been more different. My soft, graying, perfect landlady being followed by a prim woman—her daintiness made her look years younger than me—decked fully in starched white, and with pink lipstick on a mouth that turned up just slightly to show her teeth, which gleamed in the moonlight. Her little hands with long, curved fingers pawed at my pillow to fluff it, but I could barely feel the movement through all my roughed-up and aching bones.

"Your mother is going to have to go home," she said in a pipsqueak voice. "No visitors on the ward."

"No," was all I could groan. I'd never been in a hospital overnight—not even when I was born—and the idea of sleeping in a wide, open room alone was giving me the flutters. Janitors, workers, family, and all sorts of people could find their way in.

Mrs. K patted my hand. "You rest."

As my only comfort moved away in the dark toward the exit, the nurse drew herself up to her full height, her spine as straight as a pin, every seam of her white uniform aligned. "No good man likes a chippy who stays out late," she said down her nose. She bustled after Mrs. Kovalenko and left me in the dark.

★ ★ ★

"So"—a voice rang through my head—"have a bit of excitement last night, Miss Valentine?" The click of a lighter preceded the stink of a burning cigarette.

The pain in my head had moved its way to my rear—and now my least favorite pain in the ass was waking me up.

"Seriously, Lawson. I'm supposed to be resting." I opened my eyes to see the detective paging through my medical file, an ashing cigarette dangling from his lower lip. "Or do you want me to stay an invalid?"

"Imagine my horror when I heard the news that my favorite secretary in all of the five boroughs was harmed in a B and E last night."

"Mrs. K's is in the tenth precinct. You're in Midtown North." Lawson's voice was grating against my pounding temples. All the pain was making me dizzy, and the last thing I wanted to do was anything that'd show physical weakness in front of the detective. "Why on earth are you here?"

"You know, lines like that, they get a little fuzzy sometimes," Lawson said, flipping the page to read more about what might be causing my unending aches and pains. "Huh. Wouldn't'a guessed five feet seven inches tall and that weight. And please, consider my concern and appearance at your bedside a favor. For Tommy." He took a long draw from his cigarette and let two wisps of smoke trail from his nostrils as he continued to pour over my chart.

"Yeah, 'cause you two are old pals."

"Yeah, exactly. You know, we have a lot of history together. He'd want me to look out for you while he can't. The Chief and I would really like to have a chat with him anyhow." Lawson wasn't finding what he was looking for in my folder, and he angrily stubbed out his smoke in a metal ashtray attached to the wall by the door to the ward. "And rumor has it you were in some pretty distinguished company. You don't find too many heiresses in Chelsea."

I saw the heads of the women closest to me in the ward whip in my direction. If the smoking, louche detective didn't already have their attention, the mention of *heiresses* definitely grabbed it.

"Keep your voice down, Lawson. This is confidential, isn't it?" I asked. "Her father hired Tommy. I delivered something to him at his place uptown last night. Tally dropped me off home."

"Tally?"

"Miss Blackstone." The woman in the bed to my left squeaked, and I could see her scrabbling for a pen, but her ability to reach the table next to her was hindered by her leg being in full traction.

"So, did you and *Miss Blackstone* go anywhere between her father's home and Mrs. Kovalenko's last night?" A blue Gitanes cigarette box emerged from his person, and he plucked out a fresh French cigarette, an engraved Zippo lighter from his pocket, the metal clacking against a pure gold pinky ring now adorning his hand. A click, a whiff of smoke, and a deep breath. As more smoke whirled around the ward, more eyes went from their *Life* magazines and get-well-soon cards to our little charade.

"What's it to you?" I pulled myself upright in my hospital bed and tried to sit up as tall as I could, breathing deeply in an attempt to calm myself and not to vomit from the pain and the stink of European cigarettes. My hair was flat, my head poked to death by hairpins, and the heavy makeup Phyllis had caked on hours and hours ago was still smeared on my face, even though Tally had wiped off as much as she could.

"'What it is' is my case. The mystery meat left for dead in Tommy's office, you getting knocked halfway to the moon by a thug—who was waiting for you to get home and was just a few closed and presumably *unlocked* doors away from the pretty little chickadees you live with. Either way," Lawson said, walking closer to me and sitting on the end of my bed, "you're not safe right now. And this is a public ward."

I groaned and wished I could roll over to hide my face, but there was no way my screaming muscles would let me. "Lawson, I hate it when you make sense. But there's no need to scare these girls."

"Okay, okay. So, why don't you tell me what Blackstone has you working on?"

The lurch in my stomach was a combination of cold blintzes and the world's biggest fathead detective creeping in on Tommy's case.

"I can't do that," I said. "At least not until Tommy gives me the go-ahead."

"Throw me a bone here, Viviana." He looked more exasperated than angry. "Tommy's a wanted man, and you can be charged as an accessory, you know."

I realized he wouldn't threaten me with cuffs unless some higher-up had told him it was a possibility. And knowing Tommy, it was the last thing he'd ever want.

"Fine. Hold your horses on that, boy-o. I'll cooperate. I'll tell you what Miss Blackstone and I were up to last night. I promise, though you might not believe me, there were no scandals."

Detective Lawson whistled, and Officer Leary entered the ward, pencil and notebook in hand. His eyes stayed cast to the ground.

"For cripes' sake, Leary, I'm decent—you can look up." The boy blushed while Lawson laughed.

"Okay, start from the beginning," the detective commanded. "Leary—good, take notes."

"By now you know ol' Tommy Boy's got some work from Blackstone," I said while Leary nodded. "Tommy's the best PI in the city—you said so yourself, and everyone knows it. It's not all that queer to get some of the upper crust coming in with odd jobs—cheating wives, missing earrings worth millions, other little fights that only the well-to-do can waste their time on. Though I have to say, Blackstone is by far the richest client of Tommy's that *I've* ever met."

"Sure. Believe it or not, I do also care about the crimes of the rich and the famous."

"Now, I'm not leaking the particulars, like I said, but I'll give you that this isn't the most dangerous gig Tommy's ever taken."

"I'll believe you, for now."

"Believe me or don't, but I'm telling you the God's honest. Anyway, because he's a *client*, I ran uptown to give Blackstone a progress report while Tommy's incommunicado."

"I doubt Blackstone liked *that* very much."

"How'd you guess? He's a real piece of work."

"I've heard." Lawson reached over and tapped his cigarette on the edge of my water cup, now that he was too far away from the ashtray on the wall. The cup's murky plastic was dull from thousands of washings and I could barely see the ash floating on top.

"So I got to his great big uptown penthouse, where I was greeted with a cold shoulder from Mr. Blackstone and a whole lot of noses in the air from the rest of his dinner guests. You know how they are."

"Actually, I don't," Lawson retorted. "You can imagine I don't deal a whole lot with the highbrow muckety-mucks in my precinct." Since I knew the detective as well as I did, I would venture to say he was jealous.

"Good point. Maybe you should consider leaving public service, Detective."

"Don't tempt me, Valentine. Anyway—what's going on with the daughter?"

"I mean, I feel real bad for the girl," I admitted. "She's getting a raw deal. The money's not hers, and Daddy dearest dangles the carrot in front of her to try to control her. We fled her papa's party and went to Coney Island."

"You went to the amusement park?"

"Yeah, did the Wonder Wheel and all that. She'd never been."

"And then what? Speakeasy? After-hours party? Jewel heist? I don't know what those types get up to after call time."

"We went and had blintzes in the East Village."

"And then what else?"

"And then what else *what*? I got a ride home because Tallulah took out her dad's Cadillac—I don't know if she has a driver's license, so you might be able to ticket her for joyriding, if that's even considered a crime anymore—and getting a ride back was easier than taking a cab."

Lawson pulled at his pencil-thin mustache, clearly trying to discern whether I was lying. "What else."

"There was a black Nash sedan following us a good part of the way," I said, "but good luck tracking that lead down when there are thousands in Manhattan alone. Then Miss Blackstone dropped me off on the curb, and I went inside, where I got rushed by a creep and ended up here. If you want to know what happened between me getting knocked out and my arrival at the hospital, you'll have to ask Mrs. K."

"And where was Miss Blackstone in all of this?"

"Long gone by that point, I'd guess," I fibbed. "What was she going to do—spend time jawing with a secretary in her windowless room?" When said out loud, it sounded absolutely pathetic.

Leary stopped scribbling with his stub of yellow pencil. "Your room doesn't have any windows?"

"It's three dollars less a week to have no windows," I explained. "My room's the middle one on the hall. Betty has the big front room with the front window, and Dottie has the back room with the back window and the fire escape down to the alley. Phyllis is upstairs, with the whole floor. Since Mrs. K's house shares a wall with the neighboring brownstone, I got no window."

"And this intruder—did you get a look at all?" Leary pressed.

"No, not one bit. It was pretty late. Mrs. K doesn't make us stick to a curfew—that's one of the reasons I like her place so much; some other places are strict—and the girls all shut their doors and were light's out. We can all make it through the house with our eyes closed, and if I turn on the light, it wakes everyone up," I explained. "I feel blessed to have the housemates I do, Detective, but you've never dealt with Betty after she's been awoken in the night."

"The prowler—did he say anything? Anything at all, before running downstairs?"

"Nope. All I heard was someone creeping around on the landing—then footsteps. I thought it was one of the girls, nature calling or what have you—my room is next to the bathroom upstairs. Whoever it was clocked me good and proper when I was halfway up the stairs. Must've gotten me square in the jaw, by the feel of it. Thank goodness not when I was at the top, or else I'd've been kaput."

"Any witnesses?"

"Betty—in the front room—stuck her head out when she heard the running. But I don't know how much she could see. Like I said, the house was dark. I even turned off the porch light when I came in, like I always do. I don't want to besmirch our reputations, but it's usually me or Phyllis who are out the latest, but she didn't have a date last night."

"Leary, make a note that we have to talk to the dames at the boarding house. Today's your lucky day." Lawson smiled.

"And no one's telling me nothin', so lay it to me straight, Lawson—what does my chart say, since you were snooping through it? Anything broken? Will I have to be here long?"

"Nothing you've got to worry about too bad, baby. But you're gonna have to mind that caboose of yours for at least a few days. Or have someone mind it for you." A furious blush came over my own cheeks—and, from what I could see, young Officer Leary's—as Lawson turned to him and snapped his fingers. "Come on, kid. We've got some girls to see."

* * *

The same self-righteous rodent of a nurse came toward me once Detective Lawson left, bearing a gray-brown tray dotted with various slimy foods and a bowl of bright green Jell-O for a kicky pop of color. The smell of everything together was earthy, burnt, and sour, and there was no way any of it was going to pass my lips.

"That young officer looked concerned for you," she said, her voice softening. Officer Leary's worry and blushing had convinced her that my reputation wasn't a foregone conclusion, even though I was now associated with a known harlot the likes of Tallulah Blackstone.

"Sure did," I agreed. "Excuse me, but is there any chance I could see my doctor?"

"Oh, don't worry about that, dear," the nurse tut-tutted at me. "He's told the *detective* all about your condition. You'll be free to return home with your mother later this morning." The tray was dropped on the table next to me like a dead halibut, and she carried on with her rounds, ignoring that same damn custodian who came in, mopping the floor, his sleeves rolled up. I sighed and shut my eyes.

* * *

Mrs. Kovalenko's teenage boy met our cab at the curb, greeting me with a large, paper-wrapped sandwich and an offer to help me inside.

"You look like ground liver," he said, giving me a burly arm on which I steadied myself with two hands. He was only seventeen but over six feet tall, built like a brick icehouse.

"I bet you say that to all the girls, Oleks."

"Only you, Viv—you know you're my favorite." He barked out a laugh, and the sound reverberated in his barrel chest.

Two steps into the foyer and I was already exhausted.

"Not to be forward, but do you want me to carry you up?" For the second time today a young man was blushing at me, but at least I'd known this one since he was in short pants.

"You know what? Knock yourself out." He handed me my food, then crouched down low and swung his arms beneath my knees, lifting me up like I weighed as much as sparrow. "You been practicing?" I asked, pulling on his ear.

This time the blush traveled from his hairline all the way beneath his T-shirt collar, and I got no smart response.

"I'm kidding, I'm kidding," I said as he deposited me at the top of the stairs. "Can I give you a holler if I need anything?"

"Always can." He smoothed his blond hair back with his palm before making a hasty retreat to his mother's apartment in the basement.

Betty descended on me like a hungry wolf, still in her summer pajamas.

"Oh my God! Are you okay? Are you hurt? I'm amazed you aren't dead!"

The words tumbled out of her mouth a mile a minute, and her voice was so high I imagined she'd soon be calling dogs to the front stoop.

"I'm fine, healthy as a horse—don't worry." I turned the knob on my door, but it didn't budge.

"Maybe it's stuck in the humidity. Betty, be a dear and knock this open for me?"

She planted her feet and jiggled the door, but it didn't budge. "Got your keys? It feels locked."

"That's strange." I fished around in my handbag to find my ring, jangling with the keys for all of Tommy's secret compartments and my own. Selecting an old-fashioned skeleton model, I slipped it into the lock and it turned with a bit of prying, hoping the thin shaft of the key wouldn't snap off in the usually unused lock. "Home sweet home."

"Do you need some company?" Betty's eyes were like fire, and I had a feeling she wasn't overly concerned with my health.

"I need a nap, Betts," I assured her. "I need to eat this sub and then sleep for as long as I possibly can. Once I wake up . . . then you can ask me about Tally."

"Okay, sleep tight!" She skittered off to her room to wait me out.

★　★　★

Either Gene Krupa was practicing on my door, or it was dinnertime and Betty was not going to let me sleep any longer without sharing the dirt. I hadn't meant to sleep like the dead, but since I was in a bed that smelled like me and not like industrial bleach, my body decided to remain in slumber land for at least a few hours.

"All right, I heard ya!" The knocking stopped. "I'll be down in a minute."

The hall was empty as I emerged to go to the bathroom, cold cream in hand to finally take off the paint Phyllis had put on me a whole day ago. My body ached something awful, so I was all decked out in nothing but my summer nightshift and robe, hair in a kerchief. It took three rounds of Ponds to get it all off, but I left the bathroom with my whole new angel face.

It took a few minutes to get downstairs to the kitchen, creeping all the way, with my hands gripping the bannister, and Betty met me at the door.

"There is not a single man worth looking at in the whole hospital," she said through furrowed brows. "And now two *more* of your Casanovas swing by?"

I swung my head around the doorframe to Mrs. K's dining room, and lo and behold, Detective Lawson and Officer Leary were there, sitting like they owned the place, sipping coffee and eating cookies, surrounded by my housemates. Even Dottie was staring at Detective Lawson like he was Alan goddamn Ladd.

"The tough-guy charm wears off around the third time one of them bleeds on your shoes," I said. "What do they want, anyhow?"

"Just asked about what we saw last night, and I told 'em what I saw—basically nothing."

"Basically?"

"You were home, you were on the stairs, someone was prowling in the hall and knocked you flat when they were fleeing the scene."

"Good girl."

"Wanna swing by . . ."

"Yes, Betty, I want to swing by. Gimme a minute, will ya?"

Lawson and Leary had already seen me, so there was no sense in going up to change out of my nightclothes.

"Where's O'Malley?" I purred, rounding the door. "Honestly, I'm getting tired of seeing the same two faces."

Officer Leary stood so fast to greet me, his chair fell over backward. Phyllis and Dottie each suppressed giggles, and Lawson graciously began scribbling in his notebook to hide his smile.

"I choose who I work with," was all Lawson would say once he regained composure. "Viviana. Have a seat."

I didn't much care for being invited to sit in my own dining room, but I wordlessly pulled out a chair at the other end of Mrs. K's table, and the girls left the room in a single file. Mrs. K bustled in with a glass of iced tea for me and a refill on the cops' coffees. Then, I was alone.

"The girls all corroborate your story," Lawson started in, punctuating his statement with a sip of black coffee. Leary was scribbling, eyes cast down on his own notebook now.

"Go figure."

"Does the boarding house get a lot of prowlers?"

"No . . .," I said slowly. "I've lived here for years, and Mrs. K runs a tight ship. I phoned after eleven o'clock last night and told Dottie for Mrs. K to lock the front door because I had my keys, and I assumed she had."

"That's what she said. And yeah, I checked police records. The Kovalenko residence hasn't once called the police in the fifteen years the boarding house has been at this address."

"I've never felt ill at ease here. At Tommy's, of course." I swirled my glass, tinkling my ice cubes, thinking. "All types come swinging by there, and I try to be safe. If I'm alone, I'll lock the door. If there's an irate customer, Tommy always gets them out the door. But never here. Never once at Mrs. K's."

"And you make the one-mile walk to Hell's Kitchen every day?"

"Every workday, unless it's snowing or raining cats and dogs; then I take a cab and Tommy pays for it. Sometimes I go on weekend days, if Tommy asks specifically. You know this isn't a strict nine-to-five, even though I think Mrs. K would prefer it if I did something a little less . . . colorful."

"Do you take the same route? To and from work?"

"Usually. It's the safest way I've found—well lit, no walking past bars or rowdy places. But not in the past few days," I said. "I've been all over the map the past few days."

"But before Wednesday, someone coulda tracked you. Someone who wanted to take a roundabout way to hurt Tommy."

It wasn't a question from Lawson, and I felt hot tears spring to my eyes.

"I'm such a fool," I said through a sniffle. I was too tired, too sore, and too damn grouchy to keep my cool. "Any number of goons who harbored a grudge against Tommy coulda eyed me. I've been a sitting duck!"

"We've fingerprinted the front door and the bannister, but no dice," Lawson said. "Everything's too goofy for us to get a clean break."

"So you got nothing?"

Lawson downed his steaming coffee in a gulp. "I wouldn't say nothing, but not a lot to go on."

"You've got nothing here, and I know you've got nothing on Tommy. Nothing incriminating, no evidence to convict. And so you're still keen to pin him?"

"I'm not *keen* to do anything, Viv," Lawson said. "But the commish sees it as the logical conclusion—there is a warrant out for his arrest, and juries have sent men to the chair with less to go on. And if Tommy gets brought in, I gotta follow the law."

"That's a pretty big *if*," I said, my teeth chattering, even though it was plenty warm in Mrs. K's dining room. "Tommy can be a pretty slippery fish."

"Let's hope," Lawson said.

"And if you manage to get other leads?"

"If they're solid, then Tommy gets off the hook. That's how the law works."

"How it *should* work," I said in response.

"Don't start with me on this again, Viviana," Lawson said.

"Tommy came to you with all the evidence you needed."

"And I'm sorry his brother went and got fitted for a pair of cement shoes, but you know that I couldn't submit that evidence in court. What he gave me was hearsay."

"That's up to the district attorney."

"Who I *asked*," Lawson said again. "He got me no names, no photos, nothing to go on. He thinks he knows who killed his brother, but the courts wouldn't be convinced."

"But this is enough to get him fried?"

"Courts are tricky things, Viv. Not fair, just tricky."

I sat in silence.

"Well, you know where to reach me if you get any news. Leary," Lawson barked at the boy. "You're staying here."

"Detective?"

"You're staying here. For the night. Keep an eye on things."

"Yes, sir."

My face was as hot as Lawson's coffee, and from the looks of it, Leary was about as pleased with the arrangement. The detective was out the door of the dining room before I mustered up the courage to ask the question that'd been eating at my brain.

"Lawson!"

"Yeah, baby?" He peeked out from underneath his summer hat.

"*You* know our intruder here has something to do with what happened in Tommy's office, right?"

"Either him or someone who works for 'im."

My stomach dropped again as Lawson pointed at his officer.

"Leary!"

"Yes, sir?"

"Don't fall asleep on this one."

The front door of the house opened and I was blinded by the sunlight as Lawson's awful—but, at least, familiar—face disappeared in a shadow.

I was left standing with Officer Leary in the silence.

"This is a lousy assignment," I said. "But you might not find it so bad."

"Oh?"

"You'll have at least two girls up until sunrise flirting your face off," I said. Without a doubt, Betty would be down in the dining room, talking sweet to the young man in uniform. And Phyllis always liked to get in some practice whenever she could. Prepping for either major or minor du Ponts.

"I shouldn't get too distracted," Leary countered.

"Sorry, you lummox. You'll need to beat 'em off with a stick." The officer blushed. "Anything I can get you to make your overnight a little more comfortable?"

"No, no, I should be fine," he assured me.

"There's a powder room down the hall if you need it, and I'm going back upstairs to try to catch some more winks. Holler at me or Mrs. K if you can think of anything."

I beat feet as fast as I could away from Officer Leary, left standing stock-still in the dining room like a cigar store chief. Up the stairs as fast as my bruised buttocks could carry me, straight to Betty's front room.

"Viv!" Betty's eyes were wide. "What did the detective want?"

I fell face-first onto her twin bed and groaned.

"I feel like everything's about to go belly-up," I moaned into the comforter.

"Sit up," she groaned, pulling me up by the arm. "I'm getting the girls."

Tears were streaming down my face as my housemate left, then returned shortly with the other pretty faces, who were now in danger because of me. They arranged themselves around the room, Phyllis stretched across the floor like a cat in a black leotard and Dottie there in her beige culottes, a worried crease stretched across her forehead and a red correcting pencil still sticking out of her bun.

"I don't even know where to start," I said through sniffles. Dottie pulled out a handkerchief and handed it to me. "Thanks."

"Start at the beginning," Betty chimed in. "Just go step by step."

"Okay, to start—Tommy got a new case on Wednesday. Tallmadge Blackstone!"

"We knew that already, dear," Phyllis purred.

"I know, but I didn't tell you that he wanted Tommy to spy on his daughter," I explained.

"To what end?" Dottie's eyes were lighting up.

"He's afraid she won't marry her intended, Webber Harrington-Whitley, Mr. Blackstone's business partner."

"But from what I know, he's ancient!" Betty's hands went over her mouth.

"He *is*. He's something like sixty years old! And Tally's just eighteen!"

"Oh no! That poor little chickadee!" Betty was having none of this. I scanned the room and realized that, while all of us were years older than Tally, not a single resident of Mrs. K's boarding house would've even been an appropriate match for a man of that age, not even Mrs. K herself.

"Tommy was there on the boat Wednesday night," I said, turning to Phyllis, "keeping an eye on Tally. He must have gone away that night, and I haven't heard a peep from him since. I can't imagine at all what he's chasing after."

"Is that strange?" Dottie pulled the pencil from her hair and was taking notes on the back of an envelope she'd pulled from under Betty's bed.

"What makes it strange is that I found a body in Tommy's office Thursday morning."

"A body!" It was Dottie's turn to pale.

"He wasn't dead," I assured them. "But he's not alive either. I went to the hospital on Friday morning and got the scoop—he's not waking up. He got walloped pretty hard." I left out all of his other, more distinguishing features. I didn't want to upset them more.

"Oh, Viviana! That's terrible!" The murmurings around the room were grave.

"That's what brought Lawson and his flatfoots into this," I explained. "Tommy and I can handle a lot, but we sure as sugar don't take on bodies showing up in our locked office without calling the fuzz."

"You did the right thing," Phyllis soothed. "But bodies don't just happen in offices, Viviana."

"I know that," I said. "But I can't think Tommy would just disappear. That's just not the man I know."

"You don't attack a man in your own office and then leave him for dead—that would be awfully boneheaded," Dottie agreed. "And everyone would believe Tommy if he said it was in self-defense. He's in a very dangerous line of work."

"Exactly! Tommy's thrown a lot of punches to save his own hide," I said. "But I don't think he's ever once abandoned a man down."

"For as long as you've known him," Phyllis whispered, but I ignored her.

Dottie spoke up. "Viviana, is there any chance that Tommy was also hurt in the fracas?"

"Whaddya mean?"

"Tommy might've been in the office when that man showed up, but with others. Certainly there was an injured man left in the office, but perhaps the reason you can't find Mr. Fortuna is because he's been taken by the man's compatriots."

I began to shake. "That could explain how the office was locked up tight," I said. "They took Tommy and his keys and tried to pin all this on him?"

"That's certainly logical," Dottie said.

"But how does this tie into the other thing?" Betty asked.

"I don't know!" I said. "Blackstone wanted an update on *his* case Friday night, so I went to his townhouse, as you know."

"Yeah, and I am going to need that dress back soon," Phyllis said. "Not to be a nudge."

"You're not. I'll figure that out as quickly as I can," I assured her. "And obviously, I didn't have a whole lot to tell the mister. He let me stay at the party after I told him all I could. But Tally was super friendly. I don't think she's ever had a friend before."

"She sure has a lot of boyfriends," Betty said.

"Don't be a prude," Phyllis shot back, and I caught Betty making a quick, knowing wink in my direction, though I had to admit I was on Phyllis's side.

"So, we went on an adventure. A real-life exciting night on the town! But not what you'd think for Tally Blackstone. We went to Coney Island in her daddy's Cadillac, then to a diner. It was casual, like you'd do with any friend you ever had, so long as that friend had a car and endless dollars to pay the way," I explained. "And she was real . . . I don't want to say *scared*, but *reluctant* to head back to her daddy's house that night."

"Viviana," Dottie said, looking up from her writing, "do you think he's hurting her?"

"I can't say." A new pit grew in my stomach. "I don't think so. I think in his own way, he thinks he's protecting her. But at the same time, I think she's just tired of it all. Tired and sad and lonely."

"I was wondering who was screaming." Phyllis had pieced the whole thing together.

"I think at least some of that was me, girls," Betty admitted.

"Truth be told, I was gonna sneak her in overnight—I doubted anyone would mind."

"No, I would love to have breakfast with an heiress!" Betty was still hung up on Tally's glamour, and I wondered what it was like to always have people see you in terms of dollar signs and never as a person.

"She's real sweet, more normal than you'd ever expect," I said. "She'd've liked every single one of you."

"What happened to her, though?" Phyllis wasn't as swoony, since she was much better acquainted with New York's jet set.

"I guess she ran off when I went flying." My feelings were hurt, almost as much as my backside, and a silence traveled around the circle of girls.

"So . . ." Dottie was the first one to ask the question we all had: "The body, then. The prowler?"

"Lawson, that son of a gun—he's thinking the person responsible for that is also the guy who was breaking and entering here. But that's just Lawson. Everyone higher up on the chain thinks Tommy nailed the guy in his office and took off running—they've got a warrant out for his arrest."

"Any idea who it is—either the poor man or the intruders?" Betty asked.

"Not at all!" More than my aches and pains, this was what was bothering me. "And I'm sure Tommy'd figure it out faster than those harebrained flatfoots, but I can't get ahold of him!"

"You listen to me here, Viviana Valentine." Phyllis had a stern look on her face and was kneeling, pointing her finger in my face. "You don't need anyone's help figuring this out."

"Viv? Figuring it out?" Betty squeaked.

"You better believe it," Phyllis cut back. "Viv, how many times have you solved one of Tommy's cases at the same time he did? You get all the same clues as he does."

"I've met the man, as you all have," Dottie agreed. "Sharp eyes and a sharp brain, but you are just as smart as him, Viviana."

"Thanks for the pep talk, girls, but what about Tommy?"

"He didn't leave you, Viv," Betty said, smoothing my hair. "He wouldn't do that to you. Or do anything to that man in his office."

I appreciated Betty's little speech, but inside, I wasn't so sure about that last bit.

"Will you gals help me figure all this out?" I asked.

"Of course," Phyllis said.

Dottie let out a sigh. "If those men we met today can do it for a living, how hard can it be?"

DAY 5

I woke up to the usual thump-and-bump sounds of people getting ready for the Sunday services. The hubbub lasted for a half an hour, and when I opened my door, I walked into a makeshift police department in the hallway.

"Tell us what you need," Dottie said over a stack of legal pads sitting on the floor.

"Shouldn't you all be at church?" I was groggy, sweaty, and disheveled and was in the mood for coffee, not conversation.

"The Lord will understand. He'd rather us catch an attempted murderer than listen to Father Angelo go on about all the mistakes Stengel is making in the dugout," Betty said. "What's the plan?"

"First, let me splash some water on my face." Phyllis edged out of the way of the bathroom. "Second, breakfast. Third, I need to give you all a lesson on the basics of being a private dick."

★　★　★

We were settled over cold mugs of coffee and crumbs of the blueberry muffins Mrs. K had left out for us when Dottie finally broke out her steno pad and another one of her endless supplies of fresh pencils. A new officer I didn't recognize replaced Leary at eight AM, and he posted himself on the front stoop rather than deal with the craziness of our landlady trying simultaneously to get breakfast out for her tenants and her teenage son ready for St. Volodymyr's.

"Get a move on, Teach," Dottie said, straightening herself in her chair. This mystery brought out something in her I'd never seen before, and I liked it.

"First things first," I said. "Almost every one of the boys and girls we meet is gonna be up to no good. Marks, clients—the whole roster."

Betty started looking queasy.

"But you gotta understand," I soothed. "You gals aren't gonna be coming in contact with too many goons. Neither am I, for that matter. If we go places, we go places in groups. Stick together. Watch our tails. Always have a few nickels on you for the phone, just in case."

Dottie was writing down every word I said.

"And the smartest thing to do is, no matter where you are in the city"—I grimaced as I formed the sentence—"if you get in a jam, pick up the operator and ask for Detective Lawson. The boys at Midtown North are okay."

"Why do you hate the detective so much, Viv?" Betty asked.

"Oh, just many years of pet names, pickup lines, and pinched asses," I said with a sigh. "We got the usual history. Plus that whole duty-bound-to-arrest-Tommy thing."

"I feel like I'm getting offtrack," Dottie said, smacking her pencil eraser rapidly against the table. "But if Mr. Blackstone was nervous about whether his daughter was going to go quietly into her arranged marriage—what did her intended husband feel about the situation?"

I plucked a shriveled blueberry off my plate and popped it into my mouth. "That's a real good question. I'd just assumed he'd be fine with it—I mean, we've all seen photos of her. And met men."

"I can put out feelers to the girls," Phyllis piped up. "Get some gossip and all. I'm not sure who he ran with, outside of the obvious, but someone will know."

"Will they?" Betty asked. "For a man so well-connected, I've never seen him show up in the tabs."

"The most powerful people never do," Phyllis said approvingly.

"That's a good route. I'll need reports as soon as you've got 'em," I told Phyllis. "But I might have to go directly to the source."

The girls looked at me warily, and Dottie changed the subject to something about books. The meal was quickly over and everyone disappeared to their own lives.

I got dressed, grabbed my purse and Tommy's camera, tooteled out of Mrs. K's to the closest phone booth, and flipped to the H section, scanning the hundreds of entries for a Harrington-Whitley. An apartment near Gramercy Park. Easy peasy. I looked through the smeared glass windows of the booth and, making sure no one could see, I ripped the listing page clean from its binding and folded it to fit in my sweaty palm.

My head was pounding and my entire body aching. It was my instinct to head straight for my destination alone, but I felt as if I'd already been too close to death to risk heading into the shark- (or at least Blackstone-) infested waters alone again this week. I needed someone to talk me out of my pigheadedness, so I did the only responsible thing.

Popping a nickel in the slot I slammed the plunger up and down. An operator—just a few blocks away—picked up. "How may I connect your call?"

I only had two numbers memorized, and I knew that Tommy wouldn't be there to answer one of 'em.

"Chelsea- 2- 4647, please," I said. "Calling for Svitlana Kovalenko."

The familiar pattern of Mrs. K's ring danced in my ear before a breathless Phyllis picked up. "Hello?"

"Phyl, it's me."

"Viviana?"

"Yeah, listen, I've got a couple of leads," I said, twisting the phone cable though my fingers. "I'm going to run to Tommy's to grab some files."

"And then what?"

"I just need to see something."

Phyllis's voice rose, both in pitch and volume. "Viviana Valentine, if you go anywhere alone, you're going to get killed. Don't you dare!"

I smiled as I got my tongue-lashing. "I know, I know."

"We will see you soon, right?" Her voice calmed. "And call us if you need anything in the meantime, okay, honey?"

I clicked as fast as my saddle shoes would take me to Hell's Kitchen, without arousing suspicion from anyone on the sidewalk. Not that most New Yorkers were in the habit of helping a damsel in distress, but with all the cops in my life lately, I felt all eyes of the law on me at every turn.

"Don't walk so fast, sugar," a man hollered out of a rundown Mercury. "You're gonna melt."

There was a strange lug just three strides behind me who didn't say a damn thing for my honor, so without breaking my rhythm, I blew the pig a raspberry, and I heard him chuckle to his buddy behind the wheel. "Dames these days. Can't say nothin' to 'em."

★ ★ ★

Some time away from the smell and grime, and Tommy's felt foreign to me. One of Lawson's goons had been around to clean up what was left of my crime scene, and almost all the way too—but he'd still left plenty in the waste bins for me to take out at my leisure. I knew it couldn't have been Leary. He would never make more work for me.

First things first: I hid the automatic camera in its usual spot, then went into my drawer and pulled out my incomplete case files—the flimsy one for the unconscious man, and a slightly thicker one for Tally Blackstone, now with a glittering hair clip attached to it. I pinned it into my own chignon to take home for safekeeping.

I sharpened my black marking pencil and opened up Tally's file.

BLACKSTONE, TALLULAH

CLIENT NAME: *Tallmadge Blackstone*
OCCUPATION: *Millionaire*
REQUEST: *Recognizance*
TARGET: *Tallulah "Tally" Blackstone, 18. Daughter; intended bride.*
RELATED PARTIES: *Webber Harrington-Whitley, 57. Business partner to Mr. Blackstone; intended groom.*

I scribbled a new segment in the dossier that I usually used for taking dictation while Tommy strolled around the office.

NOTES:

Switching writing instruments to a good ol' Ticonderoga number two, I jotted down everything I knew about Tally Blackstone:

- *Tallulah Blackstone spotted on Wednesday, June 21, 1950, at engagement party for a minor du Pont and his future Mrs., Cassandra (surname unknown). Ms. Blackstone tailed to location by TF.*
- *That evening, TF disappeared, with no note concerning his lead or his whereabouts.*
- *On Thursday, June 22, VV discovered a note about his absence and a hair clip (see Evidence no. 1)*
- *Evening Friday, June 23, VV attended a small get-together at the home of Mr. Blackstone, at the latter's behest. VV*

ascertained Ms. Blackstone held reservations about her
upcoming nuptials but did not express explicit designs to
not follow through with the wedding. VV overheard Mr.
Blackstone, on a call to an unknown party, asking about a
"Yangon" (unknown origin).

The weight of the past few days felt heavier now that I'd
written out everything I knew. It totaled less than half a page
of notes, and I realized I had *nothing* to go on about what
had happened to Tommy or the poor man who had been left
for dead in his office. My stomach sank like I'd jumped off a
building, but unlike the ride at Coney Island, there was no
parachute to slow my fall.

Jarring me out of my pondering over the case, the doorknob turned, and a man in a severe, custom-cut black suit
poked his head in through the crack.

"Is Mr. Fortuna in?"

I damn near fell off my chair at the shock of seeing the
relatively familiar face of our upstairs office neighbor, Mr.
McAllister, clearly here and not in Southampton.

"No, sir. I'm his secretary, though. May I leave him a message? Please come in."

The suit came forward, careful not to touch anything that
might taint him with the lower class, and grumbled. "What
are you doing here? I saw the lights on. Does he make you
work the weekends? While he's gone?"

"Uh . . . yes, sir."

"I'm the man upstairs," he said to me, despite the fact that
I passed him in the hallway once a month. "I would leave

a message with you for Mr. Fortuna, but I'm about positive he'd never get it."

"That some kind of insult?" My wired nerves sizzled.

"Miss, he owes me some money, and I haven't seen him in days."

"That doesn't mean he's a fink, Mr. McAllister. He pays all his debts."

"Are you sure about that?" The man in the hot-looking suit was getting hotter around the collar. He raised his hands to motion at Tommy's office, gold watch glinting in the light, as if it was evidence that my boss was a deadbeat. "He's running you ragged—you look terrible."

I hopped up and knit my fingers together in an attempt to keep myself from giving our upstairs neighbor my own version of sign language—to tell him where he could shove his complaint.

"Sir, you are being *extremely* rude. Mr. Fortuna is not in. I will have him reach out to you as *soon* as possible."

"Keep calm, young lady—there's no reason to act a fuss," he said. "But he *will* pay."

Clearly unable to reason with such a hysterical woman, he left as quickly as he'd entered, leaving the door open in his wake so I could hear his leather shoes tapping up the stairs back to his office. After twenty minutes of listening to him storm about his office upstairs, I'd had enough.

I picked up the phone once more and pressed the hook switch.

"Operator, how may I connect your call?"

"Hey, operator, I have a question for you," I started. "If I gave you my address, would you tell me which hospital you'd call for an ambulance?"

"Miss, do you need an ambulance?"

"No, no, no," I assured her. "I'm fine and not in any danger. I just wanted to know my closest hospital."

"Of course, miss. I can help you with that."

"Great—I'm near Ninth Avenue and West Fiftieth. What's my closest fixer-upper?"

"That'd be Roosevelt, hon."

"What about the next two?"

"You could try Lenox Hill or Mount Sinai."

"Ohh, good suggestions. Sorry for the strange questions."

"Honey, this ain't nothin.'"

I switched off.

*　*　*

Sitting in the office was giving me the heebie-jeebies. I knew it was the place to be if I were to wait for Tommy, but at this point, there was no guarantee I was gonna see his stupid mug ever again. If I didn't figure out who the stiff was and why he was rootin' around our office in the small hours, Tommy was as good as toast.

Sure it was Sunday, but I needed to see if Lady Luck had a twinkle in her eye for Tommy today.

Thirty minutes of scurrying as fast as I could in the shade of the high-rises and the bronze clock outside the Toy Center building told me that it wasn't even yet eleven in the morning.

The sixteen-story building was a sight—each of the floor-to-ceiling windows in the front of the place was filled with toy displays—footballs and trains; planes and stuffed animals; air rifles and, above all, porcelain dolls.

Through the revolving doors and I was in the lobby, the building immediately transformed from a beacon of Santa's workshop to a regular, humdrum world of business.

There was a security guard sitting at a semiround desk in front of the elevators. "Miss?"

"Good morning," I cooed. "My, I hope you can help me. I'm looking for the offices of either Lars Schaeber or Jannick Christmann?"

"What do you want with them Krauts?" he asked.

The guard had all the look of someone who'd had a bad war, and I tried not to flinch at his hostility. "Business, sir," was all I replied.

"They're in the basement." The guard hooked his head over his shoulder and motioned to a dark stairwell to the left of the elevator bank. "Mind yourself down there."

I wasn't quite sure what the warning meant in the bright sunny light of day in the lobby, but as soon as I landed at the bottom of the stairs, I gathered. The basement was dank and dimly lit, a bit too moist to be healthy, and the entire space was one large room filled with display cases of porcelain dolls.

"What in the . . .?"

"Hello?" A charming man of about forty-five stood up from between the cases, holding onto a paintbrush. He had the air of an artist and the hunched shoulders of one too.

"Oh, I'm so sorry!" I made my way toward him, eking past the cases so as to not disturb the thousands of glass eyes staring right through me. I grabbed my purse close to my body, both in completely unconscious fear of the unfeeling faces and terror that I'd knock over a stand and cause the man thousands of dollars' worth of damage to his wares, which would be rude even if they weren't deeply unsettling.

"Sir, I have a very, very strange question for you, I was hoping you could help."

He chuckled. "You've come to the correct, very, very strange place," he said. "I'm Mr. Schaeber. You are . . .?"

"Viviana Valentine, sir. I work for a private investigator."

He blanched. "Oh, I see."

"Nothing to do with you, sir, I need your expertise. Or . . . someone's expertise, if it isn't yours."

"Please, then, right this way." Mr. Schaeber showed me to his desk, which was covered in disembodied ceramic baby arms. I tried to hide my shudder.

"Sir, we've managed to come across something very odd while investigating a case," I said. It was adjacent to the truth, so easy enough to remember. "A clue that is simply, well, a ceramic face." I took the photos of the mystery man's porcelain mask from my purse and handed them over.

"This is for a person," he said, a phrasing that made the whole situation seem even worse.

"Is there anyone in the city who makes or repairs these? That you know of?"

"The work is so fine, it must be Anna's," he said. "The specialty of a woman in Boston. She was a magician while the rest of us are simply craftsmen. Her work in the medium made men human, while we just make dolls." He smiled at his stock, and I couldn't help but feel touched.

"Is there a way to get in touch with this Anna woman? To maybe find out who this mask belonged to? I need to confirm a suspicion."

"Only if you're a spiritualist," the man said. "I'm so sorry, but Anna passed in '39."

My stomach fell, and for the first time, the feeling in my gut wasn't because I felt beady eyes on my neck. "Oh. What a loss. Well, thank you for your time."

"Of course, Miss Valentine. Do come back if you have more questions."

"Thank you, Mr. Schaeber."

Disappointment and relief mixed like a martini in my stomach as I ran up the stairs. One avenue for confirming the identity of the stiff was a complete dead end, but at least I was away from those goddamn dolls.

★ ★ ★

I hailed a cab to make it back to Mrs. K's—having already schlepped a few miles in New York City summer heat with a busted keister, I was wiped, and after the warning from Lawson *about* said keister being watched on my usual commute to and from work, I thought it was maybe wise to give folks the slip by taking a taxi. Not to mention, for the second time in just a few days, one of Tommy's neighbors had managed to raise my ire. And with so many people out of town, cabs were at least now easy to hail, practically hanging out on the corner waiting for me.

As soon as I'd paid the cabbie, Oleks popped his head out of the basement window. "Need a hand up the stairs?"

"Nah, I got it." He popped his head back inside, but I could see his shadow watching me as I headed up the stoop.

Now that the whole population of the house was in on this attempted murder case with me, I didn't have to do a whole lot for myself—not even open doors.

"Phyllis told us you might do something unwise," Dottie said, pulling open the great big front door. She was wearing pink culottes and a real sourpuss on her face. "We're in the dining room."

The hot and muggy foyer of Mrs. K's was filled with foreign smells.

"Dotts, what gives?"

"Mrs. K has been cooking up a storm," she said. "It all smells rather good, *I* think."

★　★　★

I ran upstairs to change into new, less sweaty clothes before descending back down to the dining room. The twelve-person dining set was a sight. The girls sat in their usual places at the table, with legal pads, pencil cups, and mystery novels dotting the gleaming wooden surface between them—everything from the coverless pulp novels that I knew Betty hoarded in her nightstand, to a pristine leather-bound Sherlock Holmes that was definitely Dottie's. Mrs. K filled the remainder of the table with bowls and plates of unfamiliar, steaming food. The door up from the kitchen swung open, and Mrs. K was revealed wearing a spotless white apron and carrying an enormous tureen.

"Viviana. Sit," she commanded rather than asked. "This came for you."

Mrs. K handed me another folded note on tissue-thin paper. She gave me an eye that assured me she was already privy to its contents, but I smiled sweetly, snuck it into a pocket, and headed quietly for the dining-room table.

I found my spot at the end, next to Dottie. "Mrs. K? What is all this?"

"You start with *kapusnyak*," she said. "It will make you feel better, gives you strength. Eat as much as you can." She ladled a healthy dollop of a greenish soup into a bowl already at my place on the table. It was less summery than the corn on the cob we'd eaten a few days ago.

"What's in it?" Phyllis was swirling the liquid with her spoon. Sitting with her long legs curled up beneath her on her chair, she resembled an overgrown child pouting at a dinner that was definitely not what she would've ordered.

"Cabbage. Carrots. Pork," Oleks said, emerging from the basement for his own bowl and seat at the table. "They call it Ukrainian penicillin."

"Looks like what we used to call my grandmother's 'soup old shoe,'" Dottie said. She was sitting primly at the head of the table, looking excited to dig in. "*Soupe au choux* in French. She was from Montreal."

"And the rest of the meal?" Phyllis asked.

"It will put meat on your bones," Mrs. K muttered, and the model stopped reaching for what looked like a wide and skinny bagel.

Oleks obliged us with the explanation of the menu, all of it completely new to me. Dumplings filled with a million different things, a grain called *kasha* made with onions and more pork. The baked potatoes looked the same, and the fried fish meatballs were tastier than I thought they'd be.

"I've always subscribed to the theory," Dottie said, "that the best way to learn about a different culture is to sample its food."

Mrs. K beamed as we all sat back in our chairs, full to the gills—and she was right, of course, that the weakness I'd been feeling had subsided, though the bruising was definitely still there. Oleks gathered up all the plates on a giant tray, to take downstairs and wash up, and Mrs. K followed him, promising us dessert.

"Is she *kidding*?" Phyllis asked. "I have a fitting tomorrow!"

Dottie cut to the chase, moving aside her napkin and pulling a steno pad toward her. "Girls, what did we find out today? Viviana, let's start with you."

"First off, you should note I ran into both of our office building neighbors in the past few days," I said. "And both seem to have a bone to pick with Tommy."

"Are they at least handsome?" Phyllis asked.

"Old," I explained. "And rude, overworked jerks."

"Overworked?" Dottie asked.

"Both were supposed to be out on vacation. But De Lancey—that's the architect on the first floor, seemed awfully busy," I said. "He must've left the missus in the Poconos."

"Maybe he left the missus in the Poconos to meet a mistress back home," Phyllis said.

"Ugh, I hope not," I replied.

"And the second?" Dottie asked.

"An ambulance chaser named McAllister who's rich enough to afford a place in the Hamptons but was awful cranky over some money Tommy owed him," I explained.

"If the architect is so overworked, he might have been in the office late the other night," Dottie mused. "Perhaps he saw someone coming in and out of the building?"

"Ooh, good thinking!" Phyllis clapped.

"I tried to ask, but he brushed me off," I said. "I'll try again."

"And you need to find out when the lawyer got back in town," Dottie agreed.

"Maybe the next time I'm there, I can give 'em both a quick grill," I said. "I guess Betty is still at work?"

"She should be home soon," Phyllis said, checking her watch.

"Good," I said. "I need her help with something."

"Do we have any other questions? Anything you might have seen or heard that you need a different perspective on?" Phyllis said.

"Well, the other night when I was at the Blackstones'," I said, "I overheard Daddy dearest saying something in code, I think. What the heck could 'Yangon' be?"

"Burma?" Dottie looked up.

"What's that?" I felt a flutter in my stomach.

"It's a country in Asia," Dottie said, trying hard, I could tell, not to sound like she was speaking to her schoolchildren.

"Is that close to Korea?" Phyllis, a dedicated listener to WNBC radio, kept as up to date as she could on the goings-on overseas.

"Sort of," Dottie said, though I'm sure she wanted to be more accurate. "The whole region is a bit topsy-turvy at the moment."

"I wonder what it has to do with Mr. Blackstone," I mused out loud. "Dottie—do you think you can get us more facts?"

"Of course," she said, scribbling in her notebook. "Do we have any other leads or clues to point the research in the right direction?"

"Not really," I admitted. "We'll start with a basic dossier."

"Not a problem."

"Then there's Harrington-Whitley," I started. "There's even less to go on with him. I've never seen or spoken to him, and I can't go calling him up to ask questions, can I?"

"I did a small bit of sleuthing," Phyllis interjected. "With some of the other girls."

"What kind of girls are we talking about?"

"Boat party girls, first," Phyllis expanded.

"First?"

"They didn't have any specifics on Harrington-Whitley, but they did go into extensive detail on the bona fides of Blackstone," she said, clearly giddy to get to the juicer meat. "If I didn't know any better, I'd say some of them were angling to become the second missus. Or get into Tally's good graces and maybe absorb her cast-offs."

"But nothing about Harrington-Whitley?"

"None of them know him personally," she started.

"But?"

"They've heard things."

"Things? Like what—he goes to brothels?"

She threw up her hands in frustration. "Who blabbed?"

There was a collective blush and shriek at the table.

"No, but, Phyl, *what*?"

"Not all models can keep their noses as clean as I do," she added, plucking at her napkin. "Some of the girls, they come from real tough backgrounds, or they got beaus and kids they have to keep proper. Some of the girls . . . need to go to different sorts of places to pay their rent."

"Don't let Mrs. K hear that," Dottie said, a deep furrow forming between her brows. "She's not too keen on your line of work already."

"I won't, cross my heart," Phyllis added. "But there are some clubs near the Village that seem quite like respectable businesses on the outside."

"But are some real joints on the inside?"

"That's the gist. Lots of girls said the old speakeasy owners just couldn't let go of the good times," Phyllis added, "and they went into other merchandise after repeal."

"I wonder how you find these places," I asked, knowing fully well Tommy probably had them committed to memory.

"Hell if I know," Phyllis said. "I just heard about them. Figured it'd look kind of fishy to ask for the address."

"Why, Viviana?" Dottie looked concerned for my safety, and probably my virtue.

"No reason."

But the girls around me didn't look altogether convinced.

Before we could get too much further into the details, the kitchen door swung open once more, and Oleks appeared on the other side, bearing a tray with plates, a towering strawberry shortcake, and a pitcher of milk.

"I convinced Mom to keep the *yabluchnyk* downstairs," he said. "Your loss, though."

"And what about Tally?" Phyllis asked as Oleks went back down to the basement.

"What about her?" I asked back. "She just seems so lonely."

"I know you're starting to like her," she explained. "But I think you need some perspective on her life that doesn't come from her own painted lips."

I played with a dollop of whipped cream on my plate. "But who even knows her? What other source do I have?"

"We all do feel as if we are her intimate friends," Dottie said quietly. "But does she actually have any?"

"She's always alone in her snaps," I pointed out. "Unless there's a, uh, . . . companion. But the *friends* never get named."

"What about the fellas with the cameras?" Phyllis said. "They follow her everywhere."

"Does anyone know who the tabloid sleazes with the spotlights are?" I asked.

"No," she said. "Those are different photographers than the ones I work with."

"But they always put their names under pictures in the tabloids," Dottie said. "They're called credits. You never noticed?"

"No!" I said. "But you're brilliant. Phyl, go run upstairs and grab all of Betty's magazines."

"On it, boss!"

★   ★   ★

It took all of us just a few minutes to pull out all the pictorials of Tally Blackstone, with Dottie keeping a running tab of whose name got credit for each sordid snap. While the list was dozens of names long, the same three kept appearing—Rudolpho Agnellini, Marcel Hedley, and Brennan Masters.

"Think they'll meet with me and dish?" I asked the girls.

"If you pay them," Dottie reasoned.

"Tommy owes me big," I sighed. "I'll call them tomorrow."

Night 5

An hour later everyone was traipsing upstairs, and Betty was just returning home from her shift, but the sugar in the shortcake had me wired like the lights on Broadway. I knew I couldn't waste time, so I pulled Betty aside.

"Hey, I think I need to check something out tonight. Are you working in the morning?"

"No, I've got Mondays off for the rest of summer," she said. "What are you thinking about?"

"Just an evening stroll."

Betty smiled. "Give me a second to change." She sped upstairs and returned in lightning time, in pedal pushers and espadrilles.

"Put some gloves in your bag too."

"You don't wear gloves with slacks!"

"They're not for fashion," I whispered. "They're for snooping." Betty ran upstairs, and I pulled the note Mrs. K had slipped me from my pocket.

Drop me a dime, Viv. I don't like loose ends.

Before I could digest this latest bit of poetry from Sandy, my partner in crime was back downstairs and ready for her adventure.

"Shouldn't we tell the other girls where we're heading?" Betty shivered. We were heading nearly due east from Mrs. K's boarding house, and the sun was hidden behind the buildings, casting us in a cool shadow.

"We'll be fine," I promised. "We're just going to look around, and no one knows who we are."

After my embarrassment of hitting up the Blackstones' for a Friday night formal dinner, I was more than prepared for a Sunday evening stroll in Gramercy in my not-borrowed gingham sundress.

"Besides," I added, "he's in the book. If he wanted to keep a low profile, he'd be unlisted."

This seemed to calm Betty's fears, and I pulled the torn White page from my purse and tracked down Webber Harrington-Whitley's address.

Betty yammered as we walked, and I couldn't stop thinking about the note Mrs. K had slipped me. Sandy had no right behaving like this, tracking me down like a bloodhound and pestering me through my landlady. If this kept up, Mrs. K would have every right to kick me out for being an absolute pest to her and my housemates. Maybe the next time Sandy rolled through, I'd have Oleks nearby to lend some heft to the situation. And as a last resort, there was always Tommy.

But Tommy was the start of that whole war to begin with—he'd given me a tough-love tongue-lashing that led to my immediate breakup with the handsy galoot. Tommy was right, of course, and I knew he'd back me up if I needed it, no matter how much I tried not to need it. I came out of my nervous Nellie stupor as we got within sight of Gramercy. The leafy and quiet neighborhood was just the home for the four-story brown brick building with a front fire escape. The tall windows out front had no bars. They directly overlooked the park, but faced north, which I knew would make every place in the building as dark as a dungeon.

"According to the listing, he's unit number one," I said. "So, the first floor, probably."

Betty bent down to examine her sandals and retie the ribbon around her ankle. "I can make this take as long as you want, sweetie," she said in a whisper. "If you want to poke around." With a swish of her wrist, the entire contents of her purse scattered to the sidewalk.

Under the guise of chasing after a rogue lipstick, I scurried toward the building just as a woman in a prim maid's outfit pushed the black lacquered door open, and let it fall shut behind her. I shot out my hand, quick as a jackrabbit, and grabbed the handle.

"Betty!" I hissed. "Get your stuff. And your gloves!"

The focal point in the foyer of the was a pedestal table with an elaborate centerpiece of roses and ferns. The floor was black-and-white marble tile. A wide, carpeted staircase twisted to the upper floors, but, toward the rear of the entry, another black-lacquered door featured a gleaming bronze number "1."

"Nice digs," Betty whispered. "I wonder how much this costs."

"More than we'd make in twenty years, I'd guess," I hummed back. "The roses aren't even silk!"

I tapped my way toward the door in the deathly quiet building.

"I think it's open."

With a nudge of my toe, the door to Webber Harrington-Whitley's co-op swung wide.

"Do you think the maid just forgot to lock it?" Betty was pulling my arm back toward the front door, but my gut was pulling me onward.

"I don't know!"

"What if he's in and just expecting guests?"

"He doesn't strike me as the kind that invites people around for Sunday dinner."

"Not *those* kinds of guests, Viviana."

"Oh!"

"I don't want to be confused for . . . one of the girls, if you know what I mean."

"I get the concern. But—," I wrenched my arm away from Betty, and she let out a little yelp—"I don't . . . I don't hear any movement at all."

By the time I finished my sentence, I was in the door, my espadrille now landing softly on a plush Oriental rug that ran down a stretch of gleaming cherrywood floors. Compared to the Blackstone residence, this was a dinky little apartment, but it sure made Mrs. K's look like a shack.

"Viviana!"

"Put your gloves on," I hissed as I pulled my own protection out of my purse. "The coast is clear—I'm sure of it."

Betty scuttled in behind me and shut Harrington-Whitley's front door, drawing the chain. "Viviana, we are going to get in trouble!"

We weren't technically breaking and entering, and Tommy had stressed to me over the years that the punishment for trespassing, especially for chickadees like me, would be a harsh verbal reprimand from a judge. Sticks and stones, the saying goes.

"No, we're not. No one's home. And if anyone from the building asks—and a Good Humor bar says they won't—we can just pretend to be the help. The maid just didn't lock up properly. I'm sure of it." But as I turned the corner into the large, dark living room, I wasn't so sure.

That Harrington-Whitley was a bachelor was a given, considering he was betrothed to Tally Blackstone. But even if I knew nothing of the man's personal life, I could tell it by his house. There was a large, old-fashioned, floor-model radio beneath the front window—the drapes of which were plain, cheap, and closed—and an equally stately desk pushed up against the far wall, without a living room set or a coffee table between them. The room was cavernous and echoed with the footsteps of the family above and the sound of my own heartbeat thundered in my ears. Webber spent his days with his back to Gramercy Park, not even looking at the private space he paid an arm and a leg to access.

Every wooden surface of the apartment was shiny and clean. The kitchen, beyond a swinging door and equipped with a brand-new Frigidaire, looked sterile. I popped open the door and found only a soda syphon without a cartridge. Betty gave a holler from the bedroom.

"Was this guy also a monk?"

I joined her in the room and found a boring iron bedstead with white linens, and only one lonely pillow floating like an island at the headboard. The only sense of personality was a low, wooden bookshelf filled with leather-bound books. A fit of giggles erupted from my stomach.

"What?" Betty asked.

"Monk is right! Honey, Tally Blackstone, by sheer personality alone, would suffocate this poor, old man." My giggles subsided into sadness. "They would just live out the rest of their lives hating every moment of it."

"She doesn't have to marry him, does she?"

"Gosh, I hope not."

I peeked my head into the bathroom and saw gleaming white porcelain on every possible surface. There was a red toothbrush, a box of baking soda, a glass bottle of peroxide, a small dish on which to mix the two, and a small, grayish Schick electric razor with the cord wrapped up neatly in a copper-colored, hinged metal box. The room felt off-kilter and strange; all the lightbulbs were lit, and not a tile was cracked. It took me a moment to realize—it was the first washroom I'd ever seen without a mirror.

We moved back out into the sparse living room, and Betty leaned her bottom against the desk. "Why on earth would Mr. Blackstone sentence the only two people he seems to care about in life to such mismatched misery?"

"Beats me," I said. "But wait a sec—move your tush."

Betty jumped aside. The top center drawer of the desk was lopsided, and as I bent down to examine it in the darkness, I could tell the wood had been gouged in someone's attempt to pick the lock.

"Well, Dollface," I said in my best imitation of Tommy, "I don't think it was the cleaning lady who left that door ajar. Look—someone's tried to force the desk open."

"Did they manage?"

I jiggled the handle with my fingers, and the drawer stayed closed. "Not this way, but—" I reached my hand under the desk and skimmed my finger over the cool, wooden surface. Finding a small crack, I pressed it with all my might, and the *thwong* of a spring sounded from inside.

"How did you know?"

"Tommy."

"He's taught you some funny stuff."

"You don't know the half of it. But hey, look—why on earth would this need to be locked?"

The contents of the desk drawer were, like the man whose house we were in, downright boring. A nice pen, a miniature enamel frame without a back, and two gold cuff links.

"What a letdown. But hey, why'd you choose me to come with you tonight?"

I picked up the weighty cuff links, and rolled them in my palm. "'Cause for the number of times you've stolen my L'air du Temps, I knew you'd have no problem with a little breaking and entering." Betty let out a giggle just as I let out a yelp.

"What *now*?"

"It's the cuff links!" I said, my hands shaking. "Look at the design!"

"So what?" Betty asked as we hurried into the foyer, out the front door, and down the sidewalk. "There's no inlays or anything, no diamonds or stones. It's just a boring little etching." It was a Sunday evening in Gramercy, and all the respectable ladies and gentlemen of the neighborhood were inside, listening to their programs. The sidewalk was ours.

"But I've seen this boring little etching before!" I held the cuff links in my sweaty fist, half hoping they'd melt away into nothingness and leave me clueless all over again.

"Where, Viviana? Where?"

"Oh, my goodness, but how did he get into Tommy's office?"

"Who?"

"Webber Harrington-Whitley!"

"When did you see him in Tommy's office? I thought only Blackstone came to visit you." The wheels behind Betty's eyes were turning a mile a minute, but she couldn't figure out how I'd come to be in the acquaintance of Tallmadge and Tallulah Blackstone and Webber Harrington-Whitley in the matter of a few days.

"It was only Blackstone, walking and talking. It was the body in the office, on Thursday morning. That was Web!"

Betty stopped dead in her tracks, blocking the entire sidewalk, white as a sheet. "Viviana! Are you sure?"

"No, not completely, but I know that something bad is going on, and Tommy got roped right into it, the big ol' horse's ass." This was a good setup and, with Tommy going radio silent for days, I felt like he was gone—hook, line, and sinker.

"He's not a horse's ass, and he's fine, I just know it!" Betty reached out grabbed my hand, pulling me over to a stoop to sit down. "Listen, sweetie, let's just go home and call that detective. Have a cup of tea. I don't quite know what's going on, but I think we should hand it all over to the police."

My stomach roiled over and over, and I hadn't felt this uneasy since Tommy'd made me take the Staten Island Ferry last summer, and even then, my knees had been less wobbly.

The idea of Lawson being in charge of clearing Tommy's good name? It would never happen. Even if Lawson knew Tommy was innocent, he wasn't a crooked cop, and he'd have to follow the evidence—and proper procedure.

"Betty, I'll never be able to sleep a wink if I hand it over to Lawson! You don't know at all—"

"He's an investigator, Viviana. He does this for a living!" Betty was sure that Lawson's paycheck, with the seal of the city of New York printed on it, endowed him some sort of magical ability in the area of investigation.

Some things always separated me from the other girls in my building, and right now it was dawning on me that one of 'em was their infuriating trust in the good of people. And by *people*, I realized now that, first and foremost, I also meant *cops*.

"Tommy and I, we investigate for a living too—don't you forget it! And we've got a better track record to show for it! I mean, Lawson—"

"Lawson what, sweetheart?" Betty's voice was an ice-cream sundae of concern and condescension.

"Tommy plays it off okay, but . . ."

"What, sweetie?" Betty's eyes looked into mine, and then the waterworks came.

"Tommy's brother, a few years ago . . ."

"Oh." Like a reflex, her hand went to her purse to pull out an embroidered hanky.

"Yeah, he was real kind, always treated me so nice. Jimmy came out okay outta the war—nothing too bad. Was gonna go straight, you know, get a boring job upstate."

"Where's he now, Viviana?"

"By Tommy's guess? At the bottom of the East River. Got on the wrong side of some Brooklyn gangster called Tino the Conderoga."

"Oh, Viviana. That's just so awful." Betty was playing with her cuticles, uncomfortable and nervous, as if having this information suddenly made her more likely to show up on the wrong side of the law. Not even a few days ago, she had been prepared to sit on the stoop for hours just to catch Tommy's eye—and now I could tell she was afraid of just the thought of him. Tommy kept company with a lot of crooks and liars, everyone guessed, but I suppose Betty never thought he'd cross the line into battling out-and-out murderers.

"Tommy says he has all this evidence that pointed the finger at his brother's boss, who's a real no-good guy, but Lawson couldn't use it, because, ya know, Tommy works a bit outside what is strictly legal."

"A bit."

"No one could make a positive ID of the guy, or any of his made men. No photos exist anywhere, and no matter how many hours Tommy cased the joint, he could never figure out how to prove he was the one who ordered Jimmy dead."

"Do you know his real name?"

"Nope, just the Conderoga. And Tommy's just spent the last few years drinking and working and trying to forget it all ever happened. Which is not made easier by the fact that Lawson sticks his nose into Tommy's business whenever he can. And I can't tell what for. Lawson's got no respect for Tommy—none at all. And don't forget—now it's Tommy's head on the block."

Betty was silent for a long time as we sat in the twilight on some stranger's stoop. As the last tears evaporated from my face, she pulled me up with a light hug, though it let me know that something between us had cooled just a bit. "Let's go home," she urged.

We got halfway back when the streetlights flicked on. "Actually . . ." I started, and Betty pulled her gaze from the sidewalk. "Betty, there's another way you can help."

"Legally?"

"I think so," I assured. "Dottie suggested that Tommy might've been hurt by a goon squad that came to the office. Is it kosher to call hospitals and ask if he's among their patients?"

"Of course," Betty said. "How else do you send flowers?"

"Can you call Roosevelt, Lenox Hill, and Mount Sinai and see if he's in one of those three?"

"Of course, Viv. I know just what to say."

"His full name is Tommaso Antonino Fortuna," I added. "Make sure you say that. He's got a shrapnel wound on his lower hip, and a real funny birthmark on his lower back and—"

"Do I want to know how you know all this?"

"Probably not."

Betty smiled. "And you say there's nothing between you two."

★   ★   ★

We rounded the corner to Mrs. K's. It was Sunday night in Chelsea too, but while Gramercy was as silent as a grave-yard, with all the respectable people inside and keeping to themselves, it seemed as if every last house in this neighbor-hood had its windows open, with family living rooms spill-ing out onto fire escapes and stoops, and each apartment was playing a different program on the wireless at top volume. Betty spent the rest of our walk chattering away about all sorts of things—new lipsticks, a dress she saw in the windows on Fifth Avenue, her sister's upcoming wedding—every-thing to keep me from talking about the case and poor Mr. Harrington-Whitley.

"Stop for a sec," I hissed as a shadow moved on the stoop. Betty squeaked.

A tall, slender man straightened himself up and held his hands up by his chest. A familiar voice rang through the shadows.

"It's just me, Miss Valentine." Officer Leary stepped into the light of the streetlamp and Betty let out a sigh.

"Don't sneak up on girls like that," I chided. "And what are you doing here in your civvies?"

Leary was standing on the sidewalk in blue stovepipe jeans, a faded cotton work shirt, and scuffed leather boots. Betty pinched me in the arm and let out a low whistle. She was in far more comfortable territory now, the world where boys show up on a girl's doorstep in the hopes of romance.

"I'll meet you inside," she said, her voice crystal clear and hopeful. "Evening, Officer."

"Hi, Betty," he said, giving her a wave. He turned back to me. "I'm not here on duty. Officer Quinn has tonight's shift, but from the shadows, I can tell he's having the time of his life in Mrs. Kovalenko's dining room."

"It's probably strawberry shortcake." I went to the stoop to sit.

"Oh, I know it is. She already gave me two pieces. I won't fit into my uniform if this case continues much longer."

"So, what's up?" Under the pretense of putting away my keys, I tossed the evidence I'd snitched from Harrington-Whitley's apartment into the bottom of my purse. I'd clutched the two cuff links so hard they'd left red marks in the flesh of my palm.

"I was just wondering, hoping, you'd like to get a drink with me tonight?"

"Are you old enough?" It was a bit of a smart-mouth thing to say, but I couldn't help it from tumbling out.

"I'm twenty-two, Miss Valentine. Four years over drinking age."

"Please call me Viv, but don't tell O'Malley or Lawson that I let you."

"Please call me Alan," he replied. "When I'm not in uniform, I guess."

"Well, twenty-two-year-old Alan Leary"—I smiled—
"I'm not much of a drinker, but I suppose I could sit with you
for a bit and talk in the twilight."

That seemed to be good enough for the officer.

"Hope you didn't travel too far to get to Mrs. K's."

"Nah. I actually live pretty close to Tommy's."

"That where you grew up?"

"Yup."

"Not a great neighborhood there."

"No, it's not, but it's home."

"Still live with the parents?"

"No, no. They both passed away. But I got my kid sister—
but she's seventeen, so not much of a kid."

"No, not much of one. I moved here when I was sixteen."

"You did? That takes guts." His eyes lit up, and I could tell
he was genuinely impressed.

"Thanks. I didn't much care for living in the middle of
nowhere. Always had that itch to get out."

"I think the city suits you," Leary said with a charming
smile.

"I know these aren't the most glamorous digs . . ."

"But you're at home, and you seem awful comfortable
here. And at Tommy's."

"Oh, Tommy's a great boss. More considerate than some
of the jamokes that these girls have worked for," I said, hitching my thumb back at the house.

"Pays you pretty good?"

"Yeah, not bad."

"You got a hell of a piece in your locks right there."

I'd forgotten that I'd slipped that sparkly barrette—one girl's piece of evidence was another girl's piece of jewelry— into my hair for safekeeping. "Oh, yeah. Long story, but . . . it isn't mine." I pulled it out and added it to the trove of clues mounting in my purse. A curl fell in my eye, and for the second time in a week, one of New York's Finest moved to brush hair from my forehead. But this time, I didn't quite stop him.

"Awful forward, Officer Leary."

"Sometimes I get brave."

"Brave enough to chat up a suspect in an assault case under the nose of your commanding officer?"

"Aw, Lawson knows you didn't do it."

"Yeah, I know."

"And for all the tea in China, I don't think Tommy did it either." He was suddenly concentrating awful hard on pulling a thread that'd emerged from the cuff of his shirt, like he was embarrassed to tell me that he didn't think my boss was a crook. "But I feel like you should know, the case isn't looking too good for Tommy."

"Oh yeah?" My blood was boiling.

"His fingerprints were all over everything."

"It's his office!"

"Well, yeah, but we need someone else's to clear him."

"Ain't you never heard of gloves?" I felt foolish as soon as the words came out of my mouth.

"Of course we have, Viviana. But nothing was smashed for a break-in, and there are no signs that anyone other than you two were in the office."

"You check for hairs or dust or fibers?"

"Of course, Viv. But Tommy's office isn't the cleanest, and people come and go from it every day."

"Sorry I'm not a good housekeeper," I grumbled.

"We have no witnesses to say if someone else coulda been there. We have a boot print, we have motive—though everyone knows it coulda been self-defense—and opportunity. And him bugging out looks bad. Real bad. But if you say he didn't do it, I want to believe you."

"God forbid you stand up at all to Lawson," I said with a huff. Here was Alan Leary, acting like he was absolving Tommy of worldly sins like he was the pope himself, but all he'd managed to do was turn me into a cold fish. "You forget—I know the look in a man's eyes when he thinks he's got a suspect."

"What's between those two, anyhow?" Leary continued on, oblivious to me giving him the cold shoulder. It was dark now, with just the dim lamps illuminating the street. A rat scuttled through the gutter, and all I wanted to do was go inside and catch up with Betty and the girls. Without a doubt, she'd already spilled the beans on what we knew—and Tommy and Lawson's beef.

"Nothing I can share with you," I muttered. "Well, Officer, it's getting late, and I think I should head inside."

Even by the streetlights I could tell Leary was crestfallen at our little chat getting cut short, but I manufactured a shiver out of the hot night air, and a trained gentleman like himself wasn't going to make a lady sit outside on the concrete if she didn't want to anymore.

"I'm sure the detective and I will swing by tomorrow, Viv, if that's alright."

"I can't stop you."

"Good night." He paused for a moment, unsure of how to bid me goodbye. We were beyond a handshake, but anything else was, in the words of the cracked-spine romance novels that floated around the boarding house, *tawdry*. He turned away.

"Alan!"

He paused.

"Do you need money for a cab?" My fingers fumbled with the toggle on my purse.

"No, thank you, Miss Valentine."

And he disappeared into the evening.

★   ★   ★

"Oh, be nice to the young man," Mrs. Kovalenko scolded me from the dining room as I headed toward the stairs. She was pouring a sleepy-looking, white-haired officer another cup of coffee. "He is sweet on you."

"I know, Mrs. K," I said.

"He is also very handsome."

"Oh, isn't that part of the problem, Mrs. K."

Officer Quinn chuckled into his mug.

"I was worried that fall down the stairs made you blind." She whacked her dish towel on the clean table, placed the coffee pot on it, and smiled to herself. "Goodnight, pretty girl. Lock the door behind you, but do not do the chain. Oleksandr ran out."

I pivoted back down to the front door and fastened the dead bolt, then started trudging back upstairs to my room.

"Betty told us what happened!" Phyllis was on the landing, in her pajamas, with a toothbrush hanging out of her mouth, spraying Pepsodent foam all down her front in excitement.

Dottie emerged from her room with her hair in a kerchief. "I'm sorry to hear about Tally's fiancé. I'll say an extra prayer for him tonight. I'm off to bed," she said. "But I'll be visiting the school library tomorrow to research Yangon and Burma for you, Viviana. I haven't forgotten."

"Thank you, Dottie," I said to her, closing the door before turning to Betty. "You should get some sleep too."

"Not until you tell us everything that happened with that dreamboat officer of yours," Betty chided. Clearly all the details of our evening had been shared with the girls of the house.

"He asked me out for a drink, but I was too tired, so we just talked on the stairs."

"If you don't want him, I'll take him," she grumbled under her breath.

I rolled my eyes. "Goodnight, honey."

"Goodnight!"

★ ★ ★

I could still hear Betty humming to herself in the bathroom as she did her nightly rituals, but my bedroom was nice and dark and quiet, the perfect place to shut out all the hubbub of nearly dead bodies, party-girl antics, and all too handsome police officers. My bag's ill-gotten contents weighed on my mind like an elephant, so I pulled out the cufflinks and the hair clip and hid them at the bottom of my nightstand drawer, under a handful of books and my winter gloves. Then I fell face-first onto my bed and slept like the dead.

Day 6

Promptly at 6:01 AM, I snapped awake and jumped out of bed, almost directly into my girdle and sundress, stopping quickly to empty my unmentionables drawer of all my remaining cash. The house was as quiet as a church, and I was in front of Tommy's building by the time the rooster crowed seven. I had a few marks to chat up.

McAllister—judging by years of dropped pencils and loud phone calls—was an early riser, so I ran up two flights of stairs to pay a call.

"Mr. McAllister," I cooed, tapping my nails on the glass pane of his door. "Sir, are you in?" I eased open the door. There was a young man sitting at a small desk by the window. His head whipped around to catch me.

"You're the girl from downstairs!"

"You're the lookie-loo from the other day."

"I'm McAllister's neph—I mean clerk. Brian."

"Oh, I get it. Were you downstairs to ask about the cash?"

"Yeah. Unc's been losing his mind. He summoned me back from the Rockaways before I was there even two days. Are you here to pay it back?"

"Yeah, but let me see him myself, would you?"

"Be my guest." Brian pointed toward the door. I knocked and went in at the grunt.

"What have you, miss?" He still managed not to recall my name.

"Sir, I received a message from Mr. Fortuna last night," I fibbed. "He was hoping you'd be a dear and remind him of the exact figure he owed you?"

"Forty-three dollars!" McAllister roared.

It was all I could do not to call him a cheapskate straight to his face. "Oh!" I caught myself. "That's . . . what he thought. I have it here for you." I dug around in the bottom of my purse for crumpled bills.

"Thank you." The lawyer visibly calmed.

"I trust you had a good vacation?" I asked.

"Yes, yes, fine. I came back with Ronald Von Meyer in his car," he said.

The name struck a chord with me. "The city councilman?" I asked. "My, my."

"And let me tell you, I'm still not sure a motorcar is the way to travel. It was as if Country Line Road was at a standstill."

"Quite right." He was muttering to himself as I shut the door.

Friday. I repeated to myself. *Too late. But—he knows the city councilman.*

I hit the stairs to Tommy's and locked the door behind myself. Quick to my desk, I snatched up the phone receiver and clicked for the operator.

"How may I connect your call?" snapped a woman with a throaty Brooklyn accent. The private lines must've gotten the operators with smoother voices; the rest of us got locals.

"Good morning!" I chirped. "I was hoping you could help me find a connection?"

"I'll do my best," the disembodied voice replied.

"Any of the following three would be great: a Marcel Hedley, Rudolpho Agnellini, or Brennan Masters?"

"Borough?"

"Start with Manhattan, I guess."

"'Start with?' Honey, we got other calls."

"Sorry you picked up this one."

"Hang on."

The line went quiet for minutes while the operator did her search.

"I couldn't spell two of 'em, but I got your Agnellini," the voice came on.

"Of all the ones to be able to spell . . ." I muttered.

"My nonna's from Florence," she replied. "You want a direct connection or the number?"

"Number first, then connection, please,"

She obliged, and within a moment I heard a sleepy voice on the other end.

"This is Rudy," he said through a yawn.

"Tally's got a date," I whispered. Filling him in on the particulars, I added, "Masters and Hedley only," and hung up.

★　★　★

I felt like I was going 'round in circles. There were only so many places a man could be found, even in New York City, that it'd only make sense that Tommy was anywhere but here. The fuzz were definitely on the lookout for him in all his favorite hidey-holes, but I wondered if they overlooked something that only one of Tommy's intimates would notice, either here or anywhere else Tommy hung his hat.

Tommy didn't live too far from his office, that much I knew. It wasn't unheard of for him to call in the mornings with an idea and then five minutes later show up still yammering, making me wonder if he ever shut his trap during the time he was shuffling on over. Work wasn't ever scarce, so I figured he could afford nicer digs than a one-bedroom flat in Hell's Kitchen, but whatever we wanted for in luxury, he couldn't deny the convenience of location.

I scooted my way toward the river, finding a squat brownstone on the edges of DeWitt Clinton. There was no live-in super to buzz or acknowledge—Tommy didn't like to be watched—and I pulled out my key ring. The front door was twice my height and solid oak, with multiple dead bolts. Since I so rarely visited Tommy at his own abode, I knew which unused keys went to the place, but not in which order. After much trial and error, I was saved by a pale, sweaty man opening the door from the inside, running out onto the sidewalk in his shirtsleeves to light up a cigarette, showing off the needle marks on his arm for all the world to see.

Up to the top I schlepped, 'cause Tommy kept what he called the penthouse but was just a fourth-floor walk-up, and I tried not to touch anything as I went. The building was mostly asleep, but on the second floor, a door hid a man having a fight with someone who, judging by the one-sided nature of the conversation, maybe wasn't real. If this is what it meant to keep your own apartment, it looked like my future was always going to be at Mrs. K's.

In front of another massive door, I struggled for two more keys, one for each of Tommy's dead bolts. The locks popped open like they were greased, and I slipped inside.

It was like a cave; the walls were brick and dark and looming, and there was only one steel-framed window at the far end of the apartment, covered with a thick curtain. I'll give it to Tommy that he is an adult man, and it was clearly a real curtain on a rod and everything, and not just a bed blanket tacked over the frame. I found the push-button and switched the lights on, relieved to see that my boss didn't live in an apartment that matched the sty he worked in. In fact, it was downright clean—no dishes in the sink; a coffee table in front of a defunct fireplace with a few magazines; and off the living room, a bathroom that was bright and shiny and complete with a white toothbrush and a half-squeezed tube of Ipana. It felt like he could be back any moment.

Just a few more nooks to check—the door next to the bathroom led to the bedroom, which was nicely sized and had a massive brass bed in the center, big enough for two people to sprawl out. And maybe they did. But the sheets looked white and crisp and cool, and it was all I could do not to curl up on top of the covers, fall asleep, and hope Tommy'd be there when I woke up. Maybe even *he'd* make the pot of coffee this time.

The only other furniture in the room was a bureau, but I couldn't bring myself to go through the man's drawers. I did take a peek in the closet. Three pairs of shoes lined up on the floor—brown, black, and boots—with just space enough for one pair to be missing. One hanger hung in the center of the rod, naked of jacket and pants.

Wherever he was, Tommy hadn't packed.

But it was time for me to pack it in.

I left Tommy's the way I came, making sure to lock up behind me. This wasn't the kind of neighborhood where a man trusted his neighbors.

★ ★ ★

It was now well after nine AM, and Tommy still hadn't shown up at the office, so I made my peace with the fact that today was going to be another day with no information, and I beat feet back down the steps, taking a moment to take a peek at the office of Mr. De Lancey. There were no footfalls behind the door—considering he complained of Tommy's pacing, it seemed he was more of a night owl—so I removed myself from the building.

It was back to Mrs. K's, where most of the house was either gone for work or making a long, slow morning for themselves behind closed doors. Seeing no pressing errands in my future, I took off my sundress and popped my pajamas back on.

I didn't get much peace and quiet before someone decided to press the buzzer on the front door. I hurried down the stairs—my backside feeling a little bit better days after my accident—and opened up to the sight of a young man in a navy blue delivery boy's outfit, gazing at a clipboard.

"Delivery for Viviana Valentine," he declared.

"That's me."

"Thank God, I didn't want to haul this back down the steps." From his right, he dragged a giant silver rack of clothing, a full foot and a half taller than I was. On the front of it dangled the forgotten Claire McCardell dress I'd worn to the Blackstone's Friday night, with a note attached.

"Sign here, please, miss." A pen and paper was thrust into my hand, and I squiggled my receipt. "I'm required to tell you that the sender has already taken care of the gratuity," he added with puss.

Careful not to tear the dress as I plucked off the note, I recognized the soft, cream-colored paper of the notecards the Blackstone family used for their correspondence.

Viviana—

Here's your dress, along with a few others I think you and your housemates may like.

T.B.

In all the excitement of my reconnaissance of Webber Harrington-Whitley's apartment—not to mention the previous morning's adventures into Toyland—I had completely forgotten that Tallulah Blackstone, the Diamond Princess and number-one party girl of New York City, still had possession of my borrowed dress. It'd also dawned on me that she'd known that I was knocked out cold by our intruder and hadn't bothered to ring me up, but I suppose dames like that think all screwy when it comes to showing concern for the common people.

I could hear someone come down the stairs and skid to a halt on the other side of the giant rack of clothing. Peeking beneath, I saw Betty's bright pink fuzzy slippers.

"Tally. Returning the dress I left at her place," I explained.

"And *then* some!" Her voice reminded me of a kid on Christmas morning.

"Nice to get her castoffs, huh."

"Oh, be nice," Betty squeaked.

"Alright, alright. Think you can help me run this upstairs? I don't want to leave it in Mrs. K's doorway."

"You bet!"

It took us each five trips, with armfuls of clothes, to bring the loot upstairs, including a few cardboard boxes of handbags and accessories, and at least one hat that, after taking it out and noticing large feathers and a few faux gardenias attached to it, I assumed Tally meant as an apology for Mrs. K's troubles.

I scrabbled downstairs for the last box when there was another knock at the door. Flinging it open to see what else the Diamond Princess could be pawning off, it took a moment before I realized the man on the steps was Sandy and not another delivery man. He advanced at me, fist at the height of my jaw.

"I swear to God, you bitch," he said, growling. "I have tried to be nice."

"Touch me again," I dared him. I saw the white-haired officer rounding into the front hall from the dining room—and so did Sandy. His shoulders hunched, and he ran down the steps, leaving the scent of cedar in his wake.

"You want me to chase after him, miss?" the old officer asked. His eyes pleaded for me to say no, and even though nothing would bring me more joy than to see Sandy sporting some steel bracelets, I shook my head.

By this point, Phyllis had emerged from her extended beauty sleep and descended a floor to see what the noise was about. She lingered over the clothing, plucking at sheaths and shirts, pulling sundresses over her nightgown, donning hats and switching out her slippers for shiny, patent-leather pumps. Then she got a gleam in her eye.

"Viiiiviannnnnnnnnaaaaa," I heard her call. "There's something you have to try on." I wasn't in the mood to play dress-up, but clearly Phyllis had uncovered a lulu I couldn't pass up.

"What is it?"

"This!"

Phyllis's thin arm thrust through the rack, holding a delicate hanger from which dangled a mostly sheer set of camiknickers, embroidered with black lace and delicate pink flowers at all the seams. I squeaked. I'd never seen something so barely there but so obviously expensive up close in my life.

"Oh, absolutely *not*," I exclaimed.

"Oh, come *on*. It's just underwear!" I could hear Phyllis holding back her laugh.

"And it won't fit me," Betty added. "I've got too much in the bust."

"It's got to go on someone, and I think it's gotta be you, Viv," Phyllis added.

"But . . ." I looked down at my red-and-white-striped pajama shirt and pants.

"But nothing! We're just having fun," Phyllis said. "We're all girls, and you'll look just dynamite."

Realizing I wasn't getting out of this, I scurried into the bathroom and made a quick change, leaving the girls pulling even more scarves and trinkets out of the box of treasures Tally had sent over. They were so overcome, Phyllis hadn't even called her friend Jacqui yet to let her know her prized red dress was safe and sound. Such was the power of beautiful—and free—clothing on my housemates.

Truth be told, I always liked the way I looked in black, and this little ditty was no exception. It was a few inches too long in the torso, but where it fit, it fit well. The embroidery was artful and hid all the right things and revealed all that it should, given the right situation. Giving myself the up and down, I looked a bit like Ava Gardner, without the lipstick but damn near all of the *va-va-voom*. Pleased by my reflection, I flung open the bathroom door, and put my back against the frame, pushing the curls out of my eyes.

"What do you think?" I purred before noticing a conspicuous silence.

Betty and Phyllis were standing, blushing in the hallway where I had left them, covered in more accessories than the entire ladies section of Lord & Taylor's, their eyes staring not at me, but at the bottom of the stairs.

Officer Leary was planted like a statue, mouth agape, turning a shade of red I'd never seen on skin before. My arms froze against the wall, trying to keep myself from falling over, but that just left most of my skin exposed.

"I'm the day shift today, Miss Valentine," he said and ran to the dining room.

★ ★ ★

As soon as he was out of sight, I collapsed on the ground, Betty came over and flopped on top of me, her bosom heaving with gasping laughs.

"I can't wait to tell Dottie," she said, trying to speak, "He is *done* for. That poor boy is *all* yours, whether you want him to be or not."

I stayed in my room as long as I could, finishing up *Queen of Shadows* and starting on *Dames Are Deadly*. But after missing breakfast, I could only make it a few hours in solitary before my stomach was griping and I knew I'd have to go downstairs. The powers that be seemed truly to be against me; in order to get out of the house without further embarrassment, I would have to scurry like a rat past the dining room where Officer Leary had posted himself.

I darted to the bathroom and took a long shower, keeping my hair under a cap to avoid having to redo it, and dressed myself in pedal pushers and a sleeveless button-down, covering as much skin as I could without feeling like I'd suffocate in the heat. No jewelry, nothing that sparkled, and just a quick run of powder over my nose; not even a splash of lipstick would grace my face. My shoes in my hand so I wouldn't even make a footfall, I snuck downstairs at lunchtime like a girl trying to make it out after curfew.

"How goes it today, Viviana Valentine?" Detective Lawson caught me in the vestibule, and it was all I could do not to curse.

"Detective."

"Where you headed, shoes literally in hand?"

"Out for lunch."

"Oh, good. Officer Leary and I are starving. What do you say?"

"Doesn't someone have to watch Mrs. K's?" I stared at Lawson's face, bidding my blood to stay down and not rush directly to my cheeks.

"Nah, I think after the weekend the coast is clear, don't you? Probably just a random B and E, wouldn't you say?" Lawson had a gleam—an actual *gleam*—in his eye. That good-for-nothing hound.

"Whatever you say, Detective. You're the professional." I forced myself to act like nothing was up. "Where can I take you fellas? Lunch is on me, as a thank-you."

"Oh, just the diner on the corner is fine by me," Lawson said. "I'm not a man of expensive taste."

"No, I wouldn't guess that you were," I said, streaming by him and out the door.

Once on the stoop, I slipped my shoes on and led the way down the sidewalk, Lawson laughing and Leary dead silent in our strange little parade.

The cool chrome of the diner's door was glinting in the sun, and I flung it open for myself. "*Chaírete*, Miklos," I greeted the first server I saw. An older Greek gentleman, who barely came up to my shoulder, waved, grabbed three menus, and scurried us to a corner booth.

I sat down first, with Lawson plopping down across from me, in the center of his red vinyl bench, looking like a delighted pig who wasn't planning on moving from the trough. I scooted down my own seat, and was pinned between Leary and the window.

"What's good here?" Lawson asked, picking up the laminated, twenty-page menu.

"It's a diner, Detective. Everything is good. Look, they have braised goat, hamburgers, General Tso's Chicken, and breakfast all day," I explained.

A woman nearly as short as Miklos came to the table and waited silently, her pen over her pad to take our order.

"Hi, Cora—a Coke for me and . . . a cheeseburger and fries?"

"Okay. Boys?"

"Same for me," Leary muttered, not lifting his eyes from the menu.

"Same for me too, dear," Lawson added, and Cora smiled.

"Then why'd you ask what was good?"

"Just to get a rise out of you."

"At least now you're being honest with me." I couldn't suppress my smile.

"Would you return the favor?" Lawson asked pointedly.

"Depends."

Cora came and delivered our plastic cups of Coca-Cola, which immediately began sweating on the table.

"You don't know where Tommy is?" Lawson asked, tossing away his straw and slurping the soda from the cup.

"No, and at this point, if I did, I'd tell you. If he were in one of your cells, I'd at least know he was alive and breathing," I said. "He wasn't in the office this morning, though I haven't called back to check since I left last."

"My boys have," Lawson said. "He ain't there."

"Oh."

"Are you telling me everything, Viviana?"

"Yeah," I said, thinking about the cuff links and shimmering hair clip floating at the bottom of my nightstand. I forced my eyes down to the table, in a passable attempt to show my worry and hide my fib.

"Listen, you sure he wasn't on any kind of case you didn't know about?"

"I know he has some open cases, but they're all in a holding pattern right now."

"Is he still fishing around on that thing with Jimmy?"

"No, no, no." I swirled a French fry in ketchup, avoiding eye contact with the men at the table. "He stares at the file a few good hours a week, and keeps an eye on the city councilman he thinks is involved, but there's been no motion on it. Thanks to you."

"It's not thanks to me, Viv; it's thanks to the laws of the city and the state of New York," Lawson said. "All he has is a theory."

"It's not just gossip that Jimmy was doing low-level work for Tino," I said. "He told Tommy outright."

"And he was—like all the others—paid in cash. Contacted by a note in the mail, instructed to burn the letters too?"

"Of course."

"So why does Tommy think Jimmy got hit?"

"He broke a rule."

"Which rule?"

"The rule of not having a brother who's a PI, I guess. And maybe Tino finally left his hiding spot and found my boss. You ever think of that?"

"We'll find him, don't worry." Lawson suddenly sounded like he cared. As Cora delivered our burgers, he reached into his jacket and pulled a crisp five-dollar bill from his own wallet, telling the older woman to keep the change.

"I said I was gonna get it!"

Lawson waved me off.

"Listen." He grabbed his burger and wrapped half in a napkin. "I gotta jet. You," he said to Leary, "take care of her today, okay? And run home and get in plainclothes. On my orders."

★   ★   ★

"He's trying to set us up now?" I asked as I picked the last French fry off Lawson's plate. It'd been a silent meal.

"Sure seems like it," Leary replied, almost but not quite cracking a smile.

"Listen—I'm going to go home and put on a more presentable outfit. You, under your supervisor's orders, are gonna do the same. Then, why don't you show me a bit of the city from the eyes of a boy who grew up here?"

"I think I can manage that." Leary threw in his napkin. "Want me to walk you home first?"

"Of course. The mean streets of Chelsea don't sleep, even on Monday afternoons."

★   ★   ★

It took less than an hour for Leary to return, now sporting the same blue stovepipe jeans that he had worn the previous night, plus a Hawaiian shirt peppered with navy-blue palm trees. On Tommy, an outfit like that would drive me up a wall, but with Leary's slicked-back hair and beat-up boots, the effect was much more charming. Plus, his shirt complemented my butter-yellow shift dress, so we made a handsome pair. On the sidewalk, he held out his arm, and I crooked mine in it, blushing a bit as I imagined Betty spying on us from her front-facing window.

"So, where are you taking me, Officer?"

"Call me Alan, can't you?"

"You're not technically off duty, Officer," I needled him.

"Fine. Let's take a stroll this way," he said, pulling me south.

"So, when you're not at work, Officer, what do you do for fun?"

"There's not a ton of 'off-duty' time," he answered with a sigh. "I work a lot of hours so my sister can go to school."

"That's no fun."

"But I still get my kicks. I go over the river to Hoboken on the weekends, sometimes, and check out street races."

"Oh, yeah? You're a greaser?"

"Not quite. I don't have my own car. Can't keep one here."

"But a copper checking out the races!"

"They don't know I'm the fuzz," he said with a wink. "And there's no reason for 'em to know. But honestly, walking the beat isn't my thing, I'm thinking of switching to motor pool."

"Certainly less of a chance of being shot in the motor pool."

"That too. Tommy ever catch some lead poisoning?"

"Once, in the bicep. Ruined my overcoat, dress, *and* my best nylons that night, he did."

"You're a special kind of woman, Viviana Valentine."

"And don't you forget it, Alan Leary."

We strolled for a good long while, until the streets began to run into each other, and the scent of the air seemed to make a funny change.

"Is someone smoking tea?" I coughed; the cafe next to us on the sidewalk smelled like a run-over skunk.

"Do not tell me a girl like you hasn't explored the Village."

"I don't come down here, much," I admitted.

"You prefer PIs to poets?"

"I can't say that I've got a preference, I just know 'em better. Men who think with their fists are a bit easier than men who think with their hearts."

"Come in, this way, though," Leary said, pulling me yet again. "Just get a cup of coffee with me."

NIGHT 6

We trundled down into a basement shop, dark and dank and thick with the smell of so many types of cigarettes my eyes began to water. The entire room was painted black—floor, walls, and ceiling—and lit with small burning candles on the tables. The bartender greeted Leary with a convoluted handshake, which I took to mean that the young officer was no stranger to the halls of Greenwich Village or the effects of smoked herb.

"Here, over here," he said, pulling me into a dark corner.

For it being three PM on a Monday, the cafe was crowded with who I took to be the usual types. A jazz man was howling away on an alto saxophone on a small stage, and a crescent of people hung on every random note from mere feet away. It was altogether a different kind of music from Tommy's usual circuit—his kind of clubs never wanted to distract from the gambling, boozing, fighting, and women with something as brainy as music that made you think, or, depending on the player, wince.

A woman, still wearing large, round black sunglasses and a black scarf over her hair was blissed out with every run, moving her body in her chair as if she'd been taken over by a trance. The rest of the tables were dotted with groups and couples, and the booth kitty-corner to us held two men, nuzzling in the dark.

"Do you come here a lot?"

"Yeah, it's a good spot," Leary said, smiling at our waitress, dressed in head-to-toe black and clearly peeved to see her tall, handsome regular in the company of another dame. "Whiskey. Viviana?"

"I'll have the same."

"I thought you didn't drink?"

"Something changed my mind."

Our drinks arrived in small glasses smudged with fingerprints. Leary picked one up and swirled the dark amber liquid, taking a sip and grimacing a bit as it burned its way down his throat.

"I'm the right company today, but not yesterday?"

"I needed a night to sleep on it."

"And tell me," he said, punctuating his question with another sip, "do you always sleep in black lace?"

I punched him as hard as I could in the bicep as he laughed. "You have no business making that joke, not after your face this morning! You were about as red as Woody Woodpecker!"

"Shh, shh, shh," he reminded me, as my shrieks matched the yelps of that saxophone. "You just caught me off guard."

"Yeah, sure," I said. "I'll have you know I sleep in pajamas just like any other girl. I assure you, all-girl boarding houses are not just satin nighties and pillow fights."

"Don't say such horrible things!" Leary was laughing now, leaning back in his chair and so much more at ease than I'd ever seen him.

"But I just about nearly died of embarrassment," I admitted, heat flaring up in my face again. "The girls insisted I try it on."

"Be square with me, Viviana Valentine," he said.

"I am! I'm not stringing you," I said. "But wait—you're acting like you've seen loads of girls in their undies."

"We've broken up a few can houses," Leary admitted. "Where did all that even come from?"

"Oh, the girl upstairs—the model," I fibbed. "You met all of them."

"Oh, the skinny broad? Yeah. Makes sense. You got any more like that lying around?"

I rolled my eyes and laughed, declining to confirm or deny the contents of my unmentionables drawer.

We sipped in silence, and I could feel my posture starting to shift, in that subconscious way your body tells you that you wouldn't mind sitting on a fella's lap, or as close to it as you could get and still be decent. And that damned Officer Leary didn't help at all, swinging his muscular arm over the back of our bench, right behind my shoulders, still smelling like Aqua Velva.

The sax man slowed into a cool, sultry part of his set, and I felt Leary lean forward to whisper into my ear.

"Viviana Valentine, what am I going to do with you?" he asked, his lips tickling my skin, the scent of whiskey on his breath.

"Viviana!" another voice shot through the darkness. "What the hell happened to you?"

★   ★   ★

"Tally!" I shot straight out of my seat and stood, eye-to-voluptuous breastbone with Tallulah Blackstone, the woman now taking off her scarf and sunglasses. She seemed to be alone; none of the other jazz cats in the bar were standing up for her—she'd either flown the coop under Daddy's nose once again, or she had some bodyguards who were really on the dole.

"Not even a word from you in days," she chided me. "I was worried out of my mind!"

"You were *worried*?" I spat back. Leary was standing now, just to my right, his mouth hanging open. "I spent a night in the *hospital*! I could've been killed!"

"Could you *imagine* if I'd shown up at the hospital for some pretty girl?" she said. "The photographers would've been swarming until sunup. Unless you *wanted* your picture in the paper." Her words burned, and the accusation stung more than I'd expected it to. Had this girl even had an honest-to-God relationship since her mother had died?

"That's the last thing in the *world* I'd ever want!" For many reasons—my own humility and Tommy's unspoken rules on the behavior of detectives—I was telling the truth.

"And not even a word of thanks for the clothing!"

"It just arrived a few hours ago—as I was heading out. I didn't have time."

"Didn't have time, huh? Too busy running off with this lug?" The words were cold and dismissive.

I stepped in front of Leary. "What's it to you?!"

Tally was keeping it pretty cool, but I could see all her muscles tense beneath her black turtleneck, fingers curled in a fist, crushing the arms of her sunglasses. Her painted lips were pursed so hard they were almost invisible. Leary reached out to put his hand on my shoulder.

As soon as he did, Tally's weight shifted, and she slunk back on her heels.

"I . . . I'm sorry. I should just go." Manhattan's Diamond Princess backed away from me so quickly she nearly tripped over a chair. Her sunglasses and hair kerchief were on before she even left the cave of the jazz club, and I went momentarily blind as she opened the door and disappeared onto the sunlit sidewalk.

"What was all that flap about?" Leary asked me.

"Do you know who that was?" I asked.

"Yeah, Tallulah Blackstone. No one in New York doesn't know who that is."

"I forgot she likes jazz," I whispered, my heart breaking just a little as I remembered the thrill she had for Charlie Parker on the radio.

"Hey," Leary's fingers trailed down my forearm until he found my hand. "Do you want to get out of here?"

"I think so."

"Okay, follow me."

He tossed a few bills down on our table for our whiskey and gave a shrug to the bartender.

"I'm sorry I embarrassed you," I said. We popped out onto the sidewalk ourselves, and I dropped Leary's hand to paw through my purse for my own sunglasses, to shield myself from the sunlight and to keep Leary from seeing my eyes that were reddening with frustrated tears.

"Didn't embarrass me at all," he said, cracking his knuckles. "You just might want to change your hair color, grow a few inches, and maybe get a disguise, before we ever go back there."

"We?"

"What? You make a good date. Until you fight with the other patrons." He smiled, but I was ready to suffocate in the humiliation of my dustup.

"Thanks for a nice afternoon, at least. You're up that way, aren't you?" I started walking toward Mrs. K's, fully expecting to make the stroll alone.

"Hey! I don't know what the beef is between you two crazy dames, but my boss told me to keep you safe. All day," he said. "The sun hasn't even gone down yet."

"Then where to?"

"Well," he checked his watch. "It's meatloaf night."

★ ★ ★

True to his word, Leary didn't live that far from Tommy's office—just a few blocks south. He pulled a ring of keys from his pocket as we approached his building, and an older woman smiled at him.

"*Tráthnóna maith*, Alan."

"*Tráthnóna maith. An raibh lá maith agat?*"

They pattered on for a few minutes, until it was clear that I was out of the loop, and she waved him off to continue sweeping her porch.

"She likes to make sure we're okay," he said. "They all got worried after our parents died. Up this way."

Inside, the hallway was somehow both too dark and glaringly bright, the light coming from a flickering, thousand-watt bulb. The rickety wooden stairs were carpeted with a fraying, dark green rug; the bannister was lacquered in about a thousand layers of high-shine shellac. The opposite wall was missing any kind of guardrail, and thousands of hands over the years left a schmutz of grease on the flat white paint. Each stair landing led to four separate apartment doors; behind most were families laughing or arguing, or babies crying. The entire building was filled, basement up, with the sound of people who didn't get a pause from life.

"One more flight," he said, skipping up the stairs, two at a time. "Smells good, though, right?"

He burst through a door right at the top of the stairs, and nearly took out a young woman, her black hair in a ponytail, stirring some thawing frozen peas in a dented aluminum saucepan on a two-burner stove, inconveniently located right next to the front door. All the while, she was reading from a book propped up on a spice rack.

"Move it, Kitty," he said, knocking into her.

She flipped away from the stove and began pelting him with her potholder.

"Stop! We have a guest!" he said, and she stopped pelting him long enough to catch her breath.

I stood in the doorway, smiling and silent, giving the blushing teenager a bit of a wave. "Sorry. I'm Viviana," I said. "Nice to meet you."

"I'm Kitty," she said back, waving her hand with the big, quilted oven mitt on it. "Can you shut the door so I can get my idiot brother's dinner out of the oven?"

I scurried inside and shut the door behind me, feeling the lock latch automatically.

"I'm in the way," I said, trying to inch anywhere but where I was. Alan had disappeared into another room, and I was left standing awkwardly in a kitchen never meant to house one person, let alone two.

"Everything's in the way," Kitty said, tossing a dented tin loaf pan onto a scorched section of laminate countertop barely larger than the pan. "Don't worry too much."

"Smells fantastic, though."

Kitty smiled as she shimmied some peas from her pot onto three chipped plates—I didn't catch sight of so much as a single spoon or ladle. "Thanks. It's the least I can do for living rent-free."

Alan was back, plucking three warped forks from a mat on the drainboard. "We eat off our knees in the living room," he said with only an ounce of self-consciousness, jerking his head back to denote that the space just on the other side of the fridge was the living room.

"Sounds good."

Kitty handed me a plate piled high with fixin's, and the hunger in my stomach clawed.

The living room itself was a small sofa, conspicuous with stuffing falling out the bottom, piled high with patchwork quilts for cushion, and three rickety crates placed around to act as side tables. On the floor in the corner was a cracked, Bakelite tabletop radio, too small for its celebrated spot.

"We had better stuff before," Alan said as Kitty claimed her usual place on the loveseat. "We had to hock a lot of it."

Alan took a place on the floor and motioned for me to take the last bit of flat cushion.

"You don't have to explain yourself," I said. "Mrs. K's is far and away the nicest place I've ever lived."

"Your parents still here?" Kitty asked.

"Back home."

"Where's home?"

"Pennsylvania."

"You going back?" Alan asked through a mouthful of meatloaf.

"Not if I can help it." Things were getting uncomfortably close to asking the worst question of all: *Why.* "So, Kitty, what are you going to do after you graduate?"

The young girl's face lit up and she began chattering about college, about science and math, and about how she couldn't wait to sleep in a dorm room. It was all sorts of things I didn't understand and couldn't ever hope for.

And to tell the truth, it sounded divine.

★ ★ ★

"She's delightful, you know," I said as I descended the front steps of the Learys' building. "And you don't have to walk me home."

"Maybe I just want to," he replied. "But yeah, she turned out okay."

"And she got a full ride to Barnard?"

"Starting in the spring." He looked appropriately proud. "I think she'll be okay."

"Could you imagine? A college degree," I snorted.

"I dunno, I think you'd do alright. You're sharp enough."

"You're not a slouch yourself." A breeze whipped down the street, and I shivered. Leary pulled me closer as we walked quietly through the night, and the mile between his house and my own was suddenly too short a distance.

As we rounded the corner to Mrs. K's, our fifteen minutes of making eyes at each other was brought to a swift halt as some lughead came whipping down the middle of the sidewalk and smashed into the two of us with a sweaty, smelly tackle, throwing a shoulder into my companion that knocked Leary flat on his back.

"Hey!" I shouted at the fleeing figure, starting down the sidewalk in pursuit. "Get back here you son of a . . ."

"Viviana, be quiet," Leary said, picking himself off the sidewalk. "Let's get you home."

He practically dragged me the last few hundred feet, and to my surprise, but clearly not to Officer Alan Leary's, Mrs. K's door was wide open. Without stopping, I ran inside.

"I'll get the girls—you check on Mrs. K," I said.

"Gotcha."

We split up in the vestibule.

All the way at the top, Phyllis was on her bed, going over pages and pages of pictures featuring her own face. I didn't even wait for an explanation as I thundered down the stairs; Betty was out, and I flung open Dottie's door without asking to find her at her desk, pouring over her students' worksheets, red pencil in hand.

"Viviana, I went to the library—" she started.

"In a minute!" I said, and I ran back down to the dining room to meet Leary.

"They're fine, they're all fine," he said.

"Same crook who threw me down the stairs, you think?"

"Same crook," Leary agreed. "Hey, can I use your phone? I'm gonna tell Kitty to lock up tight and not expect me home tonight. And I gotta call this in to Lawson."

I brought Leary up the stairs to the girls' phone on the landing. While he rang his sister and his supervisor, I poked my head back into Dottie's room.

"I'm sorry to be rude," I said. "Officer Leary just brought me home, and the door wasn't shut—we wanted to make sure no one got in again."

"Completely logical," Dottie responded. "Perhaps we should all meet you downstairs to address this lapse in security?"

"Good call," I agreed. "Can you gather the troops?"

"Of course."

★   ★   ★

Lawson, trailed by Officer O'Malley, met Betty at the door and led everyone in the house, single file. What with three police officers, Mrs. K and Oleks, Dottie, Phyllis, Betty, and myself, the dining room felt awfully small. I stood near the head of the table, with Leary right behind me, and started talking as soon as everybody sat down.

"Something real fishy is going on here, ladies and gents," I said. "Officer Leary here was escorting me from Tommy's to make sure I got home safely, and someone knocked him over on the sidewalk. And when we got to the front door, it was flapping in the breeze. Did anyone hear someone in here, snooping around?"

"Not at all, Viviana," Dottie spoke up first. "But I had my door closed and a fan on while I was correcting."

"Me neither, but I had the radio going," Phyllis said.

"I wasn't home," Betty explained. "You saw."

"I was doing the dishes downstairs," Mrs. K explained.

"And you know we can't hear anything over that racket," Oleks followed up.

"Okay, it sounds like everyone was just up to their usual Monday night, Officers," I explained to Lawson and Leary. "No one seems to have been injured."

"Viviana," Dottie interjected, "did you check to make sure your room was undisturbed?"

I rocketed up the stairs, with Leary on my tail. I burst into my bedroom and found every last thing I owned in a pile on the floor, my pillows ripped and feathers strewn everywhere. Everything fragile in the room—my vanity mirror, empty perfume bottles, and even the glass over my Woolworth's poster—was smashed to pieces, and whoever had done it had injured himself, leaving a bloody handprint on the wall over my light switch.

"Oh!" I stepped back into Leary, and his arms wrapped around me, pulling me away.

"Detective, we've got a crime scene," he said down the stairs. "Better call it in."

* * *

Facing a few hours, if not a whole night, of police officers trudging through the house, Phyllis packed overnight bags and went to a friend's apartment. Dottie was invited downstairs to sleep on a spare sofa, which Oleks prepared with clean sheets before he and his mother retired. Betty couldn't be driven from the house if there was the promise of at least one good-looking young man in uniform to chat with, so she perched at her doorway to watch the goings-on.

Leary, either by inclination or Lawson's order, joined me at the bay window in the dining room, my head in his lap as I shook with nerves.

"Why don't you just try to get some sleep?" he asked, his fingers playing with my hair. "I can see everyone from here."

"What about you?"

"I'm fine. Promise."

DAY 7

Tuesday, June 27, 1950

I woke up only a few hours later, my head lying on a throw pillow and my body covered from the drafty window with my own blanket, which someone had boosted from the crime scene. Leary was nowhere to be found, but Dottie settled down at the table, only a few feet from my head, with a plate of flapjacks and sausage and a cup of black coffee.

"Good morning, Viviana," she said, unfurling a napkin to place across her lap. "Did you sleep?"

"A bit," I said. "And you?"

"More than you, in all likelihood," she said, cutting up a hot link. "Though Mrs. Kovalenko's son snores."

I laughed and straightened myself up. I was still in my yellow dress from yesterday, and it still smelled distinctly of meatloaf and smoked grass. "Any news?"

"Nothing in regards to your room or to who may have broken in, to the best of my knowledge, though when the officers all left this morning, they said you were welcome to go back to retrieve your belongings or change clothing."

"That's good at least." I stretched to work out the knot in my back. "No more police protection?"

"Well, they instructed us to keep the doors and windows completely locked," Dottie said. She did not look pleased with that assessment of our safety.

"I don't think Mrs. K will let the door be unlocked for years to come."

"I was wondering if I might take a moment to tell you what I found while researching at school yesterday."

"Oh! Of course! Thank you, I'd completely forgotten."

Dottie reached into her purse and pulled out a sheath of typewritten notes. "Here are the extensive details, culled from both encyclopedia and recent microfiche," she explained. My eyes goggled, and she followed up. "But let me provide you with an overview."

"Dottie, before you start, I have to ask—you went to college, right?"

"City University of New York, yes."

"Did you like it?"

"I did."

"Good."

She gave me a queer look before continuing. "As you may be aware, it's all rather jumbled up over there in Asia," she put it delicately. "Between Britain pulling out of India and China's revolution—now with Korea. It's so topsy-turvy that I believe it will be a relatively long time 'til everyone gets it sorted out."

"I mean, we're talking what? Six, seven years? Like the war?" As soon as I said it, Dottie gave me a capital-L Look that let me know that I was on the wrong track.

"Much, much longer than that. Burma especially was under British rule until a few years ago and now . . . well, disorganization, at the least. Though there are some who would likely welcome continued civil unrest."

She sliced into a sausage and ate it with the poised grace of a princess, with me waiting for her to chew and swallow and continue. She was a very good teacher.

"So why on earth was Mr. Blackstone talking about it?"

"In specific instances for Mr. Blackstone, I'm not so sure," Dottie admitted. "But considering his family's history, I imagine that a country rife with problems would be ripe for the picking by industrialists. Perhaps there are diamonds there of particular interest? Less competitive than the mines in Africa?"

"Hmm." The mention of diamonds piqued my interest. "Dottie—stay here for a sec."

"I still have to finish my breakfast," she said and took a sip of coffee.

I scurried upstairs to my bedroom, opened the door, and went directly to my nightstand. There was loads of fingerprint dust on every surface, but I grabbed a hanky and yanked it open, hoping to find the spangly barrette, but finding nothing but the two cuff links among my usual bobby pins and mittens.

I ran back downstairs with just the links and found Dottie at the dining room table. She had been joined by Mrs. K, still wearing her housecoat and with her hair in curlers, who'd set-tled down for her usual ten-minute breakfast with the *Times*.

"Well, whoever it was got something," I said, my voice cracking.

"What's missing, Viviana? Should we get the detective on the phone?"

"There was a piece of jewelry," I said. "It showed up at Tommy's one day with a note from him, saying he'd be out of town. It was a diamond hair clip. I took it home—I don't know why—it felt like the right thing to do at the time. And now it's gone!"

"Oh, Viviana, that's just awful. What can you do?"

"I don't know! If it had any identifying marks on it, I'll never know."

"You had no record of it?"

"Oh! No! I did! I took photographs of the piece and kept them in our case files!"

"But what can you tell from photographs?" Dottie asked. "There's no way to gather fingerprints or hair or other physi-cal evidence."

"No, there isn't. And I don't know anything about diamonds."

Mrs. K looked up from her paper. "Well, Viviana. Why don't you call on my brother, Sergiy? He works on Forty-eighth."

Dottie and I stared blankly.

"The Diamond District, girls. If anyone can provide information, it's him."

★ ★ ★

Mrs. K finished her own plate of scrambled eggs and bacon before bustling downstairs and ringing her brother to warn him of my arrival. I scurried upstairs to get ready, using the full measure of my stubbornness to ignore the pile of mess in the center of my room. Much to my relief, the blood above my light switch and dotting the floor was gone. I wrenched open my armoire and pulled out one of my best summer suits—a bright blue cotton number with big white buttons down the front and a pencil skirt. Accessorized with my white patent-leather heels, purse, and a smart white straw hat, I felt altogether lighter than I'd felt when I woke up.

I hailed a cab at Mrs. K's curb and jetted to Tommy's office for the photographs, assuring the driver that if he'd just wait for me, I would be back in a jiffy. In less than a minute, I ran back to the taxi, and he took me to the next address.

It wasn't until I found Sergiy Doroshenko's midtown location, filled with men in black suits, that I realized just how foolish I must've looked in my royal blue getup, decked out like a little girl in an Easter bonnet.

The building was utilitarian, eight stories of graying cement and steel window casings. The storefronts along the sidewalk had twelve-foot windows, all filled with gray carpeting and glass cases shimmering with gold and jewels—but the effect was more like a bank vault than a princess's dressing room.

A glass door between the shop fronts led to a building lobby, all gray paint and tile, the only sign of life being a dusty plastic fern. A stainless steel elevator that reeked of polish and coffee brought me to the offices upstairs, and upon a squeaky opening, I saw Mr. Doroshenko's floor was marble-printed linoleum tile, with walls painted a dull and inoffensive shade of white. The entire building was quiet. After a polite knock on the door of suite 712, I entered to find a large man, so obviously Mrs. K's brother that she looked like him in a wig, sitting behind a desk, with one bright lamp turned on, illuminating a surface covered with small black leather bags and a large swatch of black velvet right in the center.

"Excuse me, sir," I whispered, "I'm Viviana Valentine."

Mr. Doroshenko stood—and kept on standing. He was easily the same height as his doorway once he was out from behind his desk, dressed head to toe in black except for a stark white shirt. His tie tack and cuff links were even jet stone. I let out a squeak.

"Oh! Oleks is going to be huge!" I said before I could catch myself. Mr. Doroshenko let out a booming laugh, the creases next to his eyes deepening with his smile.

"No, no," he said with a thick accent and a chuckle. "His father was small. Only six foot three." A bear-sized hand extended to shake my own, and he motioned for me to take a seat.

"Goodness," I said.

"And how has my little sister been treating you all, lately? Are you well fed?"

"She's the most patient woman in the world," I said. "And yes, well fed. I'm sure she's let you know that there's been a bit of trouble lately . . ."

"Ah, yes. But do not worry—she does not blame the girls," he responded. He was polite enough not to say that Mrs. K didn't blame *me*, specifically. "As long as there has been no damage to my building?"

It dawned on me that Mrs. K and her husband—whatever he'd done for a living before he passed—probably would not have been able to scrape up the loot to buy a whole brownstone, even if it was just in Chelsea. It was a family business—or maybe the only way to make sure his widowed sister could keep a roof over her head.

"Nothing permanent so far. But I guess some of the trouble might have to do with this." I pulled the photos of the hair clip from my purse and laid them on the velvet, so carefully that it was almost like I was handing over the piece itself. In the dim light, the glossy finish of the photographs gleamed.

Mr. Doroshenko picked up the images with a tenderness I usually saw reserved for babies or small animals. He pulled his lamp closer to them, blocking my line of sight to his face with the shining bulb. Strapping on some odd-looking jeweler's glasses that connected behind his head, he silently inspected every blurry facet before speaking.

"I wonder why that could be. It is a good little piece." My stomach was in knots for the full examination, but his voice was indifferent.

"Could those diamonds have come from Burma, sir?"

"Burma? There are no diamonds in Burma," Mr. Doroshenko said. "Home to the world's most stunning rubies. Enough jade to pave the roads of China. But not diamonds."

"Interesting."

"You know, what is in this piece does not have to be diamonds."

"I'm sorry—say that again?"

Mr. Doroshenko pulled off his spectacles and moved the lamp away. My eyes couldn't refocus in the dark, and Mr. Doroshenko's face was replaced with a purple blob, which floated quietly for a moment while he tried to find the right words to explain my new evidence.

"These may not be diamonds, Miss Valentine. It is probably a piece of white gold, which is valuable enough, but set with cheap topaz—resembling platinum and diamonds, but vastly less expensive. The topaz *could* be from Burma, I suppose, though I am not that familiar with those stones." He handed me back the photos. "I'm sorry—was it a gift? I should have been more careful with my words."

"Sir, is it easy to pass topaz off as a diamond? Fooled me in person, but I'm better with watches."

Mr. Doroshenko raised an eyebrow.

"Uh, I worked in a watch store back home," I said, but he didn't look convinced.

"It is easy enough," he continued. "Topaz is almost as hard, certainly clearer. Well cut, and most customers would not notice. Unless they took them to a specialist. And unless you were suspicious, who would do that?"

"Who would do that, indeed."

"There is no maker's mark on that piece."

"No?" He took my uncertainty for ignorance and went on to explain, pulling off his wedding ring and readjusting the light. Inside of the band, there was a stamp of block, Cyrillic lettering, followed by the code *56 zolotnik*.

"A maker's mark, miss. A brand name. Same as on a dress or a handbag. It tells us who made the piece—in the case of my ring, *Feodor Louri*, from Moscow. But there are other marks for Tiffany, Cartier, Bulgari, Boucheron, and so on. Many you perhaps know from your watch—uh—*selling* days."

"Right. Rolex has a crown, Vacheron that funny little cross," I agreed.

"Yes, right, right. And often, the contents of the metal will be stamped alongside. *Zolotnik* is the Russian gold standard, similar to carats in America. This is not pure gold," he added, "but stronger and, as money does not grow on trees for all of us, more affordable."

"Well, isn't that something," I said, taking the photographs back and tucking them into my purse. "Why would there not be a maker's mark on something?"

"Possibly because it is, uh, . . . not so special. Buy from someone not so prestigious, and then resell."

"Is it easy to add a mark after the fact?"

"Yes, of course. Metal—though it feels hard to our hands—it can be stamped or marked at any time by someone who knows how. And most would want to, before sale."

"How much is this piece worth, if I had to ask? If it was all bunk?"

"Less than fifty dollars." Mr. Doroshenko waffled, as if more than half my week's pay was a drop in the bucket. "But still, it is very pretty." It was clear he was trying to save my feelings.

"One more question, if I may?" I asked, plucking another small parcel from my handbag as Mr. Doroshenko's shrugged. "What about these?" Webber Harrington-Whitley's cuff links came tumbling out onto the piece of velvet.

"No stones." Mr. Doroshenko stated the obvious. "But look here. Do you see the script? Very tiny. Cartier. But custom engraved. I've not seen this design before. Though that may not be saying much, as I deal in loose stones." He gestured to his little leather sacks, which I now realized were filled with unset diamonds.

"Expensive?"

"Yes, moderately. It is twenty-four carat, very understated. For a gentleman. A man of taste. A man who makes solid investments." He made a fist and shook it, to show he approved.

"Sir, you have helped me so much," I said, reaching out to shake his hand. "I swear it, your information has been invaluable."

★   ★   ★

I left Mr. Doroshenko's air-conditioned building and hailed a taxi on the Avenue, heading back to Tommy's office for the second time that day, to meet the glazier and replace the broken window in the door later in the afternoon. I knew I wasn't going to see my boss's smiling face there to greet me, but the pull of that squeaky fan and smelly air just had a hold on me.

There were days' worth of letters stuffed into our mail slot; but other than that, the plywood door was undisturbed. I made an effort to look at every envelope—God forbid there be anything from Tommy or some other guardian angel who wanted to shed a bit more light on my situation. But the big stack was filled with bills and advertising fliers for shoes and carpet cleaning services, and most of it went straight into the can.

I'd never owned a fine piece of jewelry in my life, but for some reason, the information that the hair clip Tommy sent was, in the grand scheme of things, worthless didn't shake me. Maybe it's because it was the first piece of evidence I'd gotten in a week that didn't involve getting my caboose busted up or cause a fight to break out; or maybe, as I sat down in my squeaky desk chair, I'd finally gotten an inkling of what was going on.

I pulled Tally's case file out of my top drawer and grabbed the nearest pencil.

BLACKSTONE, TALLULAH

CLIENT NAME: *Tallmadge Blackstone*
OCCUPATION: *Millionaire*
REQUEST: *Recognizance*
TARGET: *Tallulah "Tally" Blackstone, 18. Daughter; intended bride.*
RELATED PARTIES: *Webber Harrington-Whitley, 57. Business partner to Mr. Blackstone; intended groom.*

I licked my pencil and added a new note to RELATED PARTIES.

Webber Harrington-Whitley, fifty-seven. Business partner to Mr. Blackstone; intended groom. In hospital. Prognosis: dire.

Not having spoken to a doctor, I couldn't get more specific.

Now back to the notes.

NOTES:

- *Tallulah Blackstone spotted on Wednesday, June 21, 1950, at engagement party for a minor du Pont and his future Mrs., Cassandra (surname unknown). Ms. Blackstone tailed to location by TF.*
- *That evening, TF disappeared, with no note to his lead or his whereabouts.*
- *On Thursday, June 22, VV discovered a note about his absence, and a hair clip (see Photo Evidence #1)*
- *Evening Friday, June 23, VV attended a small get-together at the home of Mr. Blackstone at his behest. VV ascertained Ms. Blackstone held reservations about her upcoming nuptials but did not express explicit designs to not follow through with the wedding. VV overhears Mr. Blackstone on a call to an unknown party, asking about a "Yangon" (unknown origin).*

I erased a bit and updated the entry with Dottie's observations.

- *Capital of country of Burma, perhaps new rich boy playground?*
- *Monday, June 26, VV incites altercation at jazz club (location: unknown) with Ms. Blackstone.*

Tommy didn't have to know, just yet, about Leary and the nightgown, I figured.

- *Tuesday, June 27, VV took evidence #1 to Diamond District for independent authentication. Item may not be platinum + diamond hair clip, instead white gold + topaz. Relatively worthless.*

I clipped the barrette photos back to the cover of the file. That was about it for Tally, so I hunted for my second case file.

UNCONSCIOUS MAN

NAME: In the conveniently blank spot, I scribbled in what I knew. *Webber Harrington-Whitley.*
OCCUPATION: *Diamond importer-exporter*
REQUEST: *Solve murder.*

I supposed he was still technically breathing, but I'd have to ask Tommy for all the ins and outs on how the state of New York treated cases of bodies alive but brain dead.

RELATED PARTIES: *Detective Jake Lawson, investigator, Midtown North*

NOTES:

- *Morning: June 1950, VV attempted identification via porcelain face mask, but found manufacturer deceased.*
- *Afternoon: June 26, VV suspects identity of deceased man, made by matching cuff links to signet ring in possessions of man in hospital.*

It wasn't a lot, but it was something. I took a long piece of Scotch tape and plastered the expensive Cartier cuff links to the front of the folder. At the mere suggestion of the stiff's identity, the cops could have someone come in and make a proper ID.

I put on the percolator and paced in the dark, waiting for the window man. Paging through every scrap of paper in the office, I managed to find a copy of the *Times* from the first day of the United Nations; a playbill from *Stagecoach*; and a backless pulp novel called *Chasing Whispers*, with a lipstick kiss on the cover, leaving me wondering what kind of dames my boss was bringing around at night after I went home.

But something was burning a hole in my stomach, and it wasn't just black coffee sitting on a rapidly depleting breakfast of toast and eggs. I picked up the phone and spun the dial.

"Midtown North," the gruff voice said.

"Is Officer Leary available?"

"Maybe," the voice barked back. "Who's askin'?"

"Viviana Valentine."

"Hold on."

There was a fumble of the receiver and some stout yelling in the background before Leary's voice came on the other end.

"Viviana?"

"Hi!"

"I'm at work," he said, sounding kind of flustered.

"Good thing this is a work question," I said, rolling my eyes. "Did you think I was the type of girl to call and whisper sweet nothings to a boy while he's on the job?"

"No, that doesn't seem like you," he admitted. "How can I help?"

"You know of any cat houses in the Village?"

I could hear him sputter. "Not off the top," he explained. "Those places have been moving to the outer boroughs."

"Just a thought."

"You gonna let me know what you're up to?"

"Certainly not."

"Just be careful."

"Am I ever not?"

Before he could answer—because frankly, I didn't want to hear it—I hung up and scurried into Tommy's dark office to begin pawing through his desk. It was mostly out of date—Tommy kept what he called a mental file, now—but in the back of the center drawer, I found an old beat-up black book filled with Tommy's block letters.

Contacts.

Settling down at my desk again to wait for the window man, I compiled a list of ten different establishments in Greenwich Village and Alphabet City that could be the potential home for Mr. Harrington-Whitley's more sordid affairs.

"The Liquor and Leave Her Lounge seems like a good place to start," I said, just as the silence was broken with a knock on the door.

"Come in!" The window guy and I went way back, so there was no sense in being polite.

"How things goin', Viv?" the window man asked. "What's it today?"

"You know, the usual, Stan the Window Man. Do you need anything from me?"

"Only fifteen dollars."

"It was fourteen and change last time!"

"Sorry, Viv," he said. "I don't set the prices. Just the glass."

The old door was plastered with so much putty over the years, it took Stan a few hours to get the pane in just right, leaving no time at all to even paint Tommy's name back on the door before it was time for him to head home for the night.

"I'll come back soon to paint the letters on," Stan promised, tossing his putty knife in his bucket.

"Don't hurry. It's bound to break at least three more times before the end of the year."

Stan chuckled as he headed back down the stairs.

★　★　★

It was nearly dusk by the time I parted with fifteen dollars (of my own hard-earned dough, racking up the figure Tommy owed *me* in expenses, including the clams I had shelled out to the schmuck upstairs) and set about my evening jaunts.

I scurried home to change, first, out of my bright blue day suit. Nothing said suspicious character in a bar quite like white patent-leather shoes, so I switched that outfit for my green nipped-waist dress and black accessories, adding a black veiled hat for an added bit of drama and anonymity. While closing up my room, I ran into Dottie in the hall.

"How was your day, Viviana?" she asked.

"Stressful," I said.

Dottie gave me a look of weary pity. "How so?"

"Just all sorts of stuff. I've checked on some leads, but they all had an alibi."

"I would say I'm sorry to hear that," Dottie said, "but we mustn't accuse innocent people of murder."

"The man I'm thinking of is not so innocent," I replied with a sigh. "He's the sourest neighbor you could get."

"Did you confirm the alibi?"

"I . . ."

"Well, he may be guilty yet."

"Wait right here." I pivoted on my heel, returning to the phone on the landing, and punched the switch to get the operator.

"Hello, I'd like to be connected to a Mr. Van Meyer's office," I said. "The councilman."

"Gimme a sec, honey," the operator said back.

"Hello!" A jolly man's voice came over the line.

"Hello, I'm calling from Mr. McAllister's office," I fibbed, realizing I didn't know McAllister's first name. "He rode with Mr. Van Meyer back from the Hamptons recently?"

"Indeed he did ride with me!" the voice confirmed. "At least he provided some company during that long dustup in Massapequa, though I think between you and me, you know it wasn't pleasant company."

"No, sir, I don't doubt that it wasn't," I said warmly into the phone. "Regardless, Mr. McAllister fears he left his hat in in your motor car, sir. He hasn't seen it since last Wednesday."

"I don't believe he did, my dear. Must've left it elsewhere as I drove him back Friday."

"Thank you, Mr. Van Meyer. I'll relay the news."

There was a click and nothing. McAllister's alibi checked out.

I turned to Dottie. "Rats."

"Viviana, I think we can say that any progress in a mystery is good, even if it removes a suspect. What do you have planned for tonight?"

"A meeting with the photographers, then the goal to scope out a bit of Harrington-Whitley's habits," I said, hoping she wouldn't infer what I meant.

"That could be dangerous." I couldn't pull the wool over Dottie's eyes.

"Yeah, well . . ." I trailed off, then I got my bright idea. "You want to come with?"

Dottie looked down at her tweedy, ankle-length skirt, button-down, and flat Oxfords. "I don't think I'm quite the kind of woman whom they expect in such establishments."

"Nah, but that's half the beauty of it, isn't it?" I explained. "We're certainly less likely to be picked up, if you know what I mean."

"I do." Dottie was getting in touch with her more daring side.

"Why don't I help you get dressed," I said. "Just a little different from your usual. C'mon, we're just looking—it'll be fun. I'll even change to something a little less flashy."

"As long as you don't expect me to wear green," Dottie said.

"Whatever color you want, I promise."

NIGHT 7

It was another hour before Dottie and I left Mrs. K's, but we looked a pair. Dottie was in a dark brown satin frock and her fancier, *heeled* Oxfords, topped with a chocolate felt turban. I'd toned down my look, donning an eggplant-purple pencil skirt and a black blouse, but I insisted on keeping the hat. In a dark bar, you'd never see us, and I liked the idea of it.

"Where are we going first?" Dottie asked, fidgeting with the toggle of her bag.

"A meeting on Bleecker," I said, cagey about information. "I have to talk to some boys."

I knew my ruse worked because three men were standing outside of a coffee joint, looking mighty shady. Each was wearing all black, and they all sported an identical pork pie hat in varying states of disintegration; a cigarette dangled from each man's lower lip. If that weren't enough of a clue, a shiny Kodak Pony dangled from a strap on every neck.

"Evening, fellas," I purred in my best imitation of a diamond debutante, and they whirled, cameras flashing. Dottie let out a small cry as she hid behind me. The cacophonous clicks of shutters slowed, and I hollered, "Your golden girl ain't comin'."

"You the dame that summoned us?" the blond man asked. I reckoned he was Masters.

"Yeah. I wanna know who's been siccing you on Tally," I said.

"What's it to you?" The dark one with the soft voice was obviously Agnellini, and I felt my heart skip a bit of a beat as his fingers caressed the knobs and bits of his camera. He was the type that Betty's romance novels would refer to as *swarthy*.

"Ten bucks for each of you for any info you've got on the source."

Dottie pulled at my elbow. "Viviana! That's a lot of money."

I shook her off while they pondered, and Agnellini piped up, sticking out his hand. Masters and Hedley followed suit, and each palm was appropriately greased in turn.

"I don't know his name," Agnellini said, as soon as he pocketed his dough. "But he's got a big, deep voice, and he ain't never been wrong."

"That's it?"

"Nah," Masters added. "And she's always alone—no bodyguard to be found." He quit talking and went back to manipulating his cigarette with his lips.

"That wasn't worth thirty bucks!"

"Shoulda started lower," was all Agnellini could say, shrugging with a wink in my direction. "See you soon, boys."

The three disappeared into the night, their cigarettes still burning and lighting the way.

★   ★   ★

"I'm sorry, Viviana," Dottie said. "Do you want to go home?"

"Nah, that's okay. That'll teach me." My pocketbook felt considerably lighter even though only three bills had flown the coop. If Tommy balked at repaying me—which I knew he wouldn't—at least I could hock the barrette if I ever got it back. "Let's get on with the night."

I looked at my list of establishments and began to walk, with Dottie keeping pace beside me. We were at our first bar within minutes, but the Liquor and Leave Her Lounge had already left. The windows were boarded up and a "For Rent" sign was pasted over the door.

"One down, nine to go," I said. "And if they're all closed, I'll still buy you a drink closer to home."

"That's kind of you."

Rather than blow all my cash on cab fare, we started a route through the streets, finding the next three joints—Miss Kitty's, The Come-On Inn, and Scarlett's Cabaret—dead and gone, either boarded up like the Lounge or replaced by more reputable establishments.

★   ★   ★

"There were only ten to choose from in Tommy's book," I explained. "From what I could tell, it hadn't been updated since '47."

"I don't mind at all," Dottie said. "It does feel so clandestine."

"Here, let's take a seat to try to figure out where to go next." I led Dottie to a bus bench and pulled my list out of my purse, studying the addresses and names, hoping that my own chicken scratch would lead me to the right joint.

"Viviana," Dottie said.

"Not yet, Dottie, I don't know where to go."

"Viviana . . ."

"I'm sorry I dragged you out on a school night."

"Viviana!" Dottie demanded my attention like I was a distracted second-grader.

"What?"

"What if we're looking at the wrong types of places?" She nodded her head down the dark, underlit sidewalk. Two men in loosely knit summer sweaters, silken pants, and loafers were walking down the street, and behind them a group of younger men—all sporting skin-tight T-shirts and dungarees, with rubber-soled shoes—had set up a radio on their front stoop and were dancing and drinking from bottles hidden in paper sacks.

"What do you mean?"

"Viviana, there is the distinct possibility that Webber Harrington-Whitley wasn't coming to the Village for girls," she said.

"I don't think it was for the tea shops, though," I responded. "Jazz?"

"Oh, Viv," Dottie laughed. She had a blush coming over her cheeks, and she rolled her eyes.

"What?"

She jerked her head over her shoulder, and the boys drinking on their porch had paired off, dancing together and touching in the shadows.

"Oh!" I exclaimed.

"It's a distinct possibility," Dottie said. "He may have just been hiding."

"Anything's possible," I said. "But why hide?"

"It's illegal!" she gasped.

"Sure, it's illegal, but here in the Village?" I asked. "Nothing's *really* illegal here."

"Nothing *you* do is really illegal in the Village. Laws may be spottily enforced, but there is always risk," Dottie said through pressed lips. "Just ask Oscar Wilde."

"The baloney guy?"

Dottie sighed. "No, Viviana. Not the baloney guy."

"It's all so unfair," I huffed.

"I imagine it's more unpleasant to live it."

"Do dames get the same treatment?" I asked. "You never see stories of cops raiding their bars and clubs in the papers."

"I don't believe the *courts* are as severe," Dottie considered. "But I shan't discuss what the police do."

"Oh, please don't—I can imagine for myself," I said.

"Granted, it wasn't until recently that women had many rights for themselves and could even choose their own paths, or whether or not to be married. I am not a lawyer, but any laws restricting people's lives don't seem just."

"When you're right, you're right," I said, pulling her up and dragging her toward Houston Street to catch a cab. "But

Webber lived by himself, so there was no reason to hide love notes in a drawer or anything, no matter who they were from. When I say there was nothing in his home, there was *nothing*. Also . . ."

"What, Viviana?"

"Dottie, I hadn't mentioned this before because I don't think it's pertinent to the case, but Webber Harrington-Whitley had an injury."

"What kind of injury? Did he have a cane?"

"No," I started. "A facial injury. He must have gotten it during his service in World War I. When I saw him at the hospital, they'd removed a mask from his face—a porcelain one, that looked just like lips and a chin. It was beautiful, in a way."

"Oh, Viviana. That's terrible."

"Explains why he was never in the papers next to the Blackstones," I said. "The poor man was missing most of his face. He must've spent most of his life trying to hide. Or being forced to. Oh, it's just so heartbreaking."

"Perhaps he chose the life he had? One unencumbered. It seems sad to us, but it does happen," Dottie said. I'd always thought of her as a lonely spinster, but with the question, I wondered if she was just someone who liked her life the way it was.

"Boy, I hope that's the case—but it's so sad that no one would even have tried to find out what happened to Mr. Harrington-Whitley if we hadn't figured out it was him," I said. "I know in my guts Tommy didn't do it, but who coulda?"

"I understand," Dottie agreed. "And I don't quite think I'm in the mood for a drink tonight."

"Me neither."

"It was nice to walk around with you, though," Dottie admitted, kicking a can down the sidewalk; I'd never before seen her behave in such a girlish way. "I feel like it's been years since I did something dangerous."

"It has been," I agreed, kicking the can again. "We really should do this more often. Preferably to nicer joints, though. Danger is only good in very, very small doses."

For the first time in a week, when I needed a taxi, one wasn't waiting at the curb. Dottie and I both stuck out our hands and after a few minutes of unladylike flailing and screaming, a cab rolled to a halt to pick us up and take us back to Mrs. K's in tired silence.

So as not to bother our landlady, Dottie and I traipsed upstairs and sat on the cold radiator in the hallway, chattering loudly until the other girls got the hint to join us in our unofficial office.

Phyllis passed around a tray of Mrs. K's chocolate chip cookies that she'd been harboring since suppertime, waiting for us to return. "So, you're telling me," she said, "that not only was poor Tally Blackstone going to be married off to a man old enough to be her grandpa, but he would have been perfectly happy to live the life of, say, desolate solitude?"

"Sounds about right," I said. "Though Dottie suggested he might have been a confirmed bachelor."

"You should've seen the place. It looked like a monastic cell," Betty added. I gave her a look, and she continued. "My grandma—*real* Catholic."

"And you don't think Blackstone knew?" Phyllis continued.

"If he knew, I doubt he would have said. He's the type that likes having other people's secrets."

"Typical despotic power machinations," Dottie muttered, and we all just blindly nodded.

"Blackstone likely gave Webber no other choice, wanting to keep absolutely everything in the family. I mean, Harrington-Whitley's apartment was pretty bare bones, nothing flashy about it," I said. "He might have had the inclination to be alone—I'm sure a young man with that large of a face injury didn't have it easy. Maybe he learned to turn off the loneliness—but maybe Blackstone made it worse."

"Hurt him further?" Betty asked.

"No, I mean, a family organization of whatever they're up to must be easier to control. Especially if you need to make sure any wealth or business gets handed down to the next generation. Tally's young enough to have kids upon kids. Her father obviously feels he should handpick her husband, and she told me herself Webber was her father's most loyal staff."

"His building was pretty buttoned-up," Betty admitted. "No one in his life was asking questions they didn't want answers to. And I bet they're all in the same circles, have the same kind of secrets."

The girls thought long and hard about that over mouthfuls of cookie, before each taking their turn to say good night and retire to peaceful sleep. Before she slipped into her room, Betty waved me over.

"Well, the intake nurses knew who he was at Roosevelt," Betty said, "which is probably a sign that he should switch to less dangerous work. But all three hospitals said there was no patient by the name of Tommy Fortuna in their wards right now, and no unnamed men fitting his description. I'm sorry, Viv."

"It's a dead end?"

"But that doesn't mean a dead boss." She gave my shoulder a squeeze and shut her door. I didn't want to be self-conscious, but I swore I heard her flip her lock too.

★ ★ ★

I was tossing and turning all night, with the tick-tock of my bedside clock ringing in my skull. I was absolutely sure that I knew everything I needed to figure out what was going on with those up-to-no-good Blackstones. But as soon as the clock hit twelve and I heard the local church bells chime, it was Wednesday—a week since Tommy'd been hired by Tallmadge Blackstone, and I was stumped.

I scurried out into the dark hall, looking for a pile of books to occupy my mind. I snagged one held together with a long stretch of masking tape—Dottie, I think, felt actual pain when she saw books mistreated. I went back into my room and flicked on a lamp, ready to kill my time until breakfast with whatever pulpy trash I'd grabbed.

The cover featured a dame in a flowy, almost see-through robe, bent in front of a vanity table, her leg cocked out like no girl ever does when she's by her lonesome, brushing her hair. I don't know if the fellas who drew these covers ever had girlfriends or wives, but they always had a funny idea in their heads about how ladies spent their time alone. But I suppose she wasn't by herself, because the artist also drew a peeping

Tom in the window, in his shirtsleeves and tattooed to the hilt. I was suddenly even gladder that my room at Mrs. K's had no window to the outside. Talk about the creeps.

The writing on the back was no less salacious than the girlie picture on the front.

"What can cause a man TO KILL?" it said in black and white.

Heiress Chastity Chase never meant to draw the attention of the Cosa Nostra Cutter—she was just an innocent girl! Or was she? Boys around town would do anything to get a touch of silken skin or grab some green. It was just a matter of time before one man tried to get too close! It's up to Detective Lance Langham to keep Chastity intact! Money! Love! Power! Intrigue!"

"God, Betty, you do love some garbage books," I said to myself, flipping open the cover and starting to read.

DAY 8

Halfway through the adventures of Chastity Chase, my mind was racing. I flipped to the last two chapters to make sure that I'd correctly guessed whodunit, and then I sat—wide awake and wired—waiting for seven o'clock in the morning. I heard Mrs. K putting out breakfast and the girls trickling out for the day, then Mrs. K and Oleks leaving, before I could run to the landing and make my calls.

"Midtown North," the gruff voice on the other end said.

"It's Viviana Valentine," I said. "I need you to get a message—"

"To Leary?" the voice cut me off.

"No, to Lawson," I said, bristling at the insinuation. "I've got business."

"Sure, Viv, go ahead."

"Tell him to meet me at Tommy's tonight, around eight PM."

"That all?"

"No, not in the least. I need you flatfoots to make sure the following people are in attendance too. You might want to grab a pencil. First up, someone's gotta go to Greenpoint . . ."

★   ★   ★

I rang off, and the operator connected me to another number. A woman's voice answered.

"Vital Records—Birth, Marriage and Death."

"Hi, Madge. It's Tommy's girl, Viv."

"Oh, hey, Viv. How can Hatch, Match, and Dispatch help ol' Tommy Boy today?"

"I need you to look up a marriage license—last name, Harrington-Whitley. And if it's there, a death certificate too." I gave her the details, and she let out a grunt of confirmation.

"Not too out of the ordinary."

"Call me at the office if you find anything, will ya?"

"You bet, sweetie."

I had the whole day to figure out the best way to corner all my guilty parties—and the whole day to get certain who those guilty parties were. I knew every piece of information I needed; the trick was getting it all to fall in obvious enough order to make Lawson believe me, but more importantly, make an arrest.

I scurried around the empty house, pilfering all the books I could find. Dottie's leather-bound Sherlock Holmes, a few cloth-bound Agatha Christies from Mrs. K's bookshelf in the dining room. Creaking open the door to the front bedroom, I spotted that Betty was out and hunted for her cache of disintegrating paperbacks. Underneath dirty laundry, clean laundry, and three months' worth of LIFE magazines, I scrabbled up *Agent of Twilight, Confessions of the Night,* and *Detectives of Destiny,* each and every one of them with a pouty-lipped heroine depicted on the cover, holding some kind of weapon—a knife, a revolver, a piece of rope—like in that new board game.

The books would have to do.

I dropped the whole pile on my bed and flipped each and every story to the last few chapters. While Sherlock Holmes often relied too often on revealing a clue that'd never been mentioned before in the story, the rest of the books gave a basic how-to. I knew I'd need a different angle from Tommy's usual M.O. since I wasn't keen on heading to a dark alley and knocking a heavy cold so I could truss him up and drag him to the cops. Though I didn't like to admit it, there could be some physical limitations to being female, and I wondered if that's why the only lady detective I could think of was that awful Miss Marple.

Weighing my options, it seemed as though calling everyone to one location and then going through the evidence was just the way to reveal what I'd found out. I rummaged through my wardrobe for a pair of slacks and a jacket that almost matched; plus a boxy button-front and modestly heeled Oxfords. I'd grab Oleks's fedora on the way out, of course, but with just a small bit of tweaks to my wardrobe, I looked like a proper private investigator, albeit a bit on the curvy side.

I scurried to Tommy's office at five o'clock, before any of the girls got home and tried to stop me. I needed to set the stage.

★　★　★

Now with an honest-to-goodness window back in the door, Tommy's felt almost right again—I didn't like the window being naked, but what was I gonna do about it? I undid all the locks and entered with a deep breath.

First things first meant hiding any potential weapons under lock and key—it was the standard procedure when Tommy was having a bit of a gathering. Letter openers, scissors, even a few good, stout lamps—all went into their usual closed drawers and cupboards. Improvised weapons were a matter of red-blooded passion, so I knew from experience no one was going to wing open the broom closet in order to get their point across. More likely, they'd throw a fist, and fists, by and large, weren't deadly. At least not in crowded rooms.

Next was to make a big enough space for all the congregants to gather. I went into Tommy's office and brought out his squeaky leather chair, and the two wooden chairs, uncomfortable as a church pew, that he made the clients sit in. I closed my roll top so no one would get the bright idea to plant their keister on my work surface, and set up a few crates so there'd be more places to sit. I wasn't sure who would show up—on their own or escorted by Lawson's men—but a good hostess is always prepared.

I set the percolator on the hotplate but kept closed the box of pastries I'd brought over, because as much as I tried, I had to admit Tommy's did have a bit of a mouse problem. Thinking about who was coming, I also nabbed a few ashtrays and placed them where I imagined Lawson would be most likely to stand. The last thing I needed was the ash of his Gitanes ground into my floorboards.

All of the overhead lights were too bright, so I flicked off a few and pulled open the blinds so the streetlight just outside would illuminate most of the room, casting threatening black-and-white barred shadows over the floor. A cab with his waiting light on at the curb slid away into the darkness.

"You better run."

I checked the wall clock, and the seconds ticked by. Just a few more minutes, and the party would arrive.

★　★　★

The phone rang and startled me out of my chair.

"Hello?"

"Vital records report—married 1911. Deceased 1918. Flu."

"Send my thanks to Madge."

The voice responded with a bureaucratic grunt, and I relaxed. Everything was settled.

★　★　★

The first to show up, of course, was Lawson, all by his lonesome.

"Hello there, baby," he crooned, not even bothering to knock before twisting the doorknob to let himself in. "Just us two?"

He was dressed in a soft, light blue, short-sleeved polo sweater with a collar; chocolate-colored pleated pants; and brown and white saddle shoes. The same plain gold pinky ring shone on his finger, and I wondered, for the first time, if he actually only had two.

"Just us for *now*, you creep, so don't get any ideas," I said. "Coffee?"

"Don't mind if I do." He was already fishing in his jacket pocket for his pack of Gitanes, lighting the cigarette before accepting a hot cup.

"You put out a search party for everyone I requested, right?"

"Of course. I can't guarantee they'll come," he said. "But who wouldn't want to indulge your whims, right, sweetheart?"

"Oh, lay off," I said. I could hear footsteps coming up the stairs.

Leary knocked politely, and then entered, followed by Tallmadge Blackstone—looking peeved as all get-out—and Tally Blackstone, in jeans and a loose summer sweater. She was glaring at Leary's back and then at me, though she ended up reconsidering and gave me a girlish wave.

"Thanks, the both of you, for coming," I greeted them. "Take a seat if you'd like—there's coffee and donuts on the table over there."

"I didn't sign up for a tea party, Miss Valentine," Blackstone said, sneering at the food as if it were contaminated.

"Nah, but Tommy's got some info for you," I said back. "And we'll expect final payment up front. Greenbacks only."

With two cops standing in the room and resolutely on my side, Blackstone pulled out a money clip and slapped a wad of bills onto my desk.

"Ah, he gave you the bastard rate, I see. Twice the regular price for your trouble." I picked up the stack and pocketed the lot of them, before any of our other visitors grew a set of sticky fingers. "Thank you."

"You'll be sure to declare all of that income, correct?" the detective grumbled.

"Of course, Officer. I ain't a cheat." I batted my lashes at him, and he smiled.

"What's going on, Viviana?" Tally asked.

"Oh, just a little project I've been working on," I assured her. "I think we can get started on the first part while we're waiting on the last two people to show up."

"Two?" Leary asked.

"Yeah, O'Malley's got the one you know about, and I'm expecting a second any moment now."

"Good," Lawson said. "I do, on occasion, like to have nights to myself."

"No, you don't," I said right back. "You're just like Tommy. The life's the job; the job's the life."

Lawson snubbed out his cigarette and lit his second with a smirk.

*　*　*

"Leary, if you could stand in front of the door, though please don't lock it," I instructed him, and I spied that he glanced at Lawson for the go-ahead.

So it was like that.

But Lawson gave a wink, and Leary did as he was told before I continued. "And Detective, I think you might want to get some pretty little bracelets on Mr. Blackstone here."

The big bull moose of a man was, as predicted, indignant, glaring at Lawson as he approached with the handcuffs.

"That son of a bitch!" he hollered, throwing his arms back and pushing everyone away from him. It felt as if he'd suddenly grown to the size of King Kong, the way his anger and sense of self-righteousness filled the room. "I am his *client*, not a suspect!"

"You're no longer a client, seeing as how you've made your final payment," I said, feeling the wad of bills in my pocket. "And truth be told, I know the answer to the question you had when you hired us. For what it's worth, you're not a suspect. I know for a fact you're a guilty party."

Tally looked a bit pale in the face, but she didn't say a word.

"Lawson, like I said—slap some cuffs on him before someone gets hurt."

Blackstone recoiled as Lawson approached, but to my surprise, he didn't swing. I wasn't sure yet if he was smart enough to know that assaulting a police officer was, at the least, a night in the tank, or if he was so pigheaded he didn't think I had the goods. Lawson ratcheted down the cuffs, and I saw the soft-handed heir to fortune wince.

"I sure hope you know what you're doing, babe," Lawson said, the cigarette pinched between his lips.

"I got a pretty good idea," I said. "Mostly, you're getting this big fish for fraud. And blackmail, I think, if I know the law."

Blackstone straightened up as if he'd been stuck with a hot poker. "That is libel!"

"This isn't a newspaper. It'd be slander," I said. "And it certainly isn't if you're guilty."

"Get to the point, Valentine," Lawson barked.

"Let's set it straight. We all know that Mr. Blackstone here started out life on easy street, don't we? Heir to a cotton and railroad fortune, he was rich enough to do whatever he wanted. He could've stuck to doing nothing, but some men aren't made to be idle. Some men think they're made for business.

"So Blackstone here went out and saw the world, collected some trinkets, and decided the right avenue for his business acumen should be something a bit flashy, a bit daring. He decided to get into diamonds, with the backing of Daddy dearest. But the diamond business is tricky, my friends, when most of the world is going through two wars and barely has enough money for food, let alone flashy stones."

Tally was staring at her father.

"Now, a man who knows business knows there's a few ways to run it if you aren't making sales," I went on. "The first way, your father's way, Mr. Blackstone, was to weather the down years, take lost profits, and hope things will turn up again. Your father sometimes lived a little bit leaner, right, Blackstone? But you were just a kid. You don't remember the hard years, just the good ones."

"My father was a brilliant man," he seethed.

"But when the going got tough again, your father wasn't around to fix it. You could've gotten by just selling some real estate or planning ahead, but you just couldn't do that."

Blackstone could only grunt at me.

"So instead, why don't you all tell us about that topaz mine you got the rights to in Burma?"

254 ⤸ Emily J. Edwards

"Bitch," he spat, and got to his feet.

I walked to my pile of folders and pulled out the photos of the sparkling hair clip.

"Tally, you were wearing this last Thursday at a yacht party in the Hudson, were you not?" I showed the photos around the room to everyone who was paying attention— basically, everyone but Mr. Blackstone.

"I was," she said quietly, and I handed the pictures to the detective.

"I got the idea from a reputable source," I explained, declining to name my landlady's brother. "It's likely that whatever sparkles ain't ice. And I think if you corral some evidence from Mr. Blackstone's clients, and perhaps his own daughter's jewelry box, you'll find out that he's been in this racket for quite a long time."

"Where's the clip now?" Lawson asked.

"It's grown some legs and walked away," I said. "But something tells me there's plenty of evidence that can be scrounged up with a few warrants to all sorts of folks who live on the Upper West Side. Maybe Connecticut too. Is it federal if it's over state lines?"

"I think that will be left up to a few district attorneys," Lawson said. The detective turned to Blackstone. "You. Sit."

"Now, Blackstone did come to us willingly with another little request, didn't you, sir?" With the crook seated in Tommy's creaky, squeaky, cracked leather chair, I was finally just a bit taller than him, and I gazed through my lashes at his purpling face. He didn't respond. "And this is where the blackmail comes in."

Out of the corner of my eye, I caught Tally sneaking toward the exit. "Leary, I thought I told you to guard that door." Tally stopped dead in her tracks.

"To the best of my knowledge, you won't be leaving here with your pa," I said to her. "And besides, you were a minor for most of this fracas."

She fidgeted.

"Tally?" Lawson asked.

"Blackstone came here and hired us to find out the exact reason why his daughter wouldn't marry the man to whom she is universally known to be betrothed, a Mr. Webber Harrington-Whitley," I explained. "Anyone with a subscription to a paper with society pages knows that much."

"True, but get on with it."

"The black*mail* comes from Black*stone* using a bit of information to force the two parties to consent," I said. "Now, I want you to promise me one thing before I continue, Lawson."

"Tell me what it is first," he said.

"I want to make sure that you only go arresting the people who are hurting others. If they aren't hurting anyone, you let them be, understand?"

"Sure, Viviana."

"At the beginning, I thought that if you searched Harrington-Whitley's personal effects, you'd find in his little black book a few entries for *discreet* gentlemen's clubs. Some associates suggested even ones exclusive to gentlemen, if you catch my drift."

"I'm catching it," the detective agreed. "Wouldn't shock me in the least. Back in the day—"

"You're going to have to spill the beans on your stories another time, Detective. But I couldn't find a book," I said. "I even went to some of the establishments listed in Tommy's old dossier of contacts to see if I could find a snitch who knew anything."

"That's awful dangerous," Lawson said. "Leary, you didn't think to stop her?"

The flatfoot just shifted and muttered something that sounded a lot like, "What makes you think I could?"

I pressed on. "So, I called up Vital Records and confirmed a suspicion."

"Which was . . .?" Lawson was growing tired. He hadn't had a sip of coffee or a fresh cigarette in minutes.

"Webber Harrington-Whitley was born Webber Whitley in 1893. He was married, once, to a woman named Hannah Harrington, in 1911. I assume she was a childhood sweetheart—he was just barely of age. She passed away in 1918. Spanish Flu, per the record. He kept a photo of her in his desk. A desk that was ransacked, likely by another one of Blackstone's goons looking for any evidence that Webber could've kept to incriminate Blackstone."

"You can't prove anything," Blackstone huffed.

"No, but she can," I said thumbing toward Tally.

"The list of men willing to take orders from *mon pére* is . . . limited," Tally said.

"Hannah waited for her husband through the war and stayed with him afterward," I said, and I saw Lawson shift on his feet. "When she died, Webber wanted to throw himself headlong into work. There weren't that many places where a man with his . . . specific issues . . . could find work—he was brilliant, but people are cruel. Eventually he found the Blackstones, who offered him plenty of work in the background. Didn't have to show his face to anyone he didn't want to. He was educated. Philips Exeter. West Point. Princeton, for business. Your father hired Webber, didn't he?"

Blackstone said nothing.

"The man was lost after Hannah died, and then Tallmadge, who Webber had watched grow up, promised him a new bride. There was a lot of shady business going on here, and I think that Blackstone was trying to force family ties into a little baby crime syndicate. Tally told me herself once—he thinks of himself as a gangster. For what it's worth, I think Webber didn't so much want Tally as a wife as he wanted to protect her the only way he could—through marriage. Once she was a wife, she wouldn't be treated like a daughter by *this* piece of work."

"Then why wouldn't she get hitched?" Lawson asked me, even though the girl in question stood in the same room.

"Tally, here—I think Daddy dearest knew she was not going to marry the man he chose for her," I said. "Tally, can I tell them?"

"You know?"

"I think so, but I don't want to say anything if it'll hurt you. We can find another way to explain it, I think."

Tally sighed. "The truth comes out eventually. But . . . does this change anything between us?"

"Not if you don't want it to." I gave her my best older-sister smile, and I meant it.

"Knock your socks off then."

With Tally's permission, I continued. "Well, she's not going to marry any man, for that matter. The inkling about Webber's romantic inclinations was the right track for Tally. She's got . . . a touch of the lavender, if you will. Girlfriends masquerading as girlfriends, if you catch my drift. Love letters hidden in a vanity drawer."

The silence in the room was so thick I could hear my heart beat in my ears. Tally didn't argue. She took a moment to push around an invisible speck on the surface of my desk.

After a moment of silence, it hit me. "Oh!"

Tally looked up.

"Cassandra!"

Tally smiled. It explained the recently engaged, future minor du Pont's blushing and Tally's cutting announcement of her "*Prince* Charming."

The men in the room looked confused.

"But anyhow, that's how you get a smart, spirited young girl who lost her mother young to do whatever you want her to do," I said to Blackstone. "You keep her in her home. Without any privacy—she told me she doesn't even have a lock on her bedroom door. You keep her under your thumb. You watch her every move and set her up for failure and shame. You ruin your own daughter's reputation so she can't ever leave you. You call your three favorite photographers to get your daughter in the papers, going wild about town with every boy you can pay off, don't you, *sir*? You manipulate the media, and at all other times you keep her surrounded by bodyguards dedicated to the family so she can't run away from you."

"God, I hope you're right about this, Valentine," Lawson said.

"That's how come the tips you gave were never wrong and how Tally showed up in the tabs week after week after week. Then you keep the real dirt in the family, so to speak. And the FBI isn't too keen on organized crime this day and age. You just wanted to marry her off to another person entirely within your control. That's about the definition of blackmail isn't it, Lawson?"

"About sums it up, yeah," he replied, his face blank. "Miss Blackstone, will you sign an affidavit stating all this as fact? That your father was forcing you into a marriage that was against your, uh, inclinations? And selling your whereabouts to the highest bidder for extortive purposes?"

"Oh, she will, Detective, as long as you keep it reasonably secret," I said. "Who do you think gave us that cheap barrette?"

"Viviana Valentine, you're one smart cookie," Tally said, a bit flustered and more than a bit impressed.

"I should say the same for you, hon."

"What are you talking about? You didn't pinch that from the boat?" Lawson's eyes were ping-ponging between me and the heiress.

"Not one bit. Stealing jewelry from teenage girls isn't really my style. The barrette showed up in an envelope, shoved underneath the door, with a note that was signed from Tommy," I said. "But it wasn't from Tommy. Tommy writes in all caps, 'cause he says his eyesight's bad. This note was written in lowercase, on the family cardstock."

"Dammit!" Tally said. "The devil really is in the details."

"So, Mr. Blackstone, to answer your question: before you could make her marry your business partner, your daughter was fixin' to send you up the river, so she could do as she pleased." I turned to Tally. "I bet you have a whole list of people who received some bunk jewels over the years. Perhaps some receipts and business records too?"

"Why, I do, indeed." Tally said, her long lashes batting at the copper despite the fact that her secret was out. "Did I break any laws, Detective?"

"Not that I can tell," Lawson said, impressed.

Leary piped up. "This would probably be a bit easier to prove if we had Harrington-Whitley's side of the story, sir."

I glared at him—as if we needed another side to the story, other than Tally's sworn statement and piles of glittering evidence.

"That's going to be awful difficult, Alan. He's been brain-dead and in the hospital for a week."

Tally gasped and let out a little cry.

"I'm sorry," I said, walking to her and holding her hand. "I should've been more tactful."

"I was never in love with him, but he was still a kind old man," she said.

"I could've figured it out sooner if you'd mentioned his injury," I said.

"I never noticed it, really," Tally said, tears coming down her cheeks. "That was just . . . him. It's not polite to bring up in conversation."

"Another part of him," I said, now trying to control my tone, "was the criminal part. I think he might have known all about your dad's business dealings. He wanted to see Tommy's notes, huh? Needed to see if the criminal enterprise he was a part of was compromised?"

Blackstone's face was set, and I got the clue.

"Oh, you sent him here, did you? I knew you had goons who'd do anything for you, but I didn't realize how high up they were on the payroll."

There was that familiar purple-faced giveaway, but this time the frustration got the better of him.

"But it must've been Fortuna who did him in!" Blackstone said. "I didn't follow him here and knock him out!"

A few more sets of footsteps were coming up the stairs, and I motioned for Leary and Tally to step away from the door.

"No, you didn't," I confirmed. "But you wanted to see if he'd gathered together Tommy's evidence, not knowing he got beaned, so you also sent a goon to his apartment to poke around. Trust me, I saw the signs. A broken picture frame and a dinged-up desk from someone trying to break the spring lock."

Blackstone pulled at his handcuffs, stretching at the steel, but couldn't break free.

"And if you want to know who clocked your accountant, the guilty party sounds like he's heading this way."

There was a scuffle outside in the stairwell, and with a crash, the office door careened open, and I winced while I eyed the brand-new pane of glass. Bumped by an experienced backside, the door stopped just before hitting the wall and wasting my fifteen hard-earned dollars. The newly set glass vibrated in its frame but didn't break.

"Hey there, ol' Tommy Boy," I said. "How was Los Angeles?"

My boss spun around and gave me a smile. Dressed in a rumpled, stained, and deeply smelly tuxedo, he looked every inch the rake, or at least like Laurence Olivier after a particularly hard night. "Evening, Dollface. Sorry I didn't call. Hope you didn't worry too much."

"It's okay—I knew you were alright. Got the perp?"

"This one?"

Tommy yanked Sandy into the room by the back of his forest-green jumpsuit. He was followed by a sheepish O'Malley, who was bleeding from the lip but somehow still smiling.

"Lawson—next time Viv tells you to round someone up, make sure the copper you send is a bit burlier. This guy was making a break for it in the hallway after headbutting poor O'Malley here."

"That's the fish I was hoping you'd catch. Santino Napolitano, or Sandy to those of us who have the bum luck to know him personally." I walked up to Sandy and mustered up my nerve to stare him in the eyes, even though on the inside, I felt a chill go right to my toes. "And Tommy? Say hello to Tino the Conderoga."

Sandy wrenched against his cuffs in a violent spasm of rage. Tommy yanked Sandy's arms harder.

"That's a pretty big accusation, Miss Valentine." Lawson said. Every other man in the office looked pale. "How do you know him?"

"I suppose you could call him an ex-beau if you were being generous," I said. "Who just so happened to come sneaking around Mrs. K's the night Blackstone here hired Tommy."

Sandy made another turn to scarper, but Tommy grabbed him by the jumpsuit before he could get too far. Leary himself stepped closer to the galoot, his own eyes slits while giving the man the once-over.

"He doesn't seem your type, babe," Lawson said.

"He isn't," I said, "but that'll teach me to be nice ever again. I felt bad for the guy, thinking he was just some no-date loser. But he and Tommy got history. Bad history."

"What'd he say to you last week, Viviana?" Leary asked.

"The girls all know I'm never gonna give this knuckle-head the time of day for as long as I live, so they ran cover while I skittered out of the way so I didn't have to talk to the creep," I said. "You saw me retreat and got real heated, but I made a mistake. I left my keys on the stoop. You knew 'em just by sight, didn't you? Not too many girls carry around the janitor ring I've got."

It was the first time Sandy decided to open his big, dumb mouth. "You were an easy catch, girl. Hooked ya as soon as I looked at ya."

"Eloquent, as always. Well, I can tell you this, Lawson," I explained. "He picked up those keys, got the right ones copied, or maybe just got 'em all, and then took 'em back to the stairs by sunup. You snatched them around dinnertime, thinking Tommy might be having a late night in the office and wouldn't be expecting visitors, so you thought you'd get the drop on him. You were using me to get at Tommy, who knew well and good Tino was the one who ordered the hit on his brother, Jimmy. But couldn't quite prove it to the satisfaction of law enforcement." I stared pointedly at the detective, whose jaw was set firmly. "Sandy knew I worked for Tommy, but Tommy had no idea that Sandy, who I was stepping out with, was Tino."

Sandy was too collected to try to fight back like Blackstone did—but the millionaire was clearly glad to not be the center of attention any longer, or fingered for murder. Sandy just shut his mouth and smirked, awfully proud of his plan.

"You snuck into Tommy's and beaned the first head you saw," I said. "There's a bookend missing from that shelf over there, Detective. I didn't notice at first because my boss isn't the tidiest, but when I was clearing the room of potential weapons for this tête-à-tête, I peeped that it was missing."

"There is," Tommy confirmed. "And—"

"And if you want O'Malley to go check the dumpster out back, you'll probably find it, covered in blood and fingerprints. Trash gets picked up late Wednesday nights—so, before this lug got Webber, but if you scurry, you'll get the goods before the trash is gone tonight. I don't know how you could've missed it before," I said, "unless you were just looking for a clean and easy way to pin this whole thing on Tommy."

Lawson ignored that last accusation but gave the young red-haired officer the thumb, and with a sigh, the junior cop went out back to dig through the garbage for evidence that was now buried underneath a week's worth of stinking, rotting New York City summer garbage.

"You'll also probably find, Officers, that he's got copies of Mrs. K's keys and that either his fingerprints or those of someone in his family match the bloody smear from my room," I said. Leary patted Sandy down and pulled two separate key rings from his front pocket. "Once I found out that the two other tenants from the building—the architect downstairs and the lawyer up—weren't on vacation, I scratched for their alibis. The lawyer upstairs had a solid, but the man downstairs didn't. But their shoes didn't match the print from the ink in the office. That's a boot print, and De Lancey only wears leather soles."

"We'd eliminated them the first day, Viviana," Lawson said. "And O'Malley there contaminated the crime scene with a print."

"Coulda shared the news and saved me some trouble!" I said. "And Tommy—make a peace offering to those fellas upstairs and down—they're real cold fish."

"Will do, Dollface."

"Now, Sandy, that first break-in at Mrs. K's, when you knocked me down the stairs—I thought at first Dottie was doing her nightly sharpening. But give him a whiff—he smells like cedar because his headquarters are at the pencil factory over in Greenpoint."

I caught Tally leaning in and giving a sniff. "Smells about right."

"Lawson here suggested that I was being followed, but I couldn't figure out how. But it was the janitors and the cabbies, wasn't it? The Nash out of Coney Island and the two guys in the diner?"

My question was met with silence.

"You gotta put those number-two tattoos in less conspicu-ous spots there, Tino. Ticonderoga number twos are the most popular pencils in America, and you can't sneak that kind of detail past a secretary."

"That's what that means? Tino the Conderoga?" Lawson piped up. "We thought it was some kind of Sicilian distinc-tion. Like duke or something."

"Just a bad pun, hon."

"Unbelievable."

"Sandy was in my room that night—and locked the door behind himself without thinking, just 'cause he had the keys—and kept coming back trying to get to Tommy. Ter-rorizing me had nothing to do with Blackstone, boys. Just a small-potatoes gangster whose plans were messed up when a lady kicked him to the curb after he tried to give her a five-finger explanation during a minor dustup. He's so used to roughing up girls, he didn't think I'd sever his link to Tommy Fortuna."

Sandy's passivity was waning, and he was starting to get awful mad that I'd gotten all his ducks in a row.

"Detective, would you and your officer please take a moment to look out that window?" Tommy asked.

"Don't mind if we do, Mr. Fortuna," Lawson responded. Tally and I stared down at my roll top, admiring the wood grain as the unmistakable sound of fists hitting meat rang through the air

"Thank you," Tommy said. Sandy was sitting, dazed, on a wooden chair, a bit red around the face and without a doubt a bit more bruised in the abdomen. Tommy knew never to hit a mark where the bruises would show. "Anyone who lays a hand on Viviana gets hands laid on them. And at least one of those was from Jimmy, you piece of shit."

"Thanks, Tommy."

"No problem, Dollface," Tommy winked at me. "So, something tells me you flatfoots will have no problem getting a search warrant for that pencil factory now. And Lawson?"

"Yeah, Tom?"

"If you're open to it, I got some evidence that'll link him to the bribery of a city councilman. And from what I know, the lawyer upstairs works for that councilman, so maybe you can slap together a warrant for his office too."

"Thanks, Tom." Lawson looked bleary.

"You knew the fink upstairs worked for the dirty politician?" I asked. "And you never said?"

"Didn't choose this office by accident. The phone lines in this building, Viv," Tommy said. "Real old. Glitchy."

"Gotcha, Tommy." I turned to Lawson and slipped the photo of the janitor out of my case file. "At any rate, I think I have a photo of at least one of Tino's henchman, if that'll help."

"Can't hurt," Lawson replied.

O'Malley emerged, panting from running up the stairs, his fingers curled around one of my favorite brass bookends, and the rest of him covered in coffee grounds, bits of wet newspaper, and more than a fair bit of cigarette ash. "Seem the one, miss?"

"Good job, hon," I replied, and he beamed like a happy setter dog.

"And where the hell were you during all of this, Fortuna?" Lawson asked.

"Apparently, missing out on a lot of fun," Tommy said. "But I won't step on your toes now, Dollface. Tell 'em."

"I think we've established by now that Miss Tallulah Blackstone isn't just some airheaded heiress," I said, giving her a smile. "You saw Tommy on the boat last Wednesday. And since you and he have shared more than a little bit of column space in the tabloids over the years, you knew exactly who he was. Decided to have a little fun, huh? Sent your private train car to Los Angeles where your dad's got a house, knowing he'd follow you like a bloodhound."

"It was just a lark, honest," she said. "I don't care for being followed, by photographers or anybody. That's not breaking a law, is it, Detective?"

"Nope," Lawson said. "I've wanted to send him on a wild goose chase a few times myself over the years. Though I think you might owe Tommy a bit of green for putting him out so bad."

"I can manage that," she said. "That alright by you, Mr. Fortuna?"

Tommy shrugged.

"Poor Tommy boy, here, did a round trip on the continental railroad in just about seven days," I explained. "He didn't even have time to pack his toothbrush before he was off. Managed to track Tally's train car all the way to L.A. before he realized she wasn't on it. You might want to give him a donut, Detective. He looks a little tired."

With Sandy and Blackstone trussed up like two Christmas turkeys, Tommy took the time to have a cup of coffee and a snack. "Thanks, Viv."

"Am I missing anything?" I asked, making eye contact with all the professional snoops in the room.

"Not that I can tell," Tommy said with a mouth full of glazed.

"Real quick, Tally—why'd you send the package if you sent Tommy packing?" I asked.

"Well, the note was just to let whoever worked with Tommy know he'd be out of town. And the hair clip—I thought someone might just pawn it, a little bit of repayment for putting you out with Tommy getting gone," she said. "After we went to Coney Island, I knew you'd keep it as evidence and follow that trail 'til the scent went cold." She stared at her father and stuck her tongue out at him like a little girl.

"I have a question, Viviana," Leary said. "How did you know Harrington-Whitley was the stiff?"

"I didn't at first," I said. "Not until I happened upon some other bits of jewelry." I unearthed the gold cuff links and handed them to Leary. "It's the Harrington family crest—he kept these in the same drawer as his photo of his deceased wife, which Blackstone's goon probably took as a trophy. Web loved her so much, he even took her name."

"That's a cockamamie idea," Lawson muttered.

"And that design was sketched in his medical records, next to personal effects, where the notes said he was wearing a signet ring, which was probably his wedding ring. The sketch was next to where it mentioned his pupils were fixed, so that meant he wasn't gonna get better, *Lawson*."

"How on earth did you know that?"

"I've been a Girl Friday for the best PI in the city for years, ya moron," I said. "You think I didn't learn a thing or two?"

THREE MONTHS LATER . . .

Friday, September 29, 1950

"You got a good thing going here with Tommy," Tally said to me, her voice dripping with more than a little bit of jealousy.

She was wearing a burnt-orange tweed suit and chocolate-brown suede pumps, the ensemble complementing her coloring perfectly, as well as reflecting the overall festive mood of New York in late September. The smell of garbage and the summer humidity had long since been replaced by the smell of slowly decaying leaves outside and the hot, dusty perfume of steam radiators inside, ours now clanging away underneath the window and topped by a reacquired mountain of paperwork.

The heiress sat in the corner as a few great big lugs in coveralls maneuvered my bulky roll top out the door.

Every last thing I'd ever collected over my years with Tommy was placed about the room—files and pens in bins on top of the cabinets, my tiny toolkit that had been relegated to the broom closet, waiting for a new home. There was a great big commotion as the descending team met two other workmen—who I knew to be hauling my new desk—coming up the stairs. A ruckus of cursing in Italian and English ensued, followed by the sound of four sets of boots and two giant wooden desks descending the stairs, and the whole thing presumably got sorted without anyone bleeding or breaking a leg.

Within a short time a new desk—matching Tommy's—came on through.

"In the back office," I said. "Fortuna and I are sharing for now. Watch the window—we just had it painted."

The lunkheads moved toward the back, and my heart soared as I read the new gilded letters on the pebbled glass:

TOMMY FORTUNA
&
VIVIANA VALENTINE
PRIVATE INVESTIGATORS

"We still have to do a bit of rearranging," I muttered to myself, making a to-do list in my head. "Gotta make more space in all the garbage we took out of Tommy's office for a new secretary desk." I put my hands on my hips and surveyed the area.

"It looks good up there," Tally said, nodding toward the door.

"What does?"

"Your name, you goose," she jabbed. "Was the test hard?"

"Not after the prep work I did with Tommy," I said. "You wanna see?"

"You bet!" Tally scurried over to me, and I opened up my purse to pluck out my wallet. Inside was an official-looking piece of cream card stock with my name and thumbprint, and the words *New York State License No. 4807, Private Investigator, bonded and insured.*

"Looks amazing!" Tally ran her fingers over the edge of the card, and I politely reclaimed it before it could get creased.

"Anyway, how's the trial going?" I asked.

"Oh, it isn't looking too good at all for *mon pére*," Tally said, staring at her hair and pulling apart her split ends with a distracted smile. "It turns out, you probably shouldn't sell bunk jewelry to a certain clientele when they can afford the best lawyers in America. And France. And maybe even Switzerland, depending on where the Niederhausers are living at the moment."

"No, that sounds like a real bonehead scam," I said. "Some people got the brains for crime, and some don't—and don't find out they don't until it's too late."

"But his assets are frozen at least, and without a doubt, most are going to be seized," she said. "The poor little rich folk with dirty diamonds will make it out of this okay."

"I'm not so worried about them," I said. "What about you?"

"Web was smart enough to put most of the real estate and land in a different company name, so the courts can't touch it," she said. "And I have trust funds from my grandparents—the elder Blackstones and Papa Leclercq, my mother's father.

Sell a good chunk of the real estate and everything will be more than fine. Plus, Webber named me as his sole heir, and he had done pretty well for himself until the end."

"And how was Web's service?"

"Good, I guess. Just small. Me and more friends than I thought he had," Tally said. "Is Sandy, uh, *Tino*, already at Sing Sing?"

"And will be for the foreseeable future," I confirmed.

"Good."

"So, those are the two biggest problems solved," I said. I shuffled some papers to fill the very tense silence of the office as we heard workmen grunt under the weight of their heavy loads.

"How did you know he took it?" Tally finally asked.

She didn't have to say his name. Between them, Tommy and Detective Lawson had scrounged up enough dirty diamonds as evidence from the Blackstone client list to put Tallmadge away for life, but my stomach was in knots not knowing what happened to the hair clip that Tally had slipped under our door. It took less than a day, but I'd finally summoned Alan Leary to my doorstep and told him I knew it was his sticky fingers that had grabbed the piece from my bedroom at Mrs. K's.

"Just the timing of it all," I said. "He was on guard duty the day you sent us that whole wardrobe of clothes. He caught me trying on that negligee, wouldn't you know it."

"He didn't!" Tally's face burned with embarrassment.

"He did! I ran back to my room to hide until everyone left for work, and once he was out of eyesight in the dining room,

I went and took a shower. He was the only other person in the house. He must've snuck upstairs and rooted through my things while the water was running."

"How did he know you had it?"

I blushed before I answered. "I'd worn it in my hair for a few days," I admitted. "You can't blame me. I'd never had anything like it before, even if it wasn't real diamonds."

"I'm the one who wore it in the first place, and *I* knew it was fake!" Tally laughed. "Did he at least give it back to you?"

"Nope."

"Where do you think it is now?"

"I'm sure in some pawn shop somewhere between here and Newark," I said, picking up a nail file and buffing my already smooth fingers.

"You're not going to tell the detective?"

"No, I don't think so," I said. "Alan's sister. She needs the money for school. But he did put in a request to be transferred to motor pool the day I called him out for his thieving."

"I swear to God, men make no sense to me," Tally said. "Stealing from a girl you got the hots for. Who does that?"

"Men do all sorts of crazy things to dames they say they adore," I said. "But what about you? What are you going to do now that all this has blown over?"

"Oh, you know. I've just got to find a way to keep myself occupied."

"What are your options?" I put on the percolator and sat down in one of Tommy's hard wooden chairs, across from Tally.

"Each of the Seven Sisters has sent a charming, refined, and forthright letter to my attention, saying they could over-look my rather informal primary education and allow me to study at their respective school," she said. "Provided I offer a sizable donation."

"College could be fun," I said.

"Imagine the trouble I could get into at Radcliffe," she said, waggling her eyebrows.

"That might be nice."

"But I was thinking I might want to get a job, at least for a little while. Stay in New York. The doors of higher education are always open provided you've got the money to grease the hinges."

"What kind of work were you thinking?" The percolator was shaking, and Tally hopped up to get it, pouring me a cup of coffee with a shaky hand.

"I thought I'd be a rather good secretary."

"Did you now?" I said. "Do you know how to type?"

"Not really."

"Invoicing?"

"Nope."

"Can you make coffee?"

"I have, once."

"What about first aid?"

"I managed to fix Dad up pretty good when he fell off his polo pony," Tally said. "Until the doctor could stop playing long enough to come to his aid."

"You sound about as prepared for the gig as I was at sixteen," I said. "But let's ask Tommy, first."

"Let's ask Tommy what?" Tommy entered from his—now *our*—office in his undershirt, his suspenders hanging from his pants, and arms flapping in the breeze. Tally looked entirely unfazed by the mostly naked man in front of her and was completely unshaken by those damn blue eyes, but I felt my stomach flutter just a bit at the sight of him.

It was good to have him home.

"We need a new secretary," I said matter-of-factly.

"We do."

"And how about one that can't type, can't keep books, can't make coffee, and doesn't know a lick about patching up bullet holes?"

"Sounds familiar, actually, Dollface," Tommy said. "But this one, from my own personal experience, is already practiced in subterfuge."

"The pay is sixty a week," I said to Tally.

"I'll do it for forty," she said.

"You'll do it for sixty," Tommy said.

"Anything that'll cover weekly cab fare from Mrs. K's." Tally shrugged.

Tommy gave me a look.

"She couldn't stay at her father's," I said. "And Phyllis moved to Paris."

"I got half the whole third floor!" Tally said, beaming. "There's a lock on the door and everything."

"I moved upstairs and got a window," I explained. "So, come to think of it, ol' Tommy boy, I think I'll need a raise in addition to this promotion."

ACKNOWLEDGMENTS

First and foremost, I must thank my husband, David, for his endless patience in listening to me babble about post-War fashion, politics, lingo, and never once batting an eye when I suggest ways to murder someone.

Heaps of gratitude for my tireless agent, Anne Tibbets, for believing in a too-short draft with a salacious title, and Donald Maass for going to bat for me.

A million thanks to my editor at Crooked Lane, Faith Black Ross, for taking a chance on Viv.

The entire team at Crooked Lane Books: Madeline Rathle, Rebecca Nelson, Dulce Botello, Melissa Rechter, and Kate McManus. I know how hard you work, and you work magic.

A special thank you to cover designer, Rui Ricardo, for capturing the essence of our Girl Friday.

And to my friends who have nudged me along the way: Andrew Rostan, Nicole Cahill, Michelle Athy, Jacqui Walpole, Taverlee Laskauskas, and Will Wallace—thank you. You are an amazing community and source of confidence.